NO HOLDS BARRED

NO HOLDS BARRED

A Daniel Whelan Mystery

Lyndon Stacey

This first world edition published 2012
in Great Britain and in the USA by
SEVERN HOUSE PUBLISHERS LTD of
9–15 High Street, Sutton, Surrey, England, SM1 1DF.
Trade paperback edition first published
in Great Britain and the USA 2012 by
SEVERN HOUSE PUBLISHERS LTD.

British Library Cataloguing in Publication Data

Stacey, Lyndon.
  No holds barred.
  1. Ex-police officers – Fiction. 2. Freight and
  Freightage – Fiction. 3. Truck drivers – Fiction.
  4. Corruption – Fiction. 5. Detective and mystery stories.
  I. Title
  823.9´2-dc22

ISBN-13: 978-0-7278-8064-2 (cased)
ISBN-13: 978-1-84751-410-3 (trade paper)

All Severn House titles are printed on acid-free paper.

Severn House Publishers support The Forest Stewardship Council [FSC],
the leading international forest certification organisation. All our titles that
are printed on Greenpeace-approved FSC-certified paper carry the FSC logo.

MIX
Paper from
responsible sources
FSC
www.fsc.org   FSC® C018575

Typeset by Palimpsest Book Production Ltd.,
Falkirk, Stirlingshire, Scotland.
Printed and bound in Great Britain by
MPG Books Ltd., Bodmin, Cornwall.

This one's with heartfelt gratitude to Jaci & Robert;
Alison, Brian & Tamzin; Judi; Di; Lynne; Rebecca;
Maggie; and Paula. They will know why.

ACKNOWLEDGEMENTS

As usual, thanks go to my good friend Mark Randle of the Wiltshire Constabulary, for his ever-patient help with my research queries.

ACKNOWLEDGEMENTS

PROLOGUE

The old brick farmhouse stood silent, its outline dark against the moonlit sky, smoke drifting from one of the tall chimney stacks, the only light a dull glow behind one of the downstairs windows.

A small bright triangle appeared as the curtain was lifted at one corner then dropped a moment later.

The woman moved away from the window, two parallel lines of worry between her brows. Flopping down into the closest armchair, she tucked a stray strand of hair behind her ear, picked up a farming magazine and began to turn the pages desultorily, blue eyes scanning the print, mind elsewhere.

Moments later, she had tossed it away and was on her feet again, drawn inexorably back to the window. Standing to one side, she peered out as she'd done dozens of times already that night.

The yard was still and deserted. Near at hand the moon gleamed on the cream roof of the Land Rover, and, further away, she could make out the outlines of the barn, the stables and the four parked lorries beyond.

All of a sudden, the security light came on, flooding the yard with brilliance, and she caught her breath.

It was a false alarm. Halfway across the open space a black and white cat froze, looking towards the house, then turned and ambled on its way.

Sighing, she let the curtain fall and began to pace the room.

He'd never stayed out so late before without telling her. Why hadn't he at least phoned?

The heavy ticking of the grandfather clock seemed to accentuate the silence.

She could have been alone in the world.

She'd had the radio on for a while, but not for long – it was too intrusive, too noisy. She was afraid of missing something.

Afraid of missing what? she asked herself impatiently. He'd gone out to investigate some lights he'd seen across the fields, that was all. More than likely he'd dropped down into the village for a quick dram at The Fox and Duck and got talking to his cronies. Typical of him not to think that she might be worrying. Or not to care, a voice in her head added.

On the rug in front of the fire, the dog stirred, stretched and looked up, perhaps sensing her anxiety. She wished he'd taken the dog, but he'd said it might get in the way, and, anyway, it would look after her and the kids while he was out.

She glanced doubtfully at the black Lab. He was top gundog material, but a guard? She wasn't so sure.

And, besides, why should she need guarding? Her imagination was running riot and that wasn't like her.

He'd left her with a spring in his step, eyes bright with the prospect of some action, even if it was nothing more than giving old Woodsmoke, the poacher, a warning off. She had an uneasy suspicion he'd been feeling bored lately. Running the business didn't tax him unduly and, although he denied it, she wondered if he was finding rural life a little tame.

Thinking of Woodsmoke, she hoped he wouldn't be too hard on the old man. The poacher was a local character who'd been around since her mother was a little girl and had never done anyone any harm, unless you happened to be a rabbit. As far as she was concerned, he was welcome to as many rabbits as he could carry.

A glance at the clock told her it was well past one o'clock. The pub would be long closed and its patrons dispersed to their respective homes.

So where was he?

The inactivity was driving her mad and, crossing to the door beside the fireplace, she went through and up the curving flight of stairs to the children's rooms.

Pausing in the doorway, she looked into the soft darkness of the first bedroom, hearing the whisper of her daughters' breathing. Two beds, two precious humps under the quilts.

All well.

She moved on to the second room, her anxiety levels falling a notch or two. Here, a young boy lay sprawled atop the bedclothes, one arm outflung, the thumb of the other hand tucked characteristically into his mouth. With a shake of her head, his mother crossed to the bedside and gently removed it before dropping a kiss on his brow and turning away.

Downstairs, the living room waited, empty save for the Labrador.

Outside, nothing had changed. The woman made herself a mug of tea, found a biscuit for the dog and settled back into the chair, drawing her feet up under her as she often told her eldest daughter not to do.

Moments later, in spite of her worry, she was asleep, tea cooling on the table at her elbow.

The whining of the dog brought her awake.

The room was filled with the soft grey light of dawn and the fire was out.

The woman uncurled her legs and sat up, cautiously flexing her stiff neck. The unwelcome reality of the situation came flooding back.

The Labrador lifted a paw and scratched at the paintwork of the doorpost, repeating the plaintive whine.

'All right, Monty, I'm coming.'

As she opened the door, the incoming air was icy cold and she saw that the clear night had left a late frost on the grass and a shimmer of ice on the Land Rover. The valley was filled with a thin, milky mist, turning the familiar vista into one of mystery. She shivered, rubbing her upper arms.

The Labrador pushed past her legs, making not for the rough grass of the home paddock as he normally did, but for the open gateway and the long gravel drive beyond. He set off at a run, ignoring her call.

On the kitchen table, her mobile began to trill, and after one last puzzled glance at the dog's fast disappearing form, she turned back and picked it up.

'Jenny? It's Sue.' The voice sounded agitated and upset. 'I'm at the top of the drive – you'd better come quickly. It's Gavin.'

'What is it? What's happened?' Jenny had started trembling violently.

'I don't know. But it's bad. He's in a bad way. I've called an ambulance.'

Jenny dropped the phone, snatched up her keys and ran out into the chill of the morning.

ONE

They came out of nowhere, engines revving noisily and horns blaring.

Daniel Whelan glanced in his rear-view mirror and saw two vehicles crowding the tailgate of his ageing silver Mercedes estate, the foremost one swerving from side to side on the narrow country road to convey an obvious message: the driver wanted to get past, and quick.

He'd seen the blue pick-up with the banks of roof-mounted spotlights and oversized wheels before. Five minutes ago, to be exact, parked to one side of the petrol station in the village where he'd refuelled his car. As an ex-copper, he couldn't quite kick the habit of making a mental note of such things.

Daniel held the crown of the road. Whatever their problem, it wasn't safe to pass and the pick-up could wait until he was good and ready to pull over.

The blue truck accelerated to within inches of his rear bumper. Its radiator grill was heavily barred, and for a moment he thought he was going to be rammed, but the driver contented himself with leaning long and hard on the horn once again.

In the back of Daniel's car, his German shepherd dog, Taz, began to bark furiously at the vehicle following, hackles up and muzzle pressed against the metal grid of the tailgate dog-guard.

Rounding a corner, Daniel spotted a pull-in on the left, one of several makeshift passing places that had naturally evolved on what was not much more than a single-track road. He pulled over and slowed to a halt.

With a roar, the pick-up accelerated past, but instead of disappearing at top speed as Daniel had expected, it swung left in front of the Mercedes and screeched to a halt, tyres smoking. A glance in his mirror showed him that the second vehicle, a pimped-up 1970s Ford Escort, had done the same behind him.

Pulse rate rising a notch or two, Daniel pressed the button for central locking and awaited developments.

As soon as the pick-up stopped moving, a young man erupted

from the far side, wearing oversized oily blue overalls, a baseball cap, wrap-around sunglasses and a truculent expression. He came round the back of the vehicle with a jaunty, swaggering step, carrying a monkey wrench. Daniel put him in his late teens or early twenties and identified him without surprise as the one who'd served him with fuel at the filling station in the village.

'How do I get to Maidstone Farm from here?' Daniel had asked as the diesel gurgled into the car's tank and the numbers on the out-of-date pump's display ticked over in maddening slow motion. The youth's manner had been confrontational, even then.

'Who wants to know?'

'I do.'

'You the new driver?'

'Why? Are you Jenny Summers?'

The young man sneered.

'Duh! Do I look like Jenny Summers?'

'I don't know. I've never met her,' Daniel had said reasonably. He wasn't spoiling for a fight but neither was he going to discuss his business with any Tom, Dick or Harry in the village.

The youth had given him a look of unmistakable dislike, replaced the pump nozzle in the machine and said rudely, 'Find it yourself,' before spoiling the gesture somewhat with the necessity of completing the fuel transaction.

Daniel paid him in cash and started the engine.

'Now, if you'd wanted to be really unhelpful,' he said, 'you could have given me the *wrong* directions.' And with a click of his tongue and a wink, he'd left the young man glowering as he drove away.

Now, freed of the constraints of his place of work, the youth came to a halt beside Daniel's car and rapped sharply on the window.

Daniel obliged by opening it three or four inches.

Having the whole of the back of the car to roam in, Taz had moved forward to just behind the front seats and was barking enthusiastically in his ear, nose pressed against the glass of the side window. Daniel had to raise his voice to be heard.

'Is there a problem?' he asked.

He could silence the dog with one sharp command, but just at the moment it suited him for Taz to make his presence known.

'Yeah, you're the problem, mister fucking smart arse!' Up close, Daniel could see a shaving rash and the remains of a nasty acne attack on the youth's chin and neck.

'And why's that? Is it a crime to ask the way around here?'

'Just shut up, OK?'

A movement on the periphery of Daniel's vision heralded the arrival of the driver of the Escort, a man perhaps a year or two older, thickset and with a somewhat bovine countenance. He came to a halt irresolutely in the region of the Merc's left wing mirror, regarding the dog warily, and looked to the spotty youth for guidance.

Heaven help us! Daniel thought.

'You,' Spotty reclaimed his attention, stabbing a dirt-grimed forefinger towards the window opening, 'need to turn round and go home. You're not needed here and you're not wanted. Got it?'

'Yeah. Got it?' came an echo from the other side.

Daniel didn't even waste a glance.

'That's enough, Taz. Quiet!' he said, and the German shepherd's barking became instead rapid, hoarse panting punctuated by the odd protesting whine. 'OK. What's this all about?'

'It's about you turning round and going back to wherever you come from.'

'But why the hell should I?'

Spotty hacked, spat and leaned closer, perhaps encouraged by Taz's quietness. He had an eyebrow stud and a small earring, Daniel noticed.

'You don't need to know why. Just do it!'

'Yeah. Just do it!' the echo said.

It was like a scene from a bad gangster movie. Daniel looked at the unhealthy skin and the thin-lipped, small mouth, vigorously chewing gum, and lost patience with the whole affair. When he'd been policing Bristol city centre on a typical Friday night, loud-mouthed troublemakers like Spotty and his friend had been two a penny.

'If you don't get back in that truck and move it in the next ten seconds, I'll open the door and let the dog out,' he told the youth.

Spotty took a step back, glancing nervously at Taz who, sensing his fear, began to rumble under his breath.

'I ain't scared of no dog.'

'Well, that's all right, then,' Daniel observed. 'You just stay there.'

'You wouldn't . . .'

'Watch me.'

Spotty wavered, clearly unwilling to back down but just as clearly wishing he was back in the safety of his pick-up.

'Five . . . Four . . .'

The man on the left turned and bolted for his car.

'Three . . . Two . . .' Daniel moved his hand towards the button.

'All right! All right!' Spotty backed away so rapidly he stumbled and almost fell. When he reached the open driver's door, he raised his voice to shout, 'You're fucking dead, man!' before prudently slipping inside and pulling the door shut.

Moments later, both vehicles had gone back the way they had come, tyres squealing dramatically, and Daniel found himself alone in the lane.

With a small sigh and a shake of his head, he put the car in gear and continued on his way.

He'd known Jenny Summers was having some trouble – after all, that was why he'd come – but he hadn't expected his arrival to provoke such an immediate and violent response. For all anyone knew, he was just another driver turning up for a job. All at once, the proposition he'd accepted primarily as a favour for a friend began to assume a more interesting slant.

'I've known Jenny Summers – or Jenny Maidstone as she was then – since she was just a kid,' Daniel's employer, Fred Bowden, had told him over after-dinner coffee, just under a week ago. 'She's a lovely girl. Though saying that, she must be nearly forty now – it's hard to believe. She's had some bad luck in her life – more than her fair share, you know how some people do?' He stopped short, a little discomfited. 'Well, Christ – yes, of course you do.'

Daniel had shrugged. It was history, now.

'Anyway, Jenny married a local lad and they took over the family farm when her father retired, but six or seven years ago Colin rolled his tractor on a steep slope and killed himself. So, there was Jenny with upwards of six hundred acres to farm and two young kids to look after.'

'That must have been tough.'

Fred nodded. 'She really loves that farm and she gave it her best shot, but, as you know, these are hard times for farmers, and eventually things got the better of her. She sold off most of her stock and laid off all but a couple of workers. It was beginning to look like she was going to have to sell up after all, but then along comes this new guy, Gavin Summers, and within a month or two they're married and he's moved in. He's not a farmer – in fact, he's in haulage, like me, and he uses the farm as a base. Anyway, it's allowed Jenny to start up her own business renting out grazing and taking horses in for livery and training, so she's happy.' He paused, taking a sip of coffee. 'At least, she was until Gavin went out after poachers one night a couple of months ago and ended up in hospital.'

Daniel's attention sharpened.

'What happened? Someone take a shot at him?'

'No. Nobody knows, really. He turned up next morning, lying on the farm track with a fractured skull.'

'And he doesn't remember anything?'

'No. He's in a coma. He hasn't spoken at all. They can't say whether he'll ever wake up. It's awful for Jenny and the kids, not knowing, and if that wasn't stressful enough, she's got all kinds of problems with the business. She rang me the other night, in tears.'

'And you're telling me because . . . ?' Daniel was pretty sure he knew the answer.

'Well, obviously *I* can't just drop everything and head off to Wiltshire, but then I thought of you. I mean, it's right up your street. You can't tell me you're not bored silly driving a delivery round for me after being a copper for ten years.'

Daniel didn't try to deny it. He had been feeling a bit restless of late.

'But I'm not a businessman,' he pointed out.

'You've got a good head on your shoulders, and, anyway, I didn't get the impression that it was the bookkeeping side of things she was having problems with. What d'you say? Will you give it a go?'

Daniel remembered the conversation now with suspicion. How much more had Fred known that he wasn't telling?

To all outward appearances, Great Ditton was a quiet Wiltshire village, much like many others Daniel had passed on his way. If there had ever been anything great about it, it had clearly been way back in its history. Now it was a straggling collection of warm brick houses and pretty cottages, interspersed with square 1960s bunga-lows, wearing their tiny plots like straitjackets. In addition to these, the village boasted a squat-towered stone church with a clipped yew hedge, two pubs hung with bright baskets of flowers, a bakery, an estate agent, the garage where he'd first made Spotty's acquaintance, and that modern rarity, a village post office and stores.

Now that he'd left the village centre behind, the road began to climb quite steeply, the houses becoming fewer and further between.

It was clearly prime farming country, and he passed the gateways to two such properties and the hexagonal roadside lodge to Great Ditton Manor before coming at last to an open five-bar gate that bore the name he'd been looking for: Maidstone Farm.

Glad that journey's end was in sight, Daniel swung the Merc into a tarmac driveway that climbed gently but steadily upward between dark banks of mixed woodland. After a couple of hundred yards, the way split, but a sign guided him to the right for the farm. A glance to the left revealed a narrow lane winding away out of sight through the woods, with a glimpse of a brick cottage off to one side.

After another hundred yards or so, the farm drive levelled out and burst from the gloom of the trees into the sunshine as it ran on between acres of grassland divided by overgrown hedgerows. Ahead of him, in a slight dip, lay the farmhouse and an untidy sprawl of barns and outbuildings including stables and a ménage.

Daniel slowed up and stopped, taking in the layout of the property. It seemed the fields of Maidstone Farm had escaped the modern trend of grubbing out hedges to create endless tracts of featureless but easily farmed land. The field on his left was grazed by a slow-moving herd of reddish-brown cattle, and, dredging the knowledge collected during his own rural upbringing, he decided they were probably Herefords. In line with what he'd learned about Jenny Summers' livery business, the fields nearer the farm buildings were smaller and supported a mixed selection of horses and ponies.

Beyond the pastureland to his left, the dark bank of woods he'd just passed through swept round in a curve that formed the horizon, effectively concealing any further Maidstone Farm land that might lie that way. On his right, the land dipped to where a willow-lined river wound its way across the flat valley bottom, beyond which a large Elizabethan house stood, partially clad in scaffolding, on a slightly raised plateau, its diamond-paned windows glinting in the sunlight.

Taking a pair of binoculars from the glove compartment, Daniel took a closer look. Evidence of building work abounded. Two new wings appeared to have been added to what was clearly a substantial house to begin with, and outside the formal gardens that surrounded the property, it looked as though extensive landscaping was underway to turn open fields into parkland, à la Capability Brown.

Daniel lowered the binoculars. It was reasonable to assume the house he was looking at was Great Ditton Manor and whoever lived there certainly had some grand ideas.

Driving on, the Merc swooped down into the valley, the lane bordered by straggling, bramble-infested blackthorn hedges before running at length between the horse paddocks and into the farmyard itself.

His arrival interrupted what appeared to be a slightly heated exchange between a well-built man in a navy-blue polo shirt and a fairly stocky woman with thick reddish-gold hair tied back off her face. They both paused to glance in Daniel's direction as he parked in front of the house next to a red and cream Land Rover and a navy blue Transit van with mirror-glass windows. He thought the woman looked stressed and unhappy.

'Hi. Daniel Whelan,' he said, getting out of the car and approaching the two of them.

For a moment, the woman looked puzzled, but then the penny dropped.

'Daniel, of course.' She mustered a smile. 'I'm Jenny. You're earlier than I expected.' She shook his hand, then gestured towards the other man. 'This is Taylor Boyd. You'll be working together. Taylor – our new driver, Daniel.'

Daniel shook hands with a man of about thirty, with an earring and dark hair made spiky with gel. His eyes were concealed behind mirrored sunglasses that hadn't come from any pound shop, and both his handclasp and expression were cool and unwelcoming. The blue shirt carried a gold logo spelling the words 'Summer Haulage'.

'Taylor, I'll speak to you later,' Jenny told him. 'But don't do anything until I've had time to think about it.'

The man accepted his dismissal with a perfunctory nod, but muttered, 'Don't take too long, then,' before turning away.

'Trouble?' Daniel asked quietly as the man moved out of range.

Jenny sighed and shook her head.

'Not really. It's OK.'

Daniel raised an eyebrow.

'Did Fred tell you why I was coming?'

She looked at him, pale blue eyes large in a freckle-dusted but rather plain face.

'Of course. I'm sorry, I was forgetting – it's just . . .'

'I know. You don't know me from Adam.'

She nodded, relieved that he understood.

'You know, I could murder a cup of tea,' Daniel said.

TWO

The kitchen at Maidstone Farm was a genuine farmhouse kitchen. Not the designers' country kitchen of the glossy magazines but the sort that had evolved over several generations of use into a comfortable and practical space.

The room was dominated by a vast range cooker that sat in an even more vast arched brick fireplace. A big flat-bottomed kettle rested on one of the hotplates and a black cat on another. Freestanding cupboards and a huge pine dresser stood against the cream painted walls, and the floor was composed of uneven flagstones. Over the family-sized stripped-pine table, a vintage clothes airer suspended from the central beam was draped with tea-towels and hung with strings of onions and bunches of herbs. Children's pictures were pinned to the American-style fridge with magnets, and a small pair of red sandals lay where they had been kicked off, next to one of the chairs.

At the opposite end of the room stood a grandfather clock and the biggest sideboard Daniel had ever seen. In front of a smaller fireplace, on a rather threadbare square of carpet, stood three mismatched armchairs, a sofa and a coffee table weighed down with magazines.

Two windows looked out over the yard, one at the carpeted end of the room and the other over the old sink with its wooden draining board. The curtains were blue and white check, the china on display also blue and white, and the whole effect was effortlessly authentic.

Jenny filled an electric kettle and switched it on, taking two mugs from a shelf and a teapot from the dresser. Taz padded round sniffing interestedly, before lying down with a sigh on the cool flags under the table.

'So, this Taylor character. What does he do, exactly?' Daniel asked.

'He's one of the drivers.' She paused. 'Well, actually, having said that, he's kind of taken charge since Gavin's been in hospital.'

'And do you always let him speak to you like that?'

Jenny flushed slightly.

'I know it's feeble, but sometimes it's just easier to pretend I haven't heard. He's basically keeping the business going. I wish I could do it myself, but what with the livery yard, and the kids, and visiting Gavin, I just haven't got the time. I put up with his attitude because I don't think I could manage without him.'

'Do you really think he'd leave if you stood up to him?'

She shrugged. 'I don't know. You think I'm being weak, but, to be honest, it's only lately he's got so bad. I wonder if he thinks . . . well, that Gavin . . .'

'That he's not coming home?'

'Well, yes.'

'I assume he didn't behave like that with your husband?'

'I shouldn't think so.' Jenny poured hot water into the pot and began to stir it with a long-handled spoon. 'But it was Gavin's business, so I don't really know. Taylor's only been working for us for about eight months. He's from a local family that have lived round here for ever – as long as my family. His father owns the scrapyard next door to the garage. They've got a bit of a reputation. I tried to warn Gavin but he said Taylor was OK. Gavin isn't from round here,' she added, as if to excuse his misjudgement.

'How is your husband now? I mean, any change?'

Jenny bowed her head and turned away, busying herself with rummaging in a cupboard.

'No. No change. The hospital can't tell me if he'll ever regain consciousness. We just have to wait.'

'That's tough.' Daniel hesitated to question her any further but he was intrigued. 'So, are the police any further forward with what happened? Fred didn't seem to think they'd got much to go on.'

'No.' Jenny poured tea and then milk into the mugs. 'It's been over two months now, and they say they're still working on it, but if they've made any progress, they certainly haven't told me.'

Daniel accepted his tea gratefully. His last stop for refreshment was a distant memory.

'I know it must be hard for you, but can you bear to tell me what happened?' he asked, sitting at the big table and reaching for the packet of biscuits.

Jenny took a chair opposite him.

'Freddy Bowden says you used to be a policeman.'

'That's right.'

'Why did you stop?'

'I trod on some high-ranking toes over an internal matter and it all got a bit messy. Basically, they made it impossible for me to stay.'

'Do you mind? I mean, still?' Jenny was watching him closely. He shook his head.

'It's history now. You either move on or waste your life being bitter.' He felt a bit of a fraud making it sound so easy. God knows, it hadn't been – still wasn't, to be honest. But they weren't here to discuss his problems. 'So, your husband . . . Fred said something about poachers.'

'Yes, well, we don't know it was anything to do with poachers. Gavin just said he'd seen some lights across the fields when he was checking on the lorries, and he was going out to investigate. I didn't think much of it at first. I mean, he was always going off in the evenings. Sometimes he'd take a gun and shoot rabbits, sometimes he'd go looking for poachers. He had a bit of a thing about them. My Dad never bothered that much when he was here. "So what if they take a few rabbits or fish," he used to say. "There's plenty to go around."'

'There's one old guy the locals call Woodsmoke – you'll know why if you ever get downwind of him. Anyway, he's been around since I was a kid and he's never done any harm, but Gavin couldn't stand him. He was determined to keep him off the farm, though how he thought he'd do it I can't imagine. Woodsmoke could run rings round him in the woods if he felt like it. I think, deep down, Gavin knew that and it made him even madder.'

'Did Gavin take the gun the night he was attacked?'

'No. He said he was just going for a look round. Like I said, I didn't think twice about it, until it started to get late. He'd sometimes go down to the village for a pint before closing and get chatting to his mates, but when it got to past midnight, I did start to worry a bit. We're early risers – have to be – and we normally go to bed quite early, too.'

'Who were his mates, particularly?'

Jenny looked a little discomfited.

'I don't really know.'

'Did you never go to the pub with him?'

'Well, when we first met, of course, but it was never easy for us both to go out, with the kids. Then when Izzy came along . . . Isobel, my youngest,' she explained. 'When she was born, it became even more difficult. I don't mind, really. I'm usually tired by the end of the day, and I'm not really a pub sort of person.'

With a decade of experience behind him when it came to hearing what people weren't actually saying, Daniel drew from her words and body language an attempt to hide the hurt of a marriage gone a little stale.

When he didn't respond immediately, Jenny tried again.

'I could have gone with him, if I'd wanted to, but, like I said, I wasn't really bothered. And, anyway, men need their "man time", don't they? They don't always want their wives and kids hanging around.'

Daniel had his own views on that but he reverted to her original tale.

'So, when it got late, what happened then? What did you do?'

'I didn't know what to do. I'd tried calling him on his mobile, but the reception is very variable round here. There's lots of places on the farm where you can't get a signal at all, so I wasn't surprised that I couldn't get him. All I could do was wait. It's daft, but I kept wishing he'd taken the dog with him, though what Monty could have done I don't know. He wasn't exactly a guarding breed, just a soft old Labrador, but you never know – if someone threatened Gavin, he might have reacted. But that night he left him behind.'

'Did he usually take him?'

Jenny shrugged. 'Sometimes. Not always.'

Daniel glanced round the kitchen, but there was no dog's bed, no bowl or toys.

'So, where's the dog now?'

'We lost him. He, um . . . wandered off.'

'When?'

'A couple of weeks ago.'

'And . . . ?' Daniel waited.

'He, um . . .' Jenny looked at the ceiling and bit her lip to stop it quivering. 'I haven't told the kids this, but they found his body a couple of days later. It looked like he'd been in a fight. They didn't want me to see, but I insisted because I couldn't believe it was really him, and it was horrible!' Tears spilled over and ran down her cheeks, and she dragged a handkerchief from the pocket of her jeans.

'You said "they". Who found him?'

She mopped at her eyes and sniffed.

'Actually, it was Liam Sellyoak's groundsman that found him. Liam lives next door, at the manor, though he's not often there.'

'Liam Sellyoak the footballer?'

'That's right. Then Taylor went round to identify Monty before telling me. He brought the body home.' Her voice cracked and she covered her eyes with her hand. 'I still don't understand why it happened. I mean, he never normally strayed far and he wasn't a fighter. He was done – you know, neutered – so it wasn't as though he was out after a bitch on heat, or something. Anyway, I couldn't tell the kids. Not after Gavin and everything. It was just too much. I didn't want them having nightmares. I told them he'd been knocked down by a car. They were devastated. They still are.'

'They'll get over it, given time. Kids are tougher than you think.'

'I know. The trouble is they keep asking when we're going to have another dog – Harry, especially. He keeps on and on about getting a puppy, but I'm scared in case something happens to that, too. I feel like nothing's safe any more. I worry about the kids all the time, too.'

'That's only natural, considering what's happened, but it will get better. Trust me.'

'You're probably right.' She sniffed and wiped her eyes. 'Sorry. Have you got kids?'

'Just one. Drew. He's nine. He lives with his mother most of the time.'

'Do you see much of him?'

'Not as much as I'd like. Amanda and I are getting a divorce, and things are difficult at the moment.' Once again, Daniel steered the conversation back to the story of her husband's attack, and, with a tenuous control on her tears, Jenny recounted the manner in which his body had been found lying on the driveway.

'Sue – she's my stable manager – found him on her way in to work and called me. I thought he was dead. There was blood coming from his nose and one ear, and he was so cold. There was a frost on the ground, but the doctors say that although he was suffering from hypothermia, the cold might actually have saved his life, stopped him bleeding to death.'

'And the police haven't any idea what happened?'

'Not really. He still had his mobile phone and wallet, so it wasn't a mugging. He had head injuries, but there was no sign that he'd been hit by a car or anything. They did say they thought he'd been moved – something to do with the grit found in the wound – but who would do that?'

'It's certainly odd. And he hasn't said anything at all since it happened?'

She shook her head. 'He's been unconscious the whole time. It's awful. He just lies there so still, and I talk to him, about the kids and the business and such, but I don't know if he can even hear me.' She fell silent, staring at the tabletop, a crease between her brows. 'I feel so guilty.'

'What have you got to feel guilty about?'

She shrugged again.

'Nothing. Everything. Things I said, things I didn't say. That sounds stupid, but things could have been better, you know? We had a few problems, a few rows, and now I might not get the chance to try and put it right.'

'You know, it's normal to feel like that,' Daniel said. 'But you have to let it go. Nobody's life or relationship is perfect all the time.'

'I suppose so.' She sighed. 'And now I don't know what to do about Taylor.'

'What were you arguing about?'

'Oh, he wants me to get rid of one of the other drivers – says he's not pulling his weight and makes mistakes.'

'And you don't agree.'

'I don't know. It's true he has made a couple of mistakes lately, but he's worked for us for ages. He used to work on the farm with Colin. The trouble is, he's sixty-two, and Taylor says he's not up to the job and it's time he retired.'

'And what do you think?'

Jenny frowned.

'I think he's probably slowed down a bit lately, but he's a good steady worker and I trust him. He's the only one of the original crew left.' She looked across at Daniel. 'I've answered my own question, haven't I?'

'Sounds like it. I think you have to do what's right for you. Follow your instincts.'

'I know you're right, but sometimes it's really hard. Things have been going wrong lately. I'm losing stock and the figures aren't adding up properly.' She hesitated. 'I suppose you wouldn't . . . ? I mean, Fred said you'd help me out. Will you take over as manager for me?'

Daniel shook his head.

'No, I don't think that would be a good idea. Not yet, anyway. I'll just drive for you and get the lie of the land. Then if anything's going on, maybe I'll be able to see what it is.'

The grandfather clock across the room whirred and chimed the hour, prompting Jenny to look at her watch and jump to her feet.

'Oh my God! I'm supposed to be at the hospital because I've got to pick the kids up from Mum's by six, and I haven't shown you the cottage yet.'

'Well, if you give me directions, I'm sure I can find the cottage,' Daniel told her. 'In fact, I might even have seen it on my way here.'

'You could have. You can see it from the fork. It's been empty since George and Marian left, but I opened it all up yesterday and gave it a quick once-over with a duster,' Jenny said, gathering up mugs and biscuits. 'And there's milk and bread and bacon and stuff in the fridge . . .'

'It'll be fine,' he assured her. 'You go.'

Seen at closer quarters, the cottage Daniel was to stay in while he worked at Maidstone Farm was a typical Victorian red-brick worker's cottage, a fact borne out by the name 'Forester's Cottage', carved into a cement square above the green painted front door.

From the outside it looked a little grim, with dingy, pale green curtains at the windows and a border of lavender and weeds between the picket fence and the building. The narrow lane carried on past it, over a cattle grid and away into the trees.

Daniel regarded the cottage with equanimity. If anything, it was a stage more welcoming than the bedsit he'd called home for the past few months.

With Taz at his heels, he let himself in with what was probably the original key. No Yale locks here.

Inside, he was faced with a tiled narrow hallway and a steep flight of stairs, carpeted in a busy pattern of brown and amber, but the thing that immediately forced itself upon his senses was an almost overpowering reek of creosote. Two doors led off immediately to his left and right, and, wrinkling his nose, he turned left into what was the cottage's sitting room. At this point, however, his complacency suffered a check.

Inside the room, the stench of wood preservative was choking and he didn't have to look far for the reason. The sage-green three-piece suite, which had doubtless served its previous owners for many years, was now upended and piled in the centre of the carpet, along with the shattered remains of what had probably been a coffee table and the broken stand of a standard lamp, its fringed shade crowning the whole like a cherry on a cupcake.

A bookcase, whose previous position was outlined in a brighter patch of the yellowing wallpaper, had been tipped over and lay atop its erstwhile contents against the Hessian-covered underside of the sofa, and everything appeared to have been liberally doused in the pungent brown liquid. The accumulated fumes, in the closed room, made the air unbreathable.

Beside him, Taz sneezed, and he pushed the dog back into the hall and shut the door. Holding his breath, he opened the window as wide as it would go, although the situation would plainly improve little until the contaminated furniture was removed. He knew from experience how the smell of creosote lingered. Unless the floorboards were replaced, it would be many weeks, if not months, before the room was inhabitable once more.

Eyes watering, he returned to the hall where Taz greeted him as if he'd been gone for a week. Ruffling the dog's fur, he went through into the room on the opposite side of the hall. This proved to be a tiny dining room, with the remains of its table and chairs piled in the centre of the faded floral carpet like a ready-to-light bonfire. These, too, were soaked in wood preservative, and it occurred to Daniel to wonder why the vandals hadn't put a match to their handiwork. After all, with the creosote it would all have gone up like a torch, and the cottage, too. The dining room contained no other furniture apart from a dark oak dresser, which had, inevitably, been tipped over, depositing a quantity of leaf-patterned china on the floor.

As in the first room, Daniel opened the windows wide and shut the door on the stench, before going along the hallway to the kitchen, mentally bracing himself for what he might find.

It wasn't as bad as he feared. Someone had emptied the contents of all the cupboards and drawers on to the floor, where crockery and glass lay shattered on the stone flags, scattered with sliced bread, liberally dusted with flour, coffee powder and sugar, and swimming in pools of milk.

Cutlery was thrown down like some weird game of culinary jackstraws on top of the mess, and something that was probably ketchup had been thrown against one brightly papered wall, but the creosote, thankfully, was absent. Also, for some reason, the electrical appliances appeared to have been left largely undamaged. This, Daniel felt, must have some significance. Surely, amid such wholesale vandalism, it could not be by accident that the inviting glass doors and fragile electrical innards had been overlooked.

He filed this piece of information away for consideration later, his attention caught by the realization that the tomato sauce on the wall had been used to write a few crudely fashioned words. He stepped closer, his shoes crunching on the carnage underfoot, and read:

Fuck off home yore not wanted here.

'You don't say,' he muttered under his breath.

THREE

'I don't believe it! I was only here yesterday.' Jenny stood in the hallway of the cottage, a handkerchief held over her nose and mouth, staring at the mess that was the sitting room. Her children, recently collected from their grandmother, waited outside in the Land Rover, where they peered through the side windows, no doubt yearning to see what was going on in the cottage.

'It probably only took them a few minutes,' Daniel said. 'It could've been done any time.'

'But who would do something like this? And why? Was it kids, do you think?'

'I don't think so. Come and have a look at this.' Daniel led the way into the kitchen, where he'd cleared up the worst of the mess on the floor, shovelling everything into black bin bags and then using a mop to deal with the residue of the milk and foodstuffs, the smaller shards of glass and the china. He had, however, left the ketchup message scrawled across the wall.

'Oh, my God!' she said.

'Who knew I was coming?'

Jenny frowned.

'Well, I told Taylor, of course, and Mum. No one else. But having said that, I expect half the village knows by now. You know how word gets round. But I don't understand why anyone would do this. It doesn't make sense. Why should anyone care about you coming here? You're not the first new driver we've taken on lately. I mean, Derek has only been with us a few months.'

'Actually, something else happened earlier this afternoon.' Daniel hadn't mentioned his run-in with the two troublemakers from the village, but now he outlined what had happened.

Jenny looked concerned.

'A blue pick-up?'

'Yes. With wide wheels and enough spotlights to light Wembley Stadium. Do you know him?'

'Ricky Boyd. Taylor's younger brother. He's a waste of space.'

'I wouldn't disagree with you there. And the other one?'

'I don't know. It might have been Scott Selby. He's a mechanic at the garage. Crazy about cars but not too bright in the other departments.'

'Mm. That sounds like our boy. Can you think of any reason they wouldn't want me here?'

She shook her head. 'No. Although, come to think of it, Ricky did ask me if I'd got any driving work for him, a few days ago, when I stopped for petrol. I didn't take him seriously. I mean, he hasn't got an HGV licence or anything. If it *was* him, he probably doesn't need a reason. He's got a real attitude problem. You only have to look at him the wrong way and there's trouble. Do you think we should call the police?'

'It's up to you, but don't do it on my account,' Daniel told her. 'It'll probably be more trouble than it's worth, even if they have a good idea who did it, and I should imagine you could do without more stress. There's nothing here that can't be sorted.'

Jenny looked round at the mess and ran a hand through her fringe. She had dark circles under her eyes and looked worn out. Daniel was sorry to have added to her worries, but it had been unavoidable.

'I suppose they've been upstairs, too?' she said after a moment.

'Yeah, 'fraid so. No creosote, but the bedding needs washing and the mattresses have been slashed.' No need to tell her that the filthy sods had emptied their bladders over everything.

'Well, you can't stay here tonight,' she said decisively. 'The creo-sote fumes would make you ill. I don't know where they got their hands on it, but I've got a horrible feeling there might have been some stored in the shed from ages ago. I mean, we always used to use it for everything before it was banned. No one knew any better.'

'We're lucky it's only in these two downstairs rooms,' Daniel said. 'I had a look while I was waiting for you. It looks as though those boards have been laid on chipboard, and there's a stone floor underneath that, so I might be able to lift the lot and just throw them away; burn them – whatever. It would be the quickest way to get rid of the smell, if you don't mind.'

'No, I don't mind. I remember now. George put those floorboards down himself, must be about fifteen years ago. He was our general handyman around the farm until he retired a couple of years ago. Marian was always complaining that the stone floor was cold and uneven.'

'Was that when they left? When he retired?'

'No. They were here until just after Christmas. I was really surprised when they said they were going. I always thought they'd be carried out in a box – or at least George would. He loved this place. But maybe Marian put pressure on him. It is very isolated here, and they weren't getting any younger. They've gone to live a couple of miles away, in Lower Ditton, in a modern bungalow. I visited them once, but it's really depressing. I should think George hates it. He didn't seem very happy.'

'And the cottage has been empty since then? What were you going to do with it?'

Jenny shrugged. 'Gavin had some sort of plan for it, but I'm not sure exactly what.'

'OK. Well, I'm happy to have a go at the floor tomorrow, if you can manage one more day with a driver short,' Daniel suggested.

'Yes, that's no problem, but are you sure? I mean, it's very kind of you, but it seems a bit much to ask . . .'

'You didn't. I offered. Now is there somewhere in the village I can get a bed for the night. A pub or somewhere?'

'There is, but you can stay at the farmhouse. We've got heaps of space.'

'Better not. Preferential treatment and all that.'

'Does that matter? It's not exactly anyone's fault, and you are a friend of Freddy Bowden's.'

'Mm. Better keep that to ourselves, if you don't mind. Might put Taylor's back up, from what I hear, and I'll learn more if I'm just one of the crew.'

Jenny looked a little bit crestfallen. 'Oh, yes, I see. Well, you'll come to supper, anyway. It'd be nice to have a bit of adult company for a change, and no one need know.'

In the event, after a pleasant evening spent with Jenny and her young family, Daniel opted to drive back to the cottage, park up and sleep in the back of his car. To avoid argument, he didn't tell Jenny, but it was no great hardship. He'd done it many a time before and kept a pillow and sleeping bag in the vehicle in case of just such an eventuality.

Letting himself into the cottage, Daniel made a mug of black tea with one of a few teabags that he'd been able to salvage from the chaos in the kitchen. Even with all the windows open, the overpowering stench of the creosote wasn't noticeably better and his eyes smarted. Using a pair of rubber gloves, he gathered up the damp bedding from the upstairs rooms, stuffed it into the surprisingly modern washing machine, added powder he'd begged from Jenny and set it going, before taking his brew and returning to the car, where Taz waited.

Nothing disturbed the peace of the woodland night except the odd fox call when Daniel took Taz for a nocturnal ramble before taking to his sleeping bag. Once there, he lay awake for a while, listening to a conversation between two owls in neighbouring trees and pondering the possible implications of the day's events.

The state of the cottage still puzzled him; not so much what *had* been done as what hadn't. He'd seen many places trashed in his police career, and the damage was often far more extreme than had been inflicted at Forester's. To have gone to the lengths they had and yet not smashed the windows or the electrical goods argued that, rather than being random, the vandalism had been carried out to a plan.

Surely the most effective way to dissuade him from staying would have been to burn the cottage down, and it would have been quicker and easier, too.

It was as though the fabric of the house had been intentionally left untouched. Did someone want it for themselves? He'd asked Jenny, but she said no one had approached her about it. And if that *was* the case, then the vandals had been a bit short-sighted when they started sloshing creosote around.

With sleep elusive, his thoughts turned to Jenny's family.

The older children, twelve-year-old Lucy and eight-year-old Harry, had the same colouring as their mother, Lucy having a blue-eyed, round-faced prettiness that might or might not mature into good looks, and Harry an expression of solemn and wide-eyed innocence that Daniel soon began to suspect was wholly misleading. It was sad to think that although Harry was just a year younger than his own son, Drew, both of them already bore the scars of life.

The youngest of the family, three-year-old Isobel, who was known as Izzy, was dark-haired and dark-eyed, apparently taking after her absent father, a fact that Jenny confirmed when she came downstairs after putting the children to bed.

'She's going to be like Gavin: adventurous and independent. She's quite a little madam already. Far more confident than Lucy was at that age. Into everything.'

'Is Gavin a sportsman?'

'He was when he was younger. Used to race motorbikes – speedway, down at Poole – and tried his hand at microlight flying and paragliding.'

'A bit of a thrill seeker,' Daniel observed.

'Before I met him. He had to give it up, though. Back trouble. His chiropractor told him if he didn't slow down, he'd end up crippled.'

'That must have been frustrating for him.'

'It was.'

'So how did he amuse himself round here? Apart from chasing poachers, I mean.'

'Well, like I said, he used to take the gun out after rabbits, or go dog racing with his mates, but I think he does get bored sometimes,' Jenny said, starting to clear the table. 'He says he isn't, but I'm not sure. He can be very short-tempered at times.'

'The kids miss him, don't they?' Daniel had picked that up clearly. He stood up and began to help gather up the dirty dishes.

'Yes. He's a good father – to all of them, not just Izzy. It's really hard on Harry and Lucy having this happen again. After Colin, I mean. It's made them very clingy. And I keep thinking . . .' She paused, her voice breaking. 'The thing is, the doctors have warned me that when Gavin comes round, if he does, he mightn't be the same. They don't know what damage may have been done.' She fished in her pocket for a handkerchief and blew her nose. 'That's the worst part – the waiting and the not knowing.'

Daniel turned over with difficulty in his sleeping bag and, with his foot, nudged Taz, who was snoring. The dog stretched and sighed before settling back against Daniel's legs once again. Moments later, the heavy breathing had resumed.

Rising early the next morning, Daniel took Taz for his morning constitutional and then drove to a farm shop café he'd noticed the day before, on the main road that ran through the neighbouring village of Lower Ditton. Tucking into a full English breakfast with a large latte at his elbow, he was able to contemplate his day's labours with fortitude, if not enthusiasm.

Out in the car, Taz gazed soulfully at the door through which Daniel had disappeared into the shop, unhappy at being excluded even though he had already been fed, and towards the end of his meal, Daniel folded half a bread roll and a rasher of bacon into a paper napkin and slid it into the pocket of his jacket to appease the dog.

Half an hour later, Daniel was back at Forester's and hard at work. An early morning foray into the shed behind the cottage had turned up a selection of tools and the discovery that someone had been there before him. The thin panels of the door had been newly splintered and the padlock that had secured it hung drunkenly on its hasp, the whole set-up entirely inadequate to keep any but the most ineffectual thief at bay.

What, if anything, they had taken, it was impossible to say, but perfectly useful tools had been left behind, so it seemed probable that someone had broken in just to see what was stored behind the locked door.

What Daniel did find, somewhat surprisingly, were two or three black bin bags absolutely bulging with empty beer bottles and cans. Had the previous occupants been heavy drinkers? From Jenny's description of them it seemed unlikely. Daniel closed the door on them and took his tools into the cottage to start work.

At around eleven o'clock, with a muzzy headache and feeling slightly sick from the creosote fumes, he made himself a cup of coffee and took it into the front garden to get some fresh air.

Taz, who had been sitting for the most part in the open back of the car, fawned round him and begged for a biscuit from a packet Daniel had bought in the village shop.

Sitting on a bench seat next to the porch, Daniel leaned against the brickwork and half closed his eyes, enjoying the warmth of the sun, which, near its zenith, found its way through the trees along the path forged by the road.

His relaxed state was rudely interrupted by Taz who suddenly scrambled to his feet and set up a furious barking, his hackles rising in a tide over his shoulders and along his back. His attention was fixed firmly on the woods on the other side of the lane.

Daniel sat up, putting a hand in Taz's collar to keep him close, and stared intently at the tree line.

Nothing. No movement and nothing that appeared out of place. A word quietened the dog to a low, continuous growl, but his gaze remained focused on the woodland and he strained against his collar. Daniel wondered if Taz could see or hear something that his own limited senses failed to, and considered letting him go to investigate.

He decided against it. After all, he had no real reason to believe that whoever was there was up to no good, and to be cornered by a large German shepherd was a terrifying experience.

The woodland was a mixture of deciduous and conifer trees, and there were probably large quantities of deer, foxes and badgers in its depths, but Daniel discounted these. He knew Taz, and the dog wouldn't have reacted in that way just for wildlife.

Putting his mug down on the doorstep, and still with a firm hold on Taz's collar, he walked down the garden path, through the open picket gateway and across the narrow tarmac lane to the edge of the wood. Here, a brief search turned up nothing to see, but Taz was quite clearly excited by what he could smell, concentrating his interest on the area beside a large oak, where closer inspection found a slight indentation in the leaf mould and a dark stain where dry leaves had been disturbed to reveal the damper layer beneath.

So someone *had* been there, but they were doubtless well on their way now. Had it been the vandals from yesterday, returning to see whether they had achieved their object?

If so, they would have been disappointed, Daniel reflected with grim satisfaction.

'Good lad,' he said, ruffling the dog's fur. He'd never have found the place without Taz. He took a soft furry toy from his pocket and tossed it to the shepherd. The squeak had long gone, but Taz enjoyed the sensation of mouthing it and it was his reward for a job well done.

*   *   *

Ripping out the floor in the old cottage took far longer than Daniel had anticipated, and by the time he'd piled all the contaminated floorboards and chipboard outside, along with the smashed furniture, the afternoon was well advanced.

Although it was tempting simply to put a match to the whole pile where it sat, the dry conditions and the proximity of the wood-land made that course of action nothing short of stupid. The creosote-soaked material was highly flammable and he lit only a small fire, painstakingly adding a little at a time and keeping a close eye on it until he'd burned it all.

By the end of the afternoon, he was bone-weary and his eyes were smarting and red-rimmed from a combination of fumes and smoke. However, the cottage was clean, and as long as he left the windows open for a few days, he felt it was safe to move in. There was hot water aplenty, courtesy of a fairly modern boiler, and Daniel ran a bath and sank into it with the intention of soaking for half an hour or so.

This pleasant plan was foiled after a scant ten minutes when the sound of a vehicle pulling to a halt outside heralded the arrival of Jenny's Land Rover, pulling a trailer piled high with an assortment of items which included, amongst other things, a small leather armchair, a mattress and a coffee table. Daniel greeted her from an upstairs window with a towel wrapped round his waist, the irritation at having his bath interrupted instantly banished by gratitude.

Dressing hastily in a clean pair of jeans and a T-shirt, he helped her unload the trailer, but she turned down his offer of coffee or tea, saying she was due at the hospital again.

'Come over for supper again?' she suggested.

'But I've got food in now.'

'You can't feel much like cooking after doing all this,' she said, looking round at the lounge with its one chair sitting incongruously on the newly exposed flagstones. 'You must be exhausted.'

Daniel couldn't deny that he was tired. He merely shrugged and pursed his lips.

'Well, anyway. The offer's there. It's only shepherd's pie, but there's plenty of it, and I thought you might like to look round the stables afterwards. Come and meet the horses.'

Daniel smiled.

'I would. Shall I come about seven?'

'Fine.' Jenny went back out to the Land Rover. Settling in the driving seat, she looked at him through the open window. 'Are you going to be all right here? I mean, it's awfully isolated. I'd hate it on my own.'

'I'm not on my own, I've got Taz,' he pointed out. 'But it wouldn't bother me, anyway. I'm used to it.'

'Don't you have any family? Brothers and sisters, I mean. And what about your parents? Where do they live?'

'Two brothers and a sister. Simon and Mark work in London. Penny lives just down the road from Mum in Dorset, and I haven't seen my father since I was eight.'

'Sorry. Am I being nosy?'

'It's all right.'

'No, it isn't. I'm dreadful. I'll see you later. Bye.' She turned the Land Rover and trailer in front of the cottage with the ease of long practice and, with a wave to Daniel, disappeared down the lane on her way to visit her husband.

FOUR

At a quarter past four the following afternoon, Daniel switched off the engine of the Iveco truck he'd been driving since eight o'clock that morning and leaned back wearily in his seat. It was not that the job differed so very greatly from the one he had been doing in Devon, but the area and the customers were unfamiliar and, in spite of the lorry's satnav, there had been one or two drops that had given him problems. Even so, he had finished his allotted schedule ahead of time, which had to be a good thing.

None of the other five drivers was back as yet and, unsure of the protocol at Summer Haulage, Daniel set about finding a hose and washing his truck down. As the weather had been dry for some days, it wasn't strictly necessary, but in Fred Bowden's depot the lorries were always kept spotless and it had become habit with Daniel, too.

This done, he checked his paperwork, posted it through the office door and let himself into the converted cowshed that now did duty as the drivers' base, with lockers, a shower room and toilet, and a sitting area known as the lounge, with microwave and facilities to make hot drinks.

There he found the television broadcasting to an empty room, presumably left on by someone who had come back at lunchtime. Daniel switched it off and, in the absence of anything else to do, made himself a cup of coffee and settled down to read the local free advertiser, the front page of which featured pictures of a protest rally against a proposed wind farm, followed on page two with a plea for information about a spate of disappearances of family pets in the area and an article bewailing the closure of yet another rural post office.

Shortly after five, he heard footsteps and voices outside, and the door opened to admit two of his fellow drivers. From the introductions earlier that day, he knew that the younger of the two, who was of medium height and build with a shaved head and tattoos on his forearms, was Derek Edwards, known to all and sundry as Dek. He led the way into the room, a half-spent cigarette drooping from his lower lip, and stopped just inside, putting a hand up to halt the man behind, who would have passed him.

'Well, well, if it isn't the new boy,' he observed. 'Putting us all to shame with his early finish and his squeaky clean truck. What do you think, Macca? D'you think he's after some brownie points with the boss?'

His companion grunted and pushed past on his way to the kitchen area. Even in the limited time he'd been around the guy, Daniel had gained the impression that Terry 'Macca' MacAlister was a man of few words. Mind you, he had no need for tough words to bolster his image. Only around five feet eight inches tall, he had a powerful physique, unnaturally bronzed skin and a short fuzz of blonde hair on his scalp. His flattened nose and one cauliflower ear bore witness to an earlier career in boxing, and now, in his early forties, he spent much of his spare time coaching the local youth, according to Jenny.

Edwards sauntered closer to Daniel.

'You're wasting your time if you're trying to impress Taylor,' he warned, in a voice that carried an indeterminate northern accent. 'Or perhaps it's the little lady you're trying to win over, is that it?'

Daniel, who had returned his attention to the newspaper after seeing who had come in, continued to ignore him.

'Is it?' Edwards repeated loudly, and his aggressive stance brought Taz out from under the coffee table, grumbling under his breath.

'I'm sorry, were you talking to me?' Daniel asked pleasantly.

The other man bristled, looking to his companion for support, but Macca was helping himself to a cup of tea and plainly not interested, so Edwards contented himself with making a short, derisive hissing noise and switching the television on once again on his way to the lockers.

Full of hot air, Daniel thought to himself, but a troublemaker nonetheless.

The next five minutes brought Taylor Boyd himself, closely followed by the youngest member of the team – an unprepossessing twenty-one-year-old who had yet to grow into his six-foot frame. His light brown hair was also shaved short, perhaps in an attempt to conform with the tougher element of the Summer Haulage crew, but, with a thin, bony face and rather weak blue eyes, all it did was emphasize his youth. Dean Stevens, who Edwards invariably referred to as Deano, was a deeply insecure and unhappy young man, desperate to fit in with his older colleagues. In Daniel's opinion, he would do far better to forge a path of his own, but it would be pointless to tell him that.

'You didn't give the new boy enough work to do,' Edwards remarked, taking up a position on the opposite sofa to Daniel. 'He was sitting here taking it easy when we got back.'

'No sense giving him too much for the first couple of days,' Boyd observed. 'Got to find his way around. Everything OK?' he added to Daniel. 'Paperwork done?'

'It's in the office.'

'Good. I wish bloody Reg was as on the ball. Where the hell's the old duffer got to?'

'Traffic, maybe,' Daniel suggested. On first meeting, Reg had seemed a likeable enough sort, and he remembered Jenny's conviction that Boyd wanted rid of him.

'I gave him an easy round, too,' Boyd grumbled on. 'I'll have a tea, Deano – when you've finished faffing about with that kettle.'

After Daniel's tour of the livery yard the previous evening, Jenny had taken him to see her pride and joy, a purebred American Quarter Horse mare with a foal at foot.

'Quarter Horse?' It was a new breed to Daniel.

'They were originally bred as stock horses to work cattle, and the cowboys would race them on their days off, up and down the main street of their local town. Because of the work they did, they were well muscled and very fast over short distances – specifically a quarter of a mile, hence the name – and eventually what started as a type of horse was developed into a breed. The Quarter Horse is actually faster over its own distance than a thoroughbred.'

'I can see what you mean by well muscled,' Daniel said. 'Even the foal looks like a bodybuilder! And the other one, is he a Quarter Horse, too?'

The mare and foal were wandering over now, followed by a smallish dark-chestnut gelding with a kindly eye.

'Yes, that's Piper. He and I go way back. It was him that got me started on Quarter Horses. He's fifteen now and getting a bit fat and lazy because I don't get time to ride him at the moment. Sue takes him out for me occasionally, but she's got her own horse to exercise.'

'I could take him out for you,' Daniel suggested, stroking Piper's velvety muzzle over the fence. 'I'd love to if you thought I could manage him. I used to ride a fair bit as a kid, and I imagine he's well up to my weight.'

'Lord, yes! He's as strong as an ox.' Jenny turned to look at Daniel. 'Do you mean it? And I'd have no worries about you managing him – he's pretty easy. Actually, that'd be brilliant. Take him out after work sometime and see how you get on.'

With this invitation in mind and the prospect of a lovely warm evening ahead of him, Daniel waited until his fellow drivers had gone home and then made his way through the farmyard and on down to the stables. Jenny had promised that Piper would be in one of the spare stables waiting for him if he decided to ride, and, sure enough, he was, contentedly munching sweet-smelling hay from a haynet.

Perched on the half-door of the adjacent empty stable was a large American stock saddle, familiar to Daniel from the endless Westerns of his youth, and his mouth curved into a slow smile. He'd always fancied trying Western riding.

'Want any help?' a voice enquired, and he turned to see a wiry, tanned, blonde-haired woman who looked to be in her late thirties, dressed in navy jodhpurs and a pale pink T-shirt. 'Hi, I'm Sue. Jenny told me you might drop by to try Piper.'

'Hi. Yes, I might need a hand. I've never put a cowboy saddle on before and the bridle looks different.'

'That's a bosal – a kind of bitless bridle. It just slips over his nose.' Sue lifted the collection of rope and leather off its hook and went into the stable, pushing Piper backwards with one lean brown hand on his chest. 'The saddle is easy enough; saddle pad, blanket and then saddle on top. The cinch does up a little like a necktie. I'll show you.'

Daniel watched as she put the bridle on and positioned the thick saddle pad and striped blanket on the horse's back, then, at her bidding, went to fetch the saddle.

'Wow, that's heavy!' he said as he swung it into position on Piper's back.

'It is heavy, but the weight is spread over a wider area, so it's actually more comfortable for the horse,' Sue explained. 'Remember, these were developed by people who rode all day long and they had to be strong enough to hold a roped steer.'

She showed him how to tighten the short cinch or girth with the thick rawhide strap that attached it to the saddle, then slapped Piper on the neck and handed the long, split reins to Daniel.

'All yours. Have fun. If you get lost, just let him have his head and he'll bring you home. He knows where his tea is.'

Piper stood like a rock as Daniel stepped into the leather stirrup and swung into the suede seat of the saddle.

'He's been well trained, so keep your movements light. Reins in one hand and lay them against his neck to turn. You can stop him by just putting a hand on his withers if you want, and don't kick him in the ribs or he'll take off like a bat out of hell and leave you sitting in the dirt! Also, if you get off and trail the reins, he'll stand still until you come back to him.'

'Right-oh, thanks.' Daniel's head whirled with all the instructions, but, keeping his touch light, managed to set off without incident. Moments later, he had left the yard with a wave to Sue and was following a grass track uphill between two fields towards a beech hanger near the ridge.

Once Daniel had got used to him, Piper was a dream to ride. The saddle was like an armchair, and the long stirrup length suited him well. When he found a stretch of inviting turf, Daniel took a handful of mane and then applied his legs firmly to the animal's sides, to test Sue's claim about his acceleration. He seemed such a calm horse; it was difficult to imagine him leaping swiftly into action.

She hadn't exaggerated. As soon as he felt the pressure, Piper bunched his muscles and shot away with a thrust like a drag racer. There was no warning – no apparent stage of speeding up. He was just suddenly running, and Daniel knew that if he hadn't been prepared, he'd certainly have been ignominiously dumped on the grass.

Leaning forward a little, he let the horse run, with Taz stretching to keep up at his side, until he came to the beech trees and roots criss-crossed the path underfoot. The lightest pressure brought Piper back to hand, and Daniel relaxed and began to enjoy himself immensely.

He'd ridden for about half an hour, and was reluctantly thinking that it was time he made his way back, when he became aware of the sound of human activity some way ahead and to his left.

He reined Piper in and sat still to listen, but for a moment all he could hear was the wind through the trees and the creaking of the saddle as the horse's sides moved with his breathing. Then, just as he thought he'd been mistaken, it came again: a faint clanking sound, as of metal being thrown against metal.

Jenny had given him the impression there was nothing in this area except hayfields and a couple of empty barns, and Daniel's curiosity was aroused. Telling the dog to stay close, he edged Piper forward. After about fifty yards or so, they topped a shallow rise and could see the brighter daylight of an open stretch of land a little way ahead.

Keeping to the soft leaf mould at the side of the pathway, he rode closer until he could see a tumbledown shed at the edge of the field and someone moving about in front of it. A familiar dark-blue van stood to one side, its rear doors open, and as he approached, two men emerged from the shed carrying something between them. Their burden was clearly heavy, and halfway to the van one of the men lost his grip and dropped it, to the accompaniment of much foul language from his companion.

'Do you want a hand?' Daniel offered, riding out of the trees.

There was quite a wind over the ridge, singing through the leaves of the beech trees, and it was clear from their reactions that neither of the men had heard his approach. As they whipped round, Daniel saw Taylor Boyd and his younger brother, Ricky – he of the blue pick-up and threatening behaviour. Neither looked particularly overjoyed to see him.

'I wondered if you wanted some help?' he said again.

Taylor recovered first.

'No, you're all right,' he said. 'We can manage.'

Daniel rode closer. 'It looks pretty heavy.'

The two men were obviously wishing him gone, and, perversely, that made him quite keen to stay. He gestured at the sizeable length of smooth, painted steel at their feet. It looked like part of some sort of farm machinery. 'So, what is that?'

'Mind your own fucking business!' Ricky flared up, but his brother told him to shut up.

'Just some scrap metal Mrs Summers wanted cleared away. It's only rusting away up here now no one's using it.'

Daniel nodded his approval.

'I expect she'll get a nice little bit for that – the price of scrap being what it is,' he said. 'Handy, your family being in the trade.'

Taylor's eyes narrowed as if he was unsure whether Daniel's remark was as ingenuous as it sounded. He apparently decided to take it at face value.

'We're all pulling together to help while the boss is in hospital. That's the kind of community it is,' he said smoothly.

'That's nice. Oh, well, if you're sure there's nothing I can do, I'll be on my way,' Daniel said, turning Piper away.

He rode until the gloom of the wood and the slope of the land made it impossible for the brothers to see him, then cut along the side of the hill and turned back up towards the shed from a different angle.

Still some way off, he reined in and stepped down from the saddle in true Western style using the stirrup, à la John Wayne. Unwilling to test Piper's much-vaunted obedience any further at this sensitive moment, he tied the long split reins to a small tree, which the horse immediately set about stripping of foliage. Using a sharp whisper, he told Taz to stay, then made his way forward, moving silently from tree to tree, his eyes on the pair by the van.

That they had been having a humdinger of an argument was plain to see, and Daniel felt it was a fair bet that he was the cause. Taking advantage of the brothers disappearing into the shed once more, he moved still closer, until he was barely twenty feet away from the van, and hunkered down under cover of a bramble bush and a decaying tree stump.

Moments later, Ricky came out again, carrying an armful of newish-looking angle-iron fence posts, followed by Taylor dragging a rusty metal roller, which squeaked in protest as it turned.

Ricky said something over his shoulder that was lost on the wind as far as Daniel was concerned, but he heard Taylor's reply.

'Well, that was bloody stupid, to start with! And what's more, it didn't work, did it?'

'That wasn't my fault,' his younger brother protested petulantly, throwing his bundle of metal into the van. 'At least I did *something*. And I'll tell you what I think—'

'I don't care what you think! You don't make the decisions; I do. And what's all the panic for? He's just a driver, that's all. Temporary. He'll probably be gone soon.'

'But he's in the house.'

'For now.'

'And anyway, I don't trust him; he's got a kind of look.'

'A look?' Taylor sounded amused. 'You're just hacked off cos he wasn't scared of you.' He turned to face the younger man. 'Listen, when the time comes – if he makes trouble, I'll take care of him. Until then, just lay off. OK?'

Ricky made a face and nodded reluctantly.

'Good. Now, give me a hand getting this bloody thing in or we'll be here all night, and I need to see a man about a very expensive dog.'

Daniel mulled over what he'd heard for much of the ride back, but he couldn't make much sense of it. Ricky's words confirmed that it wasn't so much him personally but his occupation of Forester's Cottage that was an issue, but they left him no nearer to knowing why. His brother's statement that if he made waves he would be taken care of was very interesting, and all the more so because of the calm assurance with which it was made. Taylor Boyd was definitely a man to keep an eye on.

Back in the yard, he stripped the tack off Piper and washed the sweat from his coat, giving a glowing report of his ride to Sue, who appeared as he was turning the horse out in the paddock.

'He's a cracker, isn't he?' she agreed, coming to stand beside Daniel as he leaned on the paddock fence, watching Piper roll in the dust.

'What time do you finish?' he asked, looking at his watch. It was half past seven.

'When everything's done. Why? Were you going to ask me out?' she quizzed with a sideways look of amusement.

'Well, no – I was just curious. It must be a long day for you.'

'It is, but I don't mind. I love the horses. You don't do this job if you're a nine-to-five sort. Besides, I've known Jenny for ever – we went to school together – and she really needs the support right now.'

'You're not wrong there. Actually – do you fancy getting a bite to eat?' Daniel asked.

'No, really. You don't have to. I was only teasing.'

'I know. But why not? I've got nothing much at the cottage. Of course, you've probably got family waiting for you. Stupid of me . . .'

'Just my dad, and he expects me when he sees me.' She tilted her head to one side with a smile. 'OK. Thanks. Why not?'

On Sue's recommendation, they chose The Fox and Duck for their meal. The Crown was OK, she told him, but trying too hard to be a contemporary eatery. The Fox had good home-cooked food at sensible prices, she said. It was the one the real locals used.

The first person Daniel saw, as he ducked through the low doorway, was none other than Taylor Boyd, standing at the bar with Dek Edwards.

'Whelan.' Boyd nodded curtly in Daniel's direction, then caught sight of his companion. 'Hi, Sue. All right?'

'Fine,' she replied briefly, her cheeks flushing with colour. She slipped her hand through Daniel's arm.

Lounging against the bar, Edwards leered in her direction. 'All right, Sue? You don't waste any time, do you? What's the new boy got that I haven't?'

'Manners, for a start,' she retorted, then turned to Daniel. 'Shall we go through to the other bar?'

'If you like.'

'I do.'

'I take it there's a bit of history between you and Boyd,' Daniel said as the door swung to behind them.

'What makes you say that?'

'Your body language. You seemed very keen to show him that you were with me.'

'Yeah, well, I was stupid enough to go out with him once, and once was all it took. God, I must have been desperate! Talk about an ego. Trouble is, he acts as if we're mates now, and we're so not. I don't even like him!'

'And what about Dek? What's the story there?'

'Him? No story. He's just a low-life. He's got the hots for Taylor's sister, from what I've heard. Round there at every opportunity, drooling over her like some lovesick tomcat. I'd almost feel sorry for the girl if she wasn't such a poisonous slut.'

'Wow! Don't hold back on my account,' Daniel told her.

'Sorry.' Sue had the grace to look a little sheepish. 'We have history.'

Daniel let the subject drop and she said no more about it, but she kept an eye on the door to the public bar all through the meal, leaving him to wonder whether she was dreading Boyd following or hoping he would. Daniel began to suspect that he'd been used, but he couldn't complain, for, in a way, that was just what he was doing, too.

FIVE

As a social occasion, the meal with Sue Devlin was time enjoyably spent; as a fact-finding mission, it was perhaps less worthwhile.

Gently probing, Daniel formed the impression that she didn't know Gavin Summers particularly well. He had no interest in the horses and rarely visited the stables unless it was in search of Jenny, she said, and this in itself obviously put him low in her estimation. The little information she did volunteer confirmed the notion Daniel already had of a marriage, if not in crisis, then at the very least becoming stale. He gained the impression that Sue wasn't altogether unhappy about that fact.

What also became clear was the affection that had been felt locally for Jenny's first husband, Colin Barton, killed in a tragic farming accident. This wasn't especially surprising, as Great Ditton was a close-knit community and his family had apparently been part of it for generations. As an incomer, Gavin was immediately at a disadvantage, and Daniel found himself feeling sympathy for the man.

Not entirely trusting Sue's apparent attitude towards Taylor Boyd, Daniel trod carefully in seeking information about him, merely observing that he appeared to have practically taken over the running of the haulage business in Gavin's absence and that this must be a relief to Jenny.

'Relief's not the word I would use.'

'What d'you mean?' Daniel asked, taking a sip of his after-dinner coffee.

'Well, the thing is, I don't think she trusts him a hundred per cent. Gavin took him on, see; she never would have. The family's too well known around here.'

'Well known for what?'

'Well, you know – they've got a bit of a reputation.'

'They own the garage, don't they?'

'Yeah, and the scrapyard – or salvage yard, as they like to call it. And there's some as say that not all the scrap that goes through there *is* scrap, if you know what I mean.'

Daniel did. It was a countrywide problem. With the price of raw metal being what it was, anything metallic that wasn't tied down – and some that was – went walkabout of a dark night. Lead off the church roof, copper piping, metal railings and even manhole covers were all considered fair game by the thieves, and farmers were bearing the brunt of the problem, losing oil and diesel reserves, as well as tractors and other machinery. His suspicions of that afternoon were confirmed.

'She doesn't suspect him of stealing from her, does she?' He injected shock into his tone.

'Oh, no! I mean, I shouldn't think so,' Sue said. 'It's just . . . anyone round here would be a little bit cautious where the Boyds are concerned. But if she thought he was actually stealing . . . I mean, she'd fire him, wouldn't she?'

'I suppose she would, if she had proof,' Daniel agreed. 'But you have to be a bit careful about firing people without due cause these days, I imagine. I mean, they'll have you in court at the drop of a hat.'

'Mm, and he'd be right up for that, without a doubt.'

Daniel was puzzled.

'If that's your opinion of him, what made you go out with him?'

She shrugged. 'I dunno. It was just a one-off. I thought it might be a laugh. It wasn't ever going to be serious, was it? But, I mean, he's not bad-looking and he can be quite a charmer when he wants.'

'The allure of a bad boy,' Daniel mused. 'So, what's his interest in dogs? Sorry, I overheard something and my ears always prick up when dogs are mentioned.' The phrase he'd heard Boyd use earlier that evening had lodged in the back of his ex-copper's mind, and although 'to see a man about a dog' was a common enough euphemism, the way he'd used it had seemed to imply a greater meaning. Sometimes the simplest explanation was the right one, but not, it seemed, in this case, because Sue looked genuinely baffled.

'*Dogs*? No. I mean, they've got a couple of Rottweilers at the yard, but they're more guard dogs than pets.'

'Oh, perhaps they were talking about dog racing or something,' Daniel said dismissively. Jenny had mentioned that it was one of her husband's hobbies.

'Yeah, maybe.' Sue didn't sound particularly interested. 'So, I gather someone left a welcome for you at the cottage . . . Trashed it pretty badly, by all accounts.'

'Ah, you've heard about that, then?'

'I told you, it's a small village. Everybody knows everything.'

'Including who did it?'

'I don't know about that. Most people are saying it must have been kids. There's not a lot for them to do round here of an evening or weekend. They hang around the rec usually. It wouldn't be surprising if they got up to a bit of mischief, and everyone knew that Forester's was standing empty.'

'It looked like someone might have been up there before.' Daniel told her about the beer bottles and cans. 'Maybe if they've been hanging out there, they might have been annoyed that I was moving in.'

Sue pursed her lips. 'S'pose so. Never heard tell of anyone up there. It's a bit remote.'

'Oh, well, Taz'll keep anyone away now,' Daniel said.

In due course, he paid the bill. After exchanging pecks on the cheek, they went their separate ways, Sue on foot, explaining that she only lived a few houses away from the pub, and Daniel returning to his car and the waiting dog.

As he entered the dark alleyway that led from the road to the pub car park, a deeper shadow detached itself from the wall of the building and stepped into his path.

Daniel's heart rate stepped up a notch.

'Evening, Boyd. Were you looking for me?'

He sensed a momentary hesitation from the other man and guessed he'd wrong-footed him.

'Just a word, Whelan. That's all.'

Daniel kept walking, unhurriedly but without altering his course, and Boyd gave way and stepped aside. In the lamp-lit car park, even though he was aware that Boyd was following, Daniel walked across to his car before turning round.

'Now? Can't it wait until the morning?'

'It could, but we're both here now, so why wait, eh?'

'All right.'

In the car, Taz was barking at Boyd, his muzzle scraping the glass and affording an impressive view of his teeth. Daniel quietened him with a sharp command.

'Big dog like that must cost a lot to feed,' Boyd observed. 'You interested in making a bit more money?'

Daniel played the innocent.

'What? Overtime, you mean?'

Boyd shrugged. 'In a manner of speaking. Only you'd be working for me.'

'Doing what?'

'A bit of driving, amongst other things, maybe.'

'Does Mrs Summers know about this?'

'It's nothing to do with her. Call it a bit of private enterprise, if you like. No harm done to anyone and a little extra cash in your pocket. What do you say?'

Daniel could see the gleam of Boyd's eyes in the muted light. He was watching intently, as much for Daniel's reaction as for his answer, he guessed. He deliberately kept his tone non-committal.

'I'll have to think about it. Let you know in a day or two.'

'All right, but don't take too long. And this is just between you and me, right? No need to mention our little conversation to anyone else. If I find that some little bird has been tweeting where it shouldn't . . .'

Daniel ignored the threat.

'I'll let you know,' he repeated, and got into the car.

After work the following day, with another fine evening in prospect, Daniel again found himself heading for the stables. This time he had to catch Piper from the field, and as he led him into the yard, he saw Jenny there, talking to Sue.

'Piper won't know what's hit him,' she remarked, coming over as he brushed the horse's chestnut coat to a sheen. 'Going out twice in two days.'

'You don't mind? It just seemed like such a lovely evening.'

'Of course I don't mind. I wish I could come with you.'

'Well, why don't you?'

'Because I've got three hungry children waiting for their tea. But I will one day. I just need to plan ahead. Where did you go yesterday?'

'Up the track to the beech hanger and along the ridge,' Daniel told her. He'd been debating whether to tell her of his encounter with the Boyd brothers, and now he made a snap decision. 'I saw Taylor and his brother on the other side of the wood.'

'Did you?' She frowned. 'What were they doing up there?'

'Loading some old farm machinery into their van. They gave me the impression you knew about it.'

'No, I didn't. Well, I did ask Taylor to shift some scrap for me a couple of months ago – some galvanized iron sheets from an old barn that collapsed last winter and a rusty plough from the days of horsepower – but I assumed he'd done that ages ago.'

'Mm, well, I think he may have interpreted your request as a licence to help himself,' Daniel observed, moving up to Piper's head to brush his silky forelock. He described what he'd seen.

'Oh dear, I suppose I'd better have a word with him,' Jenny said, looking as though it was a task she didn't relish.

'Actually, it might be better if you didn't, cos he'll know where the information came from, and just for now I'd rather he didn't see me as taking sides.'

'That sounds a bit serious. Do you think he's up to something?'

'Not necessarily. As far as I've seen, he's not doing too bad a job running the business – apart from having it in for Reg, as you suggested.'

'Poor old Reg. Do you think he *is* getting too old for the job?' Jenny asked.

'Well, he's always last back and Boyd makes a big fuss about him being slow, but since he has on average two more drops than the rest of us, that's not surprising, is it?'

'Wait,' Jenny caught his arm. 'He has more drops?'

'Yes. Almost always. And if not that, then he has to drive significantly further between them than we do. I asked him. He doesn't get on with the others very well, so he's never thought to ask them about their routes. He wasn't too happy when he found out.'

'But that's not fair!' Jenny exclaimed. 'Did he ask Taylor about it?'

'Yes, but he basically said Reg was talking crap and that if he wasn't happy with his job he knew what he could do.'

'So I was right.'

'Looks like it.'

'When was this? Why hasn't Reg come to me?'

'This afternoon. And I think he thinks you've got enough to deal with.'

'But why has Taylor got it in for Reg?'

Daniel shrugged. 'Maybe because Reg is old enough not to be impressed by him, and Taylor Boyd does like to control people. The youngster, Dean, is scared of him; Macca seems to respect him – God knows why – and Edwards thinks the sun shines out of his every orifice. That's the way he likes it.'

'And you?' Jenny slanted a look at him, wrinkling her nose as she squinted against the evening sun.

'He's not sure about me yet, and that suits me fine.' Daniel put down his brush and went to fetch Piper's saddle pad and blanket off the door. 'Do you give Boyd free rein in the office?' he asked, casually.

'More or less. I never meant to, but things were getting so out of hand and he offered to help. Why? Don't you think I should?'

'Within reason, I expect.'

'Well, of course I do run through the figures when I do the accounting at the end of the month,' she said.

'Fred said something about you losing stock.'

Jenny looked uncomfortable. 'I may have panicked a bit. Taylor explained what happened. It was an admin mistake – he owned up.'

'So it's all OK.'

'Yes. Well it *seems* to be. Of course, with the livery business to run as well, it's difficult to be as thorough as I'd like. God, you've got me thinking now . . .'

'I'm sorry. Look, it may be nothing, and if the business is doing OK, that's the main thing. Don't worry about it.'

'Well, we're certainly busy at the moment. In fact, Boyd is out with one of the lorries tonight, doing a bit of overtime. Whatever you think of him, you can't fault his enthusiasm.'

'Mm.' Daniel decided to sit on the previous night's conversation for the time being.

* * *

The following day was Friday, and after a long day in the cab, Daniel was making a cup of coffee for himself and one for Dean, who was so far the only other occupant of the drivers' room.

'Will he let me stroke him?' the youngster asked, looking at Taz, who characteristically lay on the room's only piece of carpet.

'I expect so, if you introduce yourself,' Daniel said, carrying the two mugs over to the sofa.

'Introduce? Seriously? No, you're having me on,' Dean's pale skin flushed with colour.

'I'm not. But I don't mean it literally – just use his name and let him see what you're about to do. Don't surprise him.'

'Oh, I see.' Dean looked at the German shepherd. 'All right, Taz?'

The dog responded by lifting his head and returning the look, and, thus encouraged, Dean leaned forward and stroked the thick fur on his head.

'He's lovely,' the youngster said reverentially.

'Do you have a dog of your own, Dean?'

'Nah, my old man won't have one in the house. When I get my own place I will, though. Can't tell me what to do then, can he?'

Daniel agreed that he couldn't.

'What made you want to work here?' he asked, after a moment.

'I love the trucks, don't I?' he said, still fussing over the dog. 'I'm qualified to drive the big ones, but Mr Summers says the insurance is too expensive while I'm so young. He says I need to get some miles under my belt first, so I just drive the van.'

'I've never met Mr Summers. What's he like?'

'He's all right. You know where you are with him and he treats you right.'

'But Taylor doesn't?'

'I didn't say that!' Dean sat up abruptly, the dog forgotten. 'You can't say I did.'

'Calm down. I'm not saying anything to anybody. It was just an observation.' Daniel took a sip of his coffee, eyeing the younger man thoughtfully. 'So you're happy here? Taylor hasn't made things difficult for you, or asked you to do anything out of the ordinary?'

'No.' Dean's pale eyes opened wide. 'I ain't got no complaints.'

'OK. That's good, then.'

A heavy silence reigned for a short while. Dean gulped his drink and looked at his feet, and Daniel just waited.

'Have you, like, heard something?' Dean said eventually. 'About Taylor, I mean.'

'No. Nothing. I was just curious. Actually, I wondered why the driver who was here before me left. Did he fall out with Taylor?' He had learned from Jenny that two drivers had left since Boyd came on the scene, and he was more than curious to find out why.

'I dunno.' His body language proclaimed it a lie as surely as any polygraph could have.

'OK. Never mind. I just wondered if you knew him.'

Dean hesitated and then, apparently deciding that no harm could come from disclosing the information, said, 'Yeah, I did. His name was Mal Fletcher. He was all right, he was. Used to live in the village but he's moved on now.'

'Oh, right.' Daniel would have liked to milk the youngster for more, but the others were due back at any moment and he could well imagine that Dean's body language would set Boyd wondering just what they'd been discussing in his absence.

'So, what are you up to this weekend? Anything interesting?' he asked instead, and he was relieved to see Dean relax as he launched into details of a golf tournament he was entering.

'Daniel. Can I have a word?'

Jenny was in the doorway of the farmhouse as he passed with Taz at his heels.

'Sure. Down at the stables?' He fancied he could feel Boyd's eyes boring into his back.

'No, I ought to hang on here for a minute. I've just put Izzy down for a nap and she's a bit restless. Come and have a cup of coffee,' she said.

Daniel resisted the temptation to look back and see if Boyd really was watching as he accepted the invitation. To do so would only make him look as if he had something to hide.

'Actually, I've just had a cup,' he said as she closed the door behind him.

Jenny made no move to put the kettle on. She turned to face him, and he thought she looked tired and stressed.

'You were right – about Taylor, I mean. He *is* up to something,' she said.

'How do you know?'

'I had to get something from the office earlier, and I remembered how you reacted when I said about him doing overtime. So I looked and there's no record of his trip last night.'

'Well, he might have forgotten to log it. Especially if he got back late,' Daniel pointed out reasonably.

'And another thing,' she went on, as if she hadn't heard. 'The fuel bills have gone through the roof – yes, I know diesel has gone up a lot lately, but this is something else. It's almost thirty per cent up on the last month Gavin was here. That can't be right, can it?'

'It does sound a bit excessive,' Daniel agreed. 'Have you said anything to Boyd?'

'Not yet. After what you said, I didn't know what to do . . .'

Daniel rubbed a hand over his tired eyes and gave it some thought.

'I reckon, mention it to him but in a non-confrontational way. Act puzzled and see what he says. If he makes some excuse, pretend to believe him. We don't want to put the wind up him at this stage.'

'Don't we?' Jenny looked unsettled.

'No, we don't,' Daniel said firmly. 'I think there might be more to this than a little low-level embezzlement, and I'd like to find out what. Let me know what he says. And, meantime, can you let me have a couple of addresses?'

Jenny didn't have a current address for the departed Mal Fletcher but suggested he ask the people who were now renting the cottage he'd vacated.

Daniel had little more luck regarding her ex-employee's reasons for leaving.

'He said he'd had a better offer and I didn't question him. I was too caught up in what was happening to Gavin,' she confessed. 'It was early days then, you see, and we didn't know if he might come round at any moment. I was at the hospital every spare moment I had.'

'That's understandable. Were you surprised Fletcher left?'

'Well, it *was* a bit sudden, but staff come and go. There's no loyalty these days. I think he knocked heads with Taylor once or twice, but he didn't seem particularly unhappy. I didn't really know him, but he seemed a nice enough guy.'

Mal Fletcher's new address, furnished in due course by the cottage's current occupant, was in Ditton Cheney, a village not five miles away, and, tucking the sheet of notepaper in his pocket, Daniel drove straight there.

A young, dark-haired woman opened the door to the brick-built terraced cottage, with a baby perched on one hip. She looked Daniel up and down and a guarded look came into her eyes. Belatedly, he remembered he was still wearing his polo shirt with the Summer Haulage logo.

'Yes?' The enquiry was abrupt.

'Is Mal around?'

'Who's asking?'

'Daniel Whelan. I work for Jenny Summers.'

'I can see that. What do you want him for?'

'Just wanted to ask him something.'

'Did Boyd send you?'

'No. He doesn't know I'm here.'

'What do you want to know?'

Daniel hesitated, but it was clear that the woman had no intention of summoning her partner. He decided to take a chance. After all, if Fletcher had knocked heads with Taylor in the past, as Jenny had suggested, he was hardly likely to go telling tales to him now. 'I want to know why Mal left Summer Haulage,' he asked.

The woman regarded him coldly. 'That's none of your business. Just go away and leave us alone.'

She started to shut the door, but Daniel put out a hand to stop it.

'I'm not here to make trouble, I promise you,' he said quickly.

'You just being here is making trouble.'

'How?'

'You obviously don't know who you're dealing with.'

'So tell me.'

'Please, go away.' Her tone had changed to pleading now. 'There's nothing more to say; it's over. We just want to be left in peace.'

'Sally?' Footsteps approached, and in a moment a burly man of around Daniel's own age appeared beside her. 'Who are you?'

Daniel started to explain, but the woman cut across him.

'He's from your old place – asking questions.'

Fletcher's eyes narrowed and he put a protective arm round her shoulders.

'About what?'

Sally stared boldly at Daniel, confident with her husband at her side. And well she might be, Daniel thought, noticing how an impressive set of biceps stretched the sleeves of the man's T-shirt.

He paused, debating his best approach, and Sally spoke for him. 'He was asking why you left.'

Immediately, Mal Fletcher's face darkened and he stabbed the air in front of Daniel's face with an angry forefinger.

'That's none of your fucking business!'

'Where are you working now?'

'That's none of your business, either.'

'Did you leave because of Boyd?'

'Get off my property.'

'I know he's up to something and I want to know what.'

'Leave us alone.'

'Wouldn't you like to get your own back?' Daniel persisted. 'If you would just tell me what happened, I might be able to help you.'

Fletcher was becoming increasingly agitated, and Sally hugged the baby close to her. 'What? Are you deaf or just stupid? What part of *leave us alone* aren't you getting?'

Daniel sighed and pulled his wallet from the back pocket of his jeans. He took out a slip of paper on which he'd written his mobile number. 'OK. Look, here's my number. If you change your mind, give me a call.'

'It won't happen.' Fletcher ignored the paper and, stepping back, pulled Sally after him and shut the door in Daniel's face.

Daniel stared at the uncompromising red paint and mentally kicked himself for mishandling the situation so badly. His visit to the former Summer Haulage employee had, in truth, been something of a long shot. He'd hoped for some kind of a reaction but he hadn't been prepared for such a violent one.

Returning to the car, he sat for a while, thinking. He'd drop his number in the post to them with a note stressing that he was on their side, and maybe when they'd had a chance to cool down, they'd think again.

He wouldn't hold his breath.

The other address Jenny had given him was that of George and Marian Coombes, who'd lived at Forester's Cottage before him.

Now, as he drew up alongside the curb outside a modern square bungalow in Lower Ditton, he checked the details again. The property was situated in a cul-de-sac containing five clones of the one he'd come to visit. Three had handrails from pavement to door, indicating elderly residents, one had a child's bicycle tumbled on the front lawn and all had brown wheelie bins parked ready for collection. A dog-waste bin adorned the nearest lamppost, and above it was pinned a notice of a fundraising coffee morning and a plea for information on a missing cat.

Jenny had said the Coombes' new home was modern, but for some reason Daniel hadn't pictured anything quite as suburban as this. He wondered how a couple who'd lived for thirty years in glorious isolation in the cottage in the woods could bear to settle in such a place.

Treading up the concrete garden path between beds of annuals that would have made the collective chests of any parks authority swell with righteous pride, Daniel pressed his finger to the doorbell button.

In due course, a chain rattled, a Yale lock clicked open and a dumpy woman stood in front of him in a shapeless, flowery dress, her plain face made all the more so by wispy grey hair pulled into an unimaginative bun. She looked him up and down and then peered past him as if expecting something or somebody else.

'Marian Coombes?'

'Have you brought the cooker?' she asked, peering at him under untidy brows. A pair of spectacles hung on a cord about her neck and Daniel thought she would do better to put them on.

'No, I'm not delivering anything, I'm from Maidstone Farm. I work for Jenny Summers.' He pointed to the logo on his shirt to back up his statement.

Marian Coombes' expression softened.

'Oh, the poor girl! How is she?'

This was a more encouraging start.

'She's coping remarkably well,' Daniel said. 'She's very brave.'

'She's a good girl. We've known her since she was a wee thing. And Mr Summers? Any change?'

'Not as far as I'm aware.'

'What's the world coming to when you're not even safe on your own land?' she asked, shaking her head and pursing her lips. 'It's frightening. Anyway, what can I do for you, Mr . . . er?'

'Daniel. I'm a friend of Jenny's, and I'm here helping out with the driving. Actually, I'm staying in your old cottage.'

'Oh, I see.' She plainly didn't.

'I wondered if I could ask you and your husband a couple of questions.'

'What about?' There again was the guarded look Daniel had seen on Sally Fletcher's face.

'Is George in?'

'He won't want to see you. He doesn't see anyone much,' she said uncompromisingly.

'Could you at least ask?'

Marian gave him a long hard look and then stood back a little.

'You'd better come in, I suppose, as you're a friend of Jenny's.'

Daniel took her up on the offer with alacrity, in case she thought better of it, and followed her down a short, carpeted hallway to a surprisingly spacious lounge, decorated and furnished with more enthusiasm than taste.

In one, pink velour-covered armchair, a small, wiry man sat staring out of the plate-glass French windows. Outside was an area of pink and grey paved patio on which stood a bird table hung with more feeders than Daniel thought he'd ever seen in one place. Beyond it a neat square of emerald lawn was bordered by brightly flowering annuals, the whole surrounded by a recently treated wooden fence.

The man looked round as they entered and regarded Daniel with a slightly puzzled expression, as if trying to place him in his memory. Above a wrinkled, weather-beaten face on which the tan was fading, a few wisps of white hair decorated an otherwise bald pate.

'Hello, Mr Coombes. We haven't met. My name's Daniel Whelan. I work for Jenny Summers,' Daniel said, going towards the man.

George Coombes ignored his outstretched hand.

'Why are you here?' he asked bitterly. 'He said he'd leave us alone if we did as he said.'

'Who did?'

'You know who. Don't act stupid! He got what he wanted and now I'm stuck in this Godforsaken place – this – this bloody concrete box with its postage stamp of a garden – until I die, which won't be long if God has any mercy!'

'Oh, George!' Tears shone in Marian's eyes.

He tossed her an impatient glance.

'Well, it's true. You know it is. Why did you let him in?'

'Taylor Boyd didn't send me,' Daniel said. 'It *is* Boyd you're talking about, isn't it?'

'Who else?'

'He forced you to leave the cottage? Tell me how? Did he threaten you?'

George shook his head.

'He said if we ever told anyone, he'd know about it and . . .'

'And?'

'Well, he'd be back, wouldn't he?'

'He'll never find out from me, I promise you,' Daniel said.

George's hooded eyes regarded him without faith. 'I don't know who you are. Why should I trust you?'

Looking at it from the old man's point of view, Daniel couldn't think of a single reason.

'Just go,' George said then. 'I don't want to talk to you. You'll just make everything worse. Please leave us alone.'

'I want to help. But I have to know what he did.'

'Please leave,' the old man repeated, returning his attention to the bird feeders once more.

Daniel had to admit defeat.

Marian showed him to the front door and opened it. 'I'm sorry, but I did warn you.'

Stepping out on to the concrete path, Daniel tried one last time.

'I wish you'd believe I only want to help,' he said, turning.

There was no reply.

He sighed. 'Well, goodbye, Mrs Coombes. Can I at least give you my number, in case you change your mind?'

'It was what he did to our cat,' she said suddenly. 'Poor little Minnie. Anyone who could do that to one of God's creatures . . .'

'What did he do?' Daniel asked gently. 'Can you tell me?'

'He left her hanging in the shed,' she said, her face crumpling with distress at the memory. 'And George found her. What was left of her.'

SIX

The night was sultry. Daniel opened his eyes in the darkness of his bedroom and wondered what had woken him.

Gradually, his night sight improved and he could make out the shapes of the wardrobe and the chair over which he had draped his clothes. There was no sound from Taz, who had taken to sleeping out on the tiny landing, no doubt getting the most from the through-draught generated by the open windows in the upstairs rooms.

In the heavy silence, Daniel could hear the ticking of his watch on the bedside chest. At some point in his short sleep, he had thrown the sheets off. Perhaps it was the heat that had made him wakeful.

Suddenly a flicker of blue light illuminated the window, outlining the frame for a fraction of a second and leaving its imprint on his retinas. He waited, listening, and presently a deep booming rumble echoed across the forest. The storm was a couple of miles away, he calculated, but no doubt that solved the mystery of what had disturbed him.

A glance at the fluorescent hands of his alarm clock told him that it was three o'clock in the morning. Turning over, Daniel closed his eyes once more, hoping the storm wouldn't come any closer. It had taken him the best part of an hour to get to sleep in the first place, the events of the day playing on his mind.

Marian's revelation about the fate of her cat was shocking. From what he had already seen and heard, Daniel had been ready to believe Boyd capable of using threatening behaviour to achieve his ends, but to find that he was prepared to resort to something so barbaric put a different slant on things.

He remembered Jenny telling him that her Labrador had been horrifically injured when he'd been found. Two mutilated animals in a short space of time – was there a link or was it coincidence? The trouble was there was no proof. For George and Marian Coombes, an anonymous letter had left them with little doubt as to Boyd's part in it, but, frustratingly, Marian told Daniel she'd burned it.

'We threw it on the fire. It was evil!' she had said, her voice shaking with emotion.

Boyd had clearly wanted the elderly couple out of the cottage; the question was why?

Daniel groaned and turned over, punching his pillow to make it more comfortable, but five minutes and half a dozen thunderclaps later, he realized his hopes of a good night's rest were to be dashed. The storm was moving slowly but steadily closer, and sleep had never been further away. He found himself thinking of his son, Drew. He'd be loving this storm, if he were here. God, he missed having him around.

A sharp crack sounded as something hit the glass of the bedroom window. Daniel lay still, frowning into the darkness. There were no trees close enough for a wind-blown branch to be responsible.

Again a crack, louder this time, and Taz padded into the room, halting beside the bed, his gaze intent on the window. Daniel sat up. It had sounded like a stone hitting the windowpane.

The third time, it was a scatter of noise, almost certainly a handful of small pebbles against the glass, and one or two found the opening and fell inside on the bare floorboards. That was enough for Taz. He threw himself forward, barking furiously, and Daniel shouted at him to lie down, for fear his enthusiasm would carry him through the open window. Grumbling, the shepherd obeyed.

In moments, Daniel was off the bed and pulling on his jeans. Crossing the room, he stood at the side of the casement and peered out. The garden was deep in shadows and he could see very little.

He waited. No more stones were thrown.

Had whoever it was given up and turned away? Unlikely, surely? If they had made the effort to come all this way in the middle of the night, it had to be important. It crossed his mind that it could conceivably be Jenny. With no telephone at the cottage, and mobile reception non-existent, he was isolated in every way, and if some catastrophe had occurred, she would have no other way of contacting him – always supposing she wanted to. But why the stone throwing? Why not bang on the door?

Taz had quietened now, apart from panting and the odd whinge, and, leaning close to the open window, Daniel looked out.

In the same instant a flash illuminated the garden, and for a split second he could see the path, the wicket gate, the lane and the wood beyond as if in daylight. He also saw the Merc, parked in the pull-in to the right of the gate, and, beside it, a man with some kind of stick or club in his hands. As darkness reclaimed the scene, there came the unmistakable sound of shattering glass.

Furious, Daniel pushed the window wider and shouted, 'Oi!'

Moments later, realizing the futility of his position, he whipped round, pushed his feet into the leather mules he wore around the house and headed for the stairs with Taz on his heels. Outside, the thunder sounded, much louder this time.

Reaching the hall, Daniel hesitated in the act of unlocking the door, caution slowing his hand. If the intention was to steal or vandalize his car, who had thrown the stones to wake him up? And why? Was someone lying in wait with a monkey wrench?

Taz was sniffing noisily at the base of the front door and whining his impatience, no such qualms afflicting his straightforward canine brain, but Daniel decided that discretion was in order and slipped his fingers through the dog's collar before opening the door.

The air outside was still and scarcely cooler on the bare skin of Daniel's torso than that inside the cottage, but he had little time to acknowledge the fact, for Taz had got wind of his quarry and launched into a lungeing, barking frenzy, throwing all of his forty-two kilos against Daniel's restraining hand.

Daniel wished he'd taken the time to clip on the dog's lead because holding Taz's collar pulled him forward, off-balance, and, in addition, Taz was hooking his nearest front paw round Daniel's leg to gain leverage. After a few battling steps, the shepherd placed another paw firmly on the back of Daniel's shoe and brought him stumbling to his knees, the torch spinning off into the darkness. One more lunge and the dog was free, racing down the path and taking the gate in his stride, while Daniel floundered, cursing, in the lavender border.

As he regained his feet, he could hear Taz barking, the tone suggesting to him that the dog had his man cornered and intended keeping him so.

'Good boy, hold him!' he yelled.

He kicked off his remaining shoe and, in two short strides, vaulted the gate and landed on the tarmac of the lane, turning towards the dark bulk of the car, ready to give his partner whatever assistance he might need. He had only been seconds behind the dog but he was already too late. As he strained to see in the gloom, the continuous barking faltered and became interspersed with a ferocious growling.

He heard a man's jeering shout and then, as a brilliant double flash lit the scene, saw Taz struggling helplessly in the mesh of some kind of net that rendered his strength and agility useless.

Desperate with fear for his dog, Daniel started forward, only to be stopped in his tracks as something hard hit him with a scything blow to the midriff and dropped him, gasping, to his knees.

Raising his head to try and see what was happening to Taz, Daniel was blinded as the area was flooded with a blaze of light from a vehicle-mounted spotlight.

Undeterred, he scrambled forward on all fours, his fingers groping in front of him for the net, but in the instant he touched it, a second blow landed across his shoulders, sending him sprawling face-down in the lane, feeling as if he might never move again.

'For Christ's sake, get that fuckin' animal outta here and deal with it!' a voice from behind Daniel growled.

Moments later, the mesh began to slide beneath Daniel's fingers. Instinctively, he curled his fingers into it to prevent its precious cargo being towed away, but as the net tugged and became taut, a booted foot stamped down with wicked force on his wrist, crushing his hand on to the tarmac.

Daniel gasped in pain, powerless to stop the net slipping through his bruised fingers and away out of reach, with Taz still held, snapping and snarling, within its folds.

Thinking only of his partner, Daniel rolled over and got to his knees, wincing as his right hand threatened to give way under his weight, but before he could bring his feet under him, he was kicked hard from the side, sending him sprawling once more, the tarmac grazing his cheekbone as he landed and rolled on to his back.

Above him, a figure loomed in the harsh light, his face concealed by a balaclava. In his hands was a baseball bat that gleamed with a metallic sheen. No prizes for guessing what he'd been clobbered with, then, but even though he couldn't see his attacker's face, he didn't think it was Ricky Boyd. The body language was wrong. Where Ricky had been all swagger and bravado, this man was full of quiet confidence. The observation brought Daniel no comfort. He would much rather have dealt with Ricky.

As he began to get up again, the man with the bat beckoned to someone behind Daniel, and before he could turn to locate this new player in the scene, his arms were grasped and pulled roughly back and upwards in one powerful movement. All at once the strain on his shoulders made it imperative that he get his feet under him as quickly as possible and he scrabbled to do so.

Another flash lit the lane, followed closely by a sharp crack of thunder almost overhead. The man behind Daniel jumped nervously before tightening his grip on Daniel's arms still further.

In the momentary brightness, there had been no sign of Taz, and Daniel suffered a stab of fear. Where was he? Had he already been 'dealt with'? Who had wielded the net?

Daniel railed inwardly at his helplessness. How many times had the German shepherd come to his rescue, and now, when the tables were turned, he was completely powerless to reciprocate. Held in an iron grip, he could only stand and wait for whatever was coming his way, but his fear was all for the dog.

He didn't have long to wait. Still hefting the bat, the first man moved forward until he stood directly in front of his captive.

Daniel was surprised how much more vulnerable he felt for having no shirt or shoes. As if a thin cotton T-shirt would have protected him in any way. With a conscious effort, he fixed his gaze on the masked face. The man clearly thrived on inflicting fear, and even if he was quaking inside, Daniel was damned if he was going to give his tormentor the satisfaction of seeing it in his face.

The balaclava leaned close and whispered in his ear.

'Why don't you be a good boy and go back where you come from? We don't want troublemakers round here.'

Daniel said nothing. He didn't get the feeling it was intended to be a conversation.

The reward for his silence was a stinging slap across the face; so quick he didn't see it coming. Moments later, another flash of lightning split the air, and as the following thunderclap reverberated around the forest, Daniel again felt the man behind him jump and his grip tighten convulsively.

All around, rain began to fall in huge, slow drops, slowly at first then gathering momentum, splashing noisily on the road, the vehicles and the hard-baked ground. They landed on Daniel's bare shoulders and head, shocking in their iciness.

'Where's Taz? Where's my dog?' he demanded through gritted teeth. The pain in his twisted shoulder muscles was beginning to bite.

The man leaned close again. 'You don't want to worry about

him,' he stated softly. 'Where he's going to he won't feel a thing. You should be worrying about yourself.'

Anxiety flared into blind fury, and Daniel smashed his head into the masked face beside his with as much force as he could muster. The man reeled back, cursing.

Caught on the hop, Daniel's captor jerked him backwards, forcing his back to arch and lifting his feet clear of the ground for a moment.

Seconds later, the first man was back, and Daniel derived some satisfaction from seeing him wiping his mouth with a leather-gloved hand.

In the next instant, no coherent thought existed as the end of the baseball bat was jabbed viciously into his stomach. Coughing, Daniel strained against the arms that held him, desperate to curl himself round the centre of his pain.

While Daniel watched with something close to despair, the shiny smooth bat was drawn back for a second blow. Aside from the natural aversion to pain, he had witnessed the results of enough fights during his police career to recognize the danger of suffering serious internal injury from such abuse. Ruptured major organs were a distinct possibility. Was this what had happened to Gavin Summers? Would Daniel, too, be found dumped on the roadside come morning?

Suddenly, lightning forked directly overhead and a tree on the edge of the wood exploded with flame as the electricity raced down its trunk to the ground.

The accompanying crack of thunder was deafening, the air crackling with the extreme heat. Feeling the involuntary spasm of fear in the arms that held him, Daniel seized the moment. With a Herculean effort, he lifted his right foot and shoved the man with the bat away from him, using the leverage to throw his own weight backwards at the same time. The move caught his captor off balance, driving him stumbling backwards into the low picket fence that marked the edge of the garden.

The old fence didn't stand a chance. Snapping like matchwood, it gave way beneath their combined weight, tipping both Daniel and the other man on to their backs amongst the straggling weeds and flowers of the border.

Falling heavily on top of his captor, Daniel heard him grunt, and the vice-like grip on his right arm loosened as the man instinctively tried to save himself. Recovering first, Daniel leaned forward, twisted as far as he was able and drove his free elbow back into the side of the other man's head.

His efforts produced a curse, but no noticeable slackening in the hold on Daniel's other arm, and aware that one or both of the others would very soon be coming to their comrade's aid, he repeated the smash, this time managing to pull clear of the man's failing grasp.

Adrenalin surging, Daniel rolled and came to his feet just as the first man stepped over the remains of the sagging fence. One-to-one combat, face to face, held no qualms for Daniel and, without further ado, he threw a hefty punch into the man's masked face.

Daniel's moment of triumph was fleeting.

A hand caught his shoulder, spinning him round, and before he could organize any form of defence, he was floored by a stunning right hook to the jaw, and lights erupted like a starburst in his skull.

Consciousness took a brief timeout, edging back with the pungent smell of lavender filling his sinuses, clearing his head like smelling salts. The left side of his face was pillowed by the springy, aromatic foliage, and for the space of a few heartbeats, it was as if nothing else existed for Daniel than the immediate vicinity and his returning senses. A woody stump was digging into his ribs, cold fat drops of rain pattered on to the bare skin of his back, and the boom of the latest thunderclap echoed endlessly in his head.

He was vaguely aware of an undercurrent of pain, but as long as he didn't move he felt he could deal with it. All he needed was to lie still and recover. He needed to be left alone.

Someone had other ideas. A booted foot was inserted under his ribcage, and with a none too gentle heave, Daniel was rolled on to his back.

As another flash illuminated the clearing, followed swiftly by yet another, the heavens opened and rain began to drive to earth in long shining silver rods, stinging Daniel's face and body and bringing him back to full consciousness in seconds. Continuing to roll away from the boot, he found himself close to the cottage wall and managed to get one knee under him and then pull himself upright with the aid of the bench that stood there.

Blinking through the rain, he saw his first attacker – now, encouragingly, minus the weapon – and, beside him, the bulky outline of another man, presumably his erstwhile captor. He also wore a balaclava, but into Daniel's mind flitted an image of his Summer Haulage colleague, Terry MacAllister, flexing his powerful arm muscles as he stretched at the end of a long day's driving. Macca would certainly be strong enough, but what had Daniel ever done to him?

Daniel slitted his eyes against the rain and waited with waning optimism for hostilities to recommence, his bruised ribs protesting with each indrawn breath. Two against one was no fun at the best of times, even though he had learned self-defence from a fellow officer in the dog unit. What wouldn't he give to have Jo-Ji Matsuki beside him now?

Another slashing flash, an instantaneous crack of thunder, and the rain turned to hail, drumming down so hard and fast that it bounced off the long-parched earth, puddling and beginning to flow like a river on the surface of the lane.

The icy water was running through Daniel's hair and down his face and body, soaking his Levis so they clung heavily to his legs, and all at once he just wanted to get it over with. He waited, feeling slightly dizzy and wanting more than anything to sit down.

'Come on, then! What are you waiting for?' he yelled suddenly, surprising even himself.

There was another brilliant searing flash, another brief blaze in the treetops across the lane, and suddenly a dark streak entered on to the stage, coming to a halt between Daniel and the two men facing him.

As the echoes of the thunder rolled away across the forest, Taz's deep bark cut through the noise of the deluge, and Daniel's heart sang.

SEVEN

With the advent of the German shepherd, apparently fit and spoiling for action, both men took a rapid step backwards.

The bigger of the two glanced nervously from the dog to the man beside him, as if for guidance, and his partner prudently decided to call it a day, gesturing over his shoulder towards the waiting vehicle.

Holding his hands out, palms forward, the man then began to back slowly away, with his burly sidekick keeping pace. Their eyes never left the dog, who matched each of their steps with a menacing forward step of his own.

In the lane, someone gunned the engine of the vehicle with the spotlights and, hearing the sound, the two men began to hurry – stumbling, with curses, over the broken fence in their efforts to beat a hasty retreat.

Daniel commanded Taz to stand, to stop him following the men out into the lane and possible danger. Moments later, he heard the vehicle's doors slam shut, and with a roar and a scream of tyres, the pick-up accelerated past the cottage and away down the road. There was another squeal of tyres as it took the corner where the roads joined, and gradually the sound of its engine faded into the night. In the absence of the spotlights, darkness descended, broken only by the sporadic flickering of the waning storm.

Taz stood barking at the departing vehicle until he could no longer hear it, then turned and began to cast around the trampled garden, snuffling excitedly at the multitude of smells.

'Hey, fella,' Daniel said gruffly. 'Come 'ere.'

His eyes were adjusting to the gloom now and he could just make out the gleam of Taz's eyes as the shepherd turned towards him. The next moment, the dog was beside him, flattening his ears with delight and butting Daniel gently with his shoulder as he fawned around his legs.

Daniel took a step backwards and sat down heavily on the bench. Throwing his arms round the dog's neck, he buried his face in the sodden fur.

'Don't you ever do that to me again, you hear? Thought I'd lost you, you old bugger!'

The dog twisted in his grasp, trying to lick his face, and suddenly Daniel found himself overbalancing sideways. He put out a hand to save himself and ended up half sitting and half lying on the cinder walk in front of the cottage. Rivulets of rainwater were streaming along the path, but Daniel's jeans couldn't get any wetter and the effort to move was all at once too great. As the adrenalin in his system ebbed away, it felt as though there wasn't an inch of his body that wasn't bruised. He leaned back against the wall, closed his eyes and listened to the steady downpour, Taz's panting and the gurgle of water bubbling into overfull drains.

'Best get inside, I reckon,' a voice suggested in a broad Wiltshire accent.

Daniel started, eyes snapping open. Not six feet away stood the shadowy figure of a shortish man wearing a wide-brimmed hat and a long, bulky coat.

His first thought was to curse his own stupidity for forgetting the man who'd wielded the net – but then logic cut in. Surely they wouldn't have left one of their number behind, and, anyway, Taz wasn't making a sound. Was it likely that he'd calmly accept the proximity of someone who had attacked him just minutes before?

'Need a hand?' The shadow moved a step or two closer, and this time Taz did growl protectively.

'I'm fine,' Daniel said with doubtful veracity. 'I can manage, thanks.'

With the aid of the bench, he made it to his knees and from there to his feet, where he stood swaying gently with one hand on the wall.

'Did you see another man around?' he asked, straining to see into the darkness. 'Round the side there?'

'Reckon I did. Took this offen 'im,' the man said, holding up what looked like a swathe of material.

The net.

Even as recognition dawned, Taz backed away with a frenzy of barking, and the man prudently tossed the mesh to one side.

'Reckon he's learned his lesson,' he observed. 'Won't get caught like that again.'

'I hope not. And thank you. Let's go in.' Daniel moved stiffly towards the door, the wet cinders squidging between his bare toes, but when he looked back, the man in the hat hadn't moved.

'Won't you come inside? Until the rain stops, at least.' In spite of the warmth of the night, Daniel had started to shiver violently and he longed to get inside and dry off.

'Reckon I don't mind the rain,' the man said, but he followed Daniel as far as the doorway nevertheless, where the light fell on gaunt, weathered features and brown eyes in the shade of the hat brim. He could have been anything from fifty to seventy years old, and was no more than five foot six tall, wearing a long stockman's coat that reached to ankles encased in worn leather walking boots.

Daniel's practised eye noted the coat's suspiciously bulging inner pockets – poachers' pockets, and never more aptly named, he suspected. He was almost certain he was looking at the locally famous Woodsmoke, of whom Jenny had spoken.

'I can do coffee,' he offered. 'But I'm afraid I haven't anything stronger.'

The wizened face split into a grin that would have had any self-respecting dentist recoiling in horror, and he patted his breast. 'I allus come prepared,' he said.

Daniel stood back and beckoned him through to the kitchen, and after a moment's hesitation, Woodsmoke stepped inside.

'Have a seat. I'll put the kettle on and then change these jeans . . .' Daniel's voice trailed away as a small, grey, lurchery face peered through the front opening of the poacher's long coat at knee level. 'Hello, little one.'

'Thass Gypsy,' Woodsmoke said with no hint of apology. 'She goes everywhere.' Carefully arranging the heavy pockets of his coat to each side, he sat himself on one of the wooden chairs and the whippet-sized bitch crept out and curled up on his feet.

Minutes later, when Daniel came back downstairs in clean jeans and a T-shirt, his hair towelled dry, the kitchen bore an aroma like a bonfire on an autumn day – an earthy mixture of leaf mould and smoke. Woodsmoke had made two mugs of coffee, and a flat-sided, green glass bottle stood on the table between them.

'Didn't put it in yourn, lessen you was one of them teetotallers.' His tone and the curl of his lip left Daniel in no doubt as to his opinion of such people.

Daniel shook his head, thanked him and, without peering too closely at the bottle, the label of which had long since disintegrated, tipped a couple of glugs into his coffee. The resulting brew made its way down his throat with a comforting burn, and for the first time since waking to hear the stones against his window, Daniel began to relax. He wished he could give Taz something similar but he guessed it was all in a night's work for the dog, who had followed him upstairs and back down, and now lay on the floor half under the table, busily washing his front paws. He and Gypsy were studiously ignoring one another.

'Reckon you need to get some ice on that.' Woodsmoke gestured at Daniel's right wrist, which was badly bruised and swollen from the forearm to the fingers.

Daniel retrieved a bag of frozen peas from the icebox of the fridge and wrapped it round his injured arm in a dishcloth.

'I can't thank you enough for what you did for Taz,' he said then, taking a seat across from Woodsmoke. 'I thought they were going to kill him.'

'If t'ad been Boyd, he would 'ave,' the poacher grunted. 'Evil that one. Pure evil.'

'Ricky, you mean?'

'No. T'other un. Taylor. You knew t'was him, spite of the masks, didn't you?'

'I guessed,' Daniel confirmed.

'Ar. They're a bad lot, the whole crowd of 'em, but Taylor's the worst. Jenny's man should never 'ave got mixed up with he.'

'Jenny says Gavin isn't from round here and didn't know the family.'

Another grunt. 'Soon learned. What's his beef with you, then?'

'He thinks I've been asking questions about him.'

'An 'ave you?'

Daniel sighed. 'One or two, maybe, on the quiet.'

Woodsmoke harrumphed. 'Not quiet enough, seemingly. Got eyes and ears everywhere, that fambly. There's not much goes on they don't hear about.'

'So it seems. So, what happened back there – with Taz, I mean?'

'Matey was gonna haul him into the tree. Didn't 'spect ter find me there, did he? Reckon I give 'im the fright of his life!' Woodsmoke chuckled appreciatively at the memory.

'Into a tree? Are you sure?'

''S'what it looked like.'

'Did you see who it was?'

'Reckon not. Come up behind 'im and put my hand on his shoulder, I did. He didn't hang around fer no introductions.'

'I don't suppose he did,' Daniel said with a slight smile.

'Reckon his heart weren't in it.'

'What makes you say that?'

'Well, Boyd, see, he woulda told 'im ter clobber the dog, not string 'im in a bloody tree! Lucky he was more interested in you, I reckon.'

'Lucky for who?' Daniel enquired morosely. Now that the sustaining effect of the adrenalin had cleared his system, a grinding discomfort was taking over, reminding him, with each movement, of the efficacy with which Boyd, if Boyd it had been, had wielded his baseball bat.

Woodsmoke grunted again. 'Woulda killed the dog, Boyd would. Seen 'im do it afore.'

'You've seen him kill a dog?' Daniel's ears pricked up. 'Whose?'

Suddenly, it seemed as if the poacher regretted having said so much. He shrugged and took a long swig of his coffee.

'Reckon I disremember.'

'I'd really like to know . . .'

'Wouldn't do yer no good, I reckon. 'S'all over an' done with.'

Sensing that the older man had said all he was going to, Daniel changed the subject, careful not to let his frustration show.

'Was it you the other day? Watching me from the wood?'

'Mighta bin.'

'Why didn't you come over?'

'Not in general sociable,' Woodsmoke said. 'Juss wanted to see what manner of man you wuz. Heard you sent the Boyd nipper packing.'

'With a little help from Taz,' Daniel admitted, adding casually, 'The Boyds have got dogs at the scrapyard, I gather. Rottweilers, aren't they?'

'The girl tell you that, did she? Sue? Never could keep her mouth shut. Bet she didn't tell you about the others though, did she? The ones you can't see.'

'What do you mean?'

'Nuthin.' All at once, Woodsmoke wouldn't meet Daniel's eyes, and this time Daniel let his exasperation show.

'But you must have meant something, else why say it?'

The older man finished his coffee in one long swallow and stood up.

'Didn't mean nuthin'. Juss ramblin'. Folks'll tell you I'm daft in the head, an' maybe they're right. Reckon you don't wanna take no notice of what I say.' He stood up and headed for the door, the little lurcher once again hidden under his coat.

Daniel followed him. 'You're no more mad than I am. What are you scared of? *Who* are you scared of? Is it Taylor Boyd?'

Woodsmoke turned sharply.

'Iss not just him! You don't know what you're messing with. There's dozens of 'em – hundreds. People you don't expect. They come from all over. There's nuthin' you can do 'cept keep your head down and pretend you don't see nor hear nuthin.'

He made to move away again, but Daniel caught hold of his coat sleeve.

'What are you talking about? What people?'

Woodsmoke paused and, without turning, said reluctantly,

'Reckon there's plenty others, but Boyd's lot calls theirselves the Butcher Boys. But I never told you that and no one can prove I did.'

As the little woodsman disappeared into the darkness, Daniel locked the front door of the cottage and returned to the kitchen. A glance at the clock told him it was a quarter to four. Hard to believe that so much had happened in such a short time.

He rinsed the mugs, turned the lights off and made his way back upstairs with Taz at his heels, feeling a dozen bruised muscles pull with every step. Tomorrow wasn't going to be much fun. It was Saturday and only a half-day, but, as luck would have it, he was one of the drivers rostered on. He searched his memory; Reg was the other one, so at least he should be spared coming face to face with Boyd for a day or two.

Lying on top of the single cotton sheet, Daniel closed his eyes and tried to sleep, but the combination of aching body and busy mind made the goal a remote one.

The Butcher Boys. A gang of some sort, by the sound of it. The way the poacher had spoken of them made them sound almost like Freemasons. Were they known to the police? If the cottage had had a telephone line and internet access, he'd have been out of bed and Googling the name right away, but, as it was, it would have to wait. Perhaps a call to Tom Bowden would turn up some information. Tom was the son of Daniel's boss in Devon, and a Detective Inspector who had helped him massively in the past.

Turning over, he punched the pillow with his good hand and wriggled so he wasn't lying on a bruise. Sleep remained stubbornly elusive. He was beginning to have some ideas about Taylor Boyd and the possible nature of the gang, and they were none of them pleasant.

The morning dawned clear with the sun climbing steeply into an azure sky. Getting up, showering and dressing was an ordeal for Daniel, whose stomach and shoulder muscles were rebelling against the treatment they'd received.

The face that looked back at him from the bathroom mirror had also seen better days. His jaw was slightly swollen and bore a bruise that was only partially visible under the night's growth of stubble, so he decided to remain unshaven. There was another bruise in his hairline, collected when he'd butted Boyd in the face. That didn't show at all, and its presence was a source of satisfaction, solely because he knew that Boyd must have come off far worse. The only immediately obvious signs of the night's unrest were the graze on his cheekbone and his painfully swollen wrist, now inexpertly bandaged.

Emerging from the cottage after a breakfast of coffee, toast and paracetamol, he found the front garden similarly the worse for wear, a substantial length of its picket fencing flattened and the borders trampled. Across the lane, the top twenty or thirty feet of one of the fir trees in the wood was blackened and split in two where the lightning had struck.

At the side of the cottage, Daniel stood and stared at the cherry tree where, according to Woodsmoke, Taz had been destined to hang helplessly tangled in the net. It looked innocent enough, its branches and twigs sparkling with raindrops, but he had no illusions as to what would have happened if things had gone differently or the poacher not turned up.

On inspection, the net had proved to be made of green nylon cord, thin but incredibly tough and with a mesh small enough to have made it extremely difficult for the dog to chew through. A red weal on Taz's muzzle bore testament to his efforts to do just that and showed how cruelly the cord could burn. Daniel thought it might be some kind of net for fruit canes, but he wasn't sure. It was in the dustbin now.

He whistled to Taz and headed for the car.

'All right. So, are you going to tell me what's going on?'

It was lunchtime. Daniel had just finished his morning's driving and thankfully returned the keys and paperwork to the office when Jenny had asked him for a word and led the way into the house. Now she squared up to him with a stance that meant business. He attempted a look of innocent enquiry in reply, but she was having none of it.

'You've got a graze on your face, a bandage on your wrist, you haven't shaved and you're moving around like a geriatric – and a none too fit one at that! Add to that, two smashed headlights on your car. Don't tell me nothing's happened, because I won't believe you.'

'OK, boss,' Daniel said contritely. 'The official line is that I went outside in the storm last night to chase away whoever was smashing my lights and fell over the dog. That's what I told Reg.'

'And the unofficial one?' Jenny turned to open the fridge, from which she produced bread, butter, cheese and a jar of pickle, and began making sandwiches.

'Well, actually, in a manner of speaking I did.' Daniel said, leaning his behind against the table. 'But smashing the lights turned out to be a decoy, to lure me out.'

'Someone attacked you?' Jenny was shocked. 'Did you see who it was?'

Daniel hesitated, unsure how much he should tell her. 'There were three of them and they were wearing masks, but I have a pretty good idea,' he said finally.

'Not Taylor?' Jenny looked as though she didn't really want to hear the answer.

Daniel nodded. 'And possibly Terry MacAllister, too.'

Jenny frowned. 'But why? I mean, what did they want?'

'I think Macca was just there as the muscle, but Boyd was delivering a message. He wants me out of the cottage and preferably out of Wiltshire, too.'

'Oh, my God! But why?' Jenny exclaimed. 'Did they hurt you? No, silly question, I can see they did. But, I mean, what's the matter with Taylor? What's he up to?'

'Well, somehow he seems to have got wind of my visit to Mal Fletcher and George and Marian Coombes yesterday. As to what he's up to, I don't know, but I'm going to make it my business to find out,' Daniel said grimly.

'But what about the police? Can't they do something? You have told them?' She scanned his face. 'You haven't, have you?'

'Er, no.'

'But why not? You should, you know. You can't just let them get away with it.'

Daniel shrugged. 'If I'd thought it would do any good, I might have, but, to be honest, there's not much point. It was dark and they were wearing masks. Legally, I'd be on a hiding to nothing, even if it ever got to court, which I doubt. I wasn't even sure who I was dealing with myself, until old Woodsmoke turned up.'

'Woodsmoke? Was he there?' Jenny looked understandably confused.

'I think he just happened to be passing. Out to bag himself a little something for his larder unless I'm much mistaken. Lucky for me and even luckier for Taz.' He outlined what had happened with the net.

Jenny picked up her knife and resumed the sandwich making.

'It seems so wrong that you can't do anything about it.'

'I know.' Daniel sighed. 'But I know the way the law works and a good lawyer would throw my testimony out in seconds. Sad but true.'

Jenny made a sound of intense frustration. 'So, what now? I mean, what do we do about Taylor?'

'Not much we can do. For the sake of working harmony, I shan't let on that I've recognized him. It'll be interesting to see how they play it on Monday.' He paused. 'How long has MacAllister worked for you?'

'Oh, he's been here a while. He was one of the first ones Gavin took on. I always thought he was one of the better ones. Why?'

'Just wondered. Tell me, have you ever heard of the Butcher Boys?'

She frowned, pursed her lips and shook her head. 'I don't think so. Who are they?'

'Well, some sort of gang, I imagine. Woodsmoke mentioned them but he wasn't too keen to elaborate. He got as far as telling me that the Boyds are involved with them, but then he dried up and wouldn't say any more.'

'A gang? What kind of gang?'

'I'm not sure yet, but I intend finding out. I tried to ring Tom Bowden earlier, but Fred tells me he's on leave and has his phone switched off. Smart move, that. The only way to get some peace – especially in his job – but not much help to me.'

'I'm sorry. I mean, when I asked for help, I never dreamed anything like this was going to happen. I didn't want anyone to get hurt. I'll understand if you've had enough – if you'd rather not stay, I mean . . .'

'Absolutely not. I've got personal reasons for wanting to get to the bottom of this, now.'

'If you're sure?' Jenny looked immeasurably relieved. 'I just feel so guilty.'

'Well, don't. It's not your fault. Taylor started it, and his reaction to my being here just serves to prove that your suspicions were right and there *is* something going on.'

'I suppose so.' Jenny put two plates of sandwiches on the table and gestured to Daniel to sit down. Sitting opposite him, she picked up a sandwich, but instead of eating it, she put it back on the plate and looked helplessly at him.

'Oh, God! How am I meant to go on dealing with Taylor and MacAllister after this?'

'Best pretend I haven't said anything,' Daniel suggested. 'I mean, you can't fire them – for the same reasons that I can't take this to the cops. And if you let on that you know, things are bound to get very awkward.'

'Things already *are* awkward.' Jenny ran a hand through her fringe distractedly. 'It's just one thing after another. How did every-thing get so complicated?'

Daniel could think of nothing comforting to say. His own life had been complicated for as long as he could remember.

'By the way, I noticed Taz has got a nasty place between his toes – probably from the net. He keeps licking it and I wouldn't mind letting a vet just take a look at it. Who do you recommend, round here?'

'Ever since I can remember, we've always had Ivor Symmonds. Both for the farm animals and the small ones. He's an absolute dear. Getting on a bit now, but I can't imagine him ever retiring. Tell him I sent you.'

Following Jenny's directions, Daniel and Taz found themselves on the doorstep of Symmonds and Son, Veterinary Surgeons, at the north end of Great Ditton's main street, just after three o'clock that afternoon.

The surgery was located in a small courtyard just off the street, the gleaming paintwork and general air of prosperity indicating that the business was doing well.

Inside, red leatherette bench seats lined two walls, and a TV screen high in one corner advertised worming and flea treatments, dog-grooming services and the benefits of pet insurance, on a continuous loop.

'Mr Symmonds won't be a moment,' the middle-aged, copper-headed receptionist said cheerily from behind a counter set in one wall. 'Take a seat.'

Instead, Daniel drifted across to the notice board and stood lazily scanning the advertisements and business cards pinned to the cork. Amongst the puppies for sale, dog groomers and walkers and house-sitters advertised there, there were no less than five notices offering rewards for the safe return of lost pets.

'This seems to be a big problem around here,' he said, turning to the receptionist.

She looked up.

'Sorry?'

'Pets going missing. There was something about it in the paper and I've seen several posters.'

'Yeah, it's awful.'

'So, what's happening? Are they stealing them for ransom, do they know?'

'Um . . . I'm not sure. There was a story in the papers a couple of months ago where this family did get their dog back. The little girl had leukaemia and she was missing the dog so much the parents offered a reward. There was a lovely picture of them all together, afterwards. Lynda found it – you know, Lynda Boyd from the garage. Said she spotted it wandering down the road. Said she was going to donate the money to the dog rescue.'

'That's nice,' Daniel said, though on recent experience he felt he'd want to see the receipt before he would credit any members of *that* family with charitable actions.

'Mr Whelan?' A tall, wiry man in his sixties had come into the reception area. He wore camel-coloured corduroy trousers and a checked shirt, and peered over wire-rimmed glasses that perched halfway down his bony, hooked nose. The whole was topped by frizzy mid-grey hair.

'Yes, that's me.' Daniel whistled to Taz and they followed the vet into his consulting room, where the dog began to pace nervously about, pausing to whine by the door. 'He's spent too much time in vets' surgeries,' Daniel explained.

'It's an inescapable fact that most of my clients would rather be somewhere else,' Symmonds observed. 'I believe I have that in common with dentists.'

Daniel smiled. 'Are you Symmonds or Son?'

'Both,' the vet replied. 'The original Symmonds was my father, so in that sense I am the son, but I also have a son myself.'

'And is he a vet, too?'

'Indeed he is. But for the moment he prefers to forge his own path. Can't blame him, I suppose. He's working in Cardiff.'

'You miss him,' Daniel was watching the older man's face.

'Of course, but one day he'll be back to stay and then I'll hang up my stethoscope.'

'Jenny said she thought you'd carry on till you dropped . . .'

'No, just till Philip takes over. Then it's the slippers and pipe for me.'

'You work on your own here?'

'I have locums. Now, let's take a look at this lad of yours. What's he been up to?'

Symmonds dealt with the cut on Taz's paw competently, finishing it off with a super-neat bandage that he recommended should stay on for at least forty-eight hours, and asking to see him again at that time.

Daniel thanked the vet for seeing him at short notice.

'That's OK. Anything for little Jenny. Known her family for years. She's been so unlucky, what with losing her first husband and now this.'

'Yes, more than her fair share.'

As the vet showed him out, Daniel paused by the notice board.

'What do you make of this, then? All these cats and dogs going missing.'

Symmonds shrugged. 'It's a bit of a mystery. But I expect you'll find some of those are probably old adverts. I don't know when the board was last sorted out.'

'I did it last week,' his receptionist spoke up indignantly from her position behind the counter.

Symmonds cast her an unreadable look.

'An organized gang, then? Stealing to order?'

'But then you'd expect them to be specific breeds – gundogs or lurchers. Some of these are just mongrels. And who'd pay for a stolen black-and-white cat? The rescues are stuffed with them.'

'Ransom, then, perhaps. I don't know. Whoever it is, I just hope the police catch up with them soon.' Symmonds shook his head sadly.

At that moment, the street door opened and the vet's expression became stony. With a hasty goodbye to Daniel, he turned on his heel and went back into his consulting room.

Surprised, Daniel looked round and saw an overweight middle-aged man with a weather-beaten face, slicked-down black hair and luxuriant sideburns. He wore navy-blue overalls and a pair of heavy-duty working boots, and as he passed Daniel, he left the smell of sump oil hanging in the air.

He disappeared into the consulting room and Daniel heard the vet say testily, 'I thought I told you to phone first!'

'But I needed some stuff for tonight, and as I was passing . . .'

'Close the bloody door!' Symmonds hissed, and the altercation was cut off as the door banged shut.

The receptionist produced an embarrassed smile.

'I'm sorry about that. He *will* turn up without an appointment.'

'Who is he?' Daniel asked, though he was pretty sure of the answer.

'Oh, don't you know?' The girl pulled a face. 'That's Norman Boyd. Godfather of the Great Ditton Mafia!'

EIGHT

Leaving the vet's and heading for his car, Daniel's eye was caught by a van parked half on the pavement, with the words *Ditton Vale Gazette* stencilled on the side and rear doors. He paused, looking up at the adjacent building. Just below one of the upper windows, the same words adorned a white board. Even though the day was bright, he could see a striplight on in the room behind the window and someone moving about.

At ground level, beside the door, were three nameplates and an intercom. Daniel pressed the buzzer and waited, and presently a rather impatient male voice informed him that the office was closed.

'OK. Your loss,' Daniel told him. 'I'm sure someone else will be interested.'

'Look, wait! Hold on a minute. What's it about?'

'You said you were closed . . .'

'I thought you were one of those bloody irritating people who want to put an advert in at the last minute. All right, look, the door's open. Come on up.'

True to his word, the door clicked and opened an inch or two, and, with Taz at his heels, Daniel accepted the invitation, finding himself at the foot of a steep flight of stairs with an arrow directing him up to the *DVG* office.

The owner of the grumpy voice turned out to be younger than Daniel expected; a lean, thin-faced individual in his early twenties, with an unhealthy pallor and a shock of frizzy, gingery hair. He was wearing faded jeans that hung on his bony hips and a T-shirt that advertised the 2005 UK tour of some rock group Daniel had never heard of.

'Er, sorry about before,' he offered as he let Daniel into the brightly lit and chaotically untidy office. 'Amy's supposed to be here – she does classifieds – but she's going to a hen do, so I let her off early, and sod's law when I do that, half a dozen people turn up at the last bloody minute with advertising forms clutched in their sticky little mitts, wanting insertion in Monday's paper – even though the deadline is Friday evening and it's now Saturday. William Faulkner, by the way. Editor.' He stuck out a long-fingered white hand.

'Annoying,' Daniel agreed, briefly clasping the hand. 'Daniel Whelan.'

'And . . . ?' He'd spotted the dog.

'Taz,' Daniel supplied. 'You don't mind, do you?'

'No, not at all. I like dogs.' He raised his eyebrows expectantly. 'So, what have you got for me?'

'Ah. I didn't actually say I had anything for you. I just implied it and you joined up the dots. I actually wanted to ask you a couple of questions.'

'Oh,' William frowned, adding with an oddly touching naivety, 'That's not exactly playing fair, is it?'

'No,' Daniel agreed candidly. 'Are you *very* busy? The thing is, I need some info and I thought you might be just the man.'

'Well, I am *pretty* busy. Actually, not so much busy as about to pack up for the day, really. What is it you want to know?'

'A couple of things. Do you have a searchable archive?'

'Absolutely. I indexed it myself.' William moved with a slouching yet energetic stride to a workstation by the window, tapped a few keys and brought up a display on the monitor. 'Pull up a pew,' he added with the wave of a hand.

Daniel gave a silent cheer. He'd struck lucky.

Whatever William's plans had been for the evening, he didn't leave the office until gone six, getting caught up in Daniel's quest for information so enthusiastically that it was Daniel himself who eventually drew the editor's attention to the lateness of the hour.

Although his visit to the *DVG* office had been completely unpremeditated, it had paid dividends. He'd arrived with a number of half-formed ideas buzzing around his head, and while it couldn't be said that he left with any definitive answers, the ideas had certainly taken a more perceptible shape.

The main thrust of his queries had been about animals reported missing in the area, but they had also gone on to search for cases of animal cruelty, which in turn led to three reports linked to dog fighting.

'You don't think the pets are being stolen for fighting?' William had asked, his face showing concern. He'd already told Daniel that he had a cat at home that he was careful to keep in at night.

'No. Not directly. The dogs used for fighting are bred specially for it – hence the name, pit bull terriers: bred for the fighting pit. Even though it's totally illegal, it's big business. Auntie Lily's Shih Tzu wouldn't be anywhere near tough enough – but they have been known to use pet dogs and cats as bait. Teasers – to raise the blood lust in the younger, untried fighting dogs. No doubt it gives the humans a cheap thrill, too. By the way – don't run any adverts for animals free to good homes in your paper. They might as well just deliver them straight to the pit bull owners.'

'But that's awful! It's disgusting!' The *DVG* editor was genuinely shocked. 'The authorities know this goes on but they can't put a stop to it?'

'It's an ongoing battle. They know it's rife, but it's very difficult to catch them at it,' Daniel said sadly. 'The dog-fighting community is a tight one and, as you might imagine, is a magnet for some really choice characters. Nobody talks lightly.'

'How do you know all this?' William was all of a sudden wary, and Daniel fell back on a version of the truth.

'I've got a mate who's a cop and he told me about it. So when I saw all the posters round here for missing pets, something started niggling in my suspicious little mind.'

'You really think it's going on in this area? Have you told your mate about it?'

'Not yet. He's on leave. But I will.'

'So you think Maisie Cooper was actually on to something, then?'

Maisie Cooper had featured in one of the search results. She had complained that her spaniel had been attacked and seriously mauled on a local footpath by a dog she swore was a pit bull terrier. When interviewed, she had said she had warned the police and the RSPCA that there were fighting dogs in the area but said they hadn't believed her. It had been her stated opinion that it would take the death of a child to stir them to action.

'I can't say for sure,' Daniel said. 'But it might be worth having a word with this Maisie, though.'

'Have a job – she's dead. Hit-and-run accident last year. Here, I'll find it for you.' William's long fingers sped over the keys and, within moments, the report of Maisie Cooper's tragic end was on the screen in front of them.

Daniel leaned forward. The article was brief, reporting her death in hospital following the accident and saying that it gave weight to local residents' calls for a speed limit on the roads around the village.

'She was a bit of a gossip,' William said. 'But kind at heart. Always there helping whenever there was a do in the village. There was a huge turnout at the funeral. They never caught the driver, though.'

Daniel's eyes narrowed thoughtfully, but a glance at the editor showed that he was taking the report at face value.

Another news item, in the *In Brief* column, had told of a joint RSPCA and police raid on a suspected dog-fighting venue that William said was about twenty miles away. Several dogs had been seized and put to sleep under the Dangerous Dogs Act, and two arrests had been made, it reported, but neither was a local man. The article was in an issue dated some eight weeks previously.

After leaving the *DVG* offices, Daniel drove to the garage for fuel and was surprised to see that the gates to the adjacent scrapyard stood wide and the swinging metal sign still showed it as open.

Mindful of the illegality of his smashed headlights, he paid for his diesel and turned the Merc's steering wheel in the direction of Boyd's Salvage Spares.

Hidden as it was behind a substantial fence of corrugated metal sheets topped with barbed wire, Daniel was unprepared for the scale of the site. As soon as he went through the gates, the rough gravel driveway passed between untidy banks of scrap metal fifteen or twenty feet high. It then continued across the centre of the vast plot with avenues branching off it on either side, before curving right-handed and culminating in a huge turning space in front of a forty-foot-long Portakabin, two large Nissen huts and a smaller shed.

Although a crudely painted sign said 'Reception', the door to the cabin had a 'Closed' sign and was locked when Daniel tried it, confirming what he'd half suspected: that the main gates had been left open by mistake. There were no signs of life, although he could hear the muffled barking of a number of dogs, which seemed to be coming from some way off. In his mind he heard Woodsmoke's voice again. *Didn't tell you about the other dogs, though, did she? The ones you can't see.*

With the Rottweilers in mind, he'd left Taz in the car, and now he heard the dog grumbling as he moved to the window of the first Nissen hut and peered in. The state of the glass made it almost impossible to see anything, but as he was met with no frenzy of barking, he concluded that there were no dogs in residence. It appeared to be a storeroom for saleable spare parts.

As he moved on to the second hut, Taz began to bark fretfully in the car.

'Can I 'elp you?' a voice enquired loudly, and Daniel spun round to see Norman Boyd approaching from a side alley leading two well-muscled dogs of medium height, one fawn, one black. They were both tailless but, clearly, neither was a Rottweiler.

'Oh, hi. I was looking for some new headlights for the Merc,' Daniel replied, going towards the man. The dogs wriggled and wagged their docked stumps in delighted anticipation; their owner made no effort to appear similarly welcoming.

'We're closed.'

'I see that now, but the gates were open, so I just drove on in.'

'Bloody Melody! Head in the bloody clouds!' the man muttered under his breath. Then, to Daniel, 'We close at five thirty. My daughter was meant to lock up on her way out.'

'Sorry,' Daniel said, but made no move to leave. 'Nice dogs. What are they? Mastiffs?'

'No. Labrador-cross-boxer.' Boyd said shortly. 'Got their papers and everything. Look, you'll have to come back on Monday, I'm afraid.'

'Yeah, I'm sorry. I thought it was odd you being open so late. Huge place you've got here. I expect you need good guard dogs.'

'These aren't guard dogs. No, we've got a couple of Rottweilers out back. These are just pets. Soft as butter.'

'I can see that,' Daniel agreed, rubbing the black dog behind its ears. Its companion pushed its head into his hand to receive the same fuss.

'Look, I'm sorry, but you'll have to leave now. I'm a busy man and I need to get that gate shut before some other punter comes breezing in.'

'Of course. Sorry about the mistake. I'll come back on Monday.'

With a final caress for the dogs, Daniel turned and went back to his car.

Outside the salvage yard gates, on the edge of the garage fore-court, he slowed to a halt and pondered his next move. It was at times like this that he most regretted the demise of his career in the police, and, more especially, the manner in which it had come about, leaving him *persona non grata* with nearly all his former colleagues.

Nearly all.

Absent-mindedly watching the progress of a woman with a pair of cocker spaniels along the pavement on the opposite side of the road, he remembered his own spaniel, Bella, a top drugs dog who'd been reallocated when he'd been pulled from the dog unit. He'd had nearly six years working with that dog. The memory brought a stab of bitterness that surprised him. He'd thought he was over it.

Resolutely, he forced himself to concentrate on the here and now. Bella had been reassigned to an Anglo-Japanese handler called Jo-Ji Matsuki – he of the martial arts skills – and commonly referred to by his peers as Joey Suzuki.

A man of few words, Joey had a reputation for level-headed reliability, and although Daniel hadn't known the man well, he had always found him pleasant. He also had a nice way with the dogs in his care, and in Daniel's opinion that counted for a lot. You could tell quite a bit about a person by the way they treated their animals. Joey might well be worth a try.

Sitting with the engine idling, Daniel searched the memory on his mobile without much optimism and was surprised to find a home number for the man. That was where his luck ran out for the time being, his call being fielded by an answering machine on which he left a brief message.

That done, he toyed with the idea of sounding out the local police on the matter of the missing pets, but Great Ditton certainly didn't have a station, and he didn't know for sure where the nearest one was or whether it would even be open on a Saturday evening. Adding to that the doubtful wisdom of turning up in a car that was clearly not roadworthy, he gave the idea up as a non-starter.

At the turning to Forester's, Daniel hesitated and then drove on down the farm drive. It was still early and a ride out on Piper was a great deal more alluring than a long evening spent at the cottage, where the only entertainment was reading or listening to the radio.

Daniel wasn't one for long periods of inactivity, and Taz could certainly do with a run now his paw was sorted.

As he drove out from the shelter of the trees on to the rise overlooking the farm, the first thing that caught Daniel's eye was the fluorescent striped livery of a police Range Rover parked in front of the house. He slowed to a stop. Had Jenny decided to report the previous night's trouble after all? If she had, he could kiss the idea of an evening ride goodbye. Irritation set in. He really wasn't in the mood for the interminable questioning that would follow.

'Bugger!' he said. There was no point in turning round now. If the police wanted to speak to him, they would catch up with him sooner or later. He drove over the rise and on down the slope to the yard, parking beside the Range Rover just as Jenny emerged from the house accompanied by two officers, one male and one female.

'Well, we'll be in touch as soon as we have any more news, Mrs Summers,' Daniel heard the man say as he got out of the car.

'Thank you. Oh, hi, Daniel. Daniel's my new driver,' Jenny told the pair. 'He's on loan from a friend to help out for a bit.'

The two officers looked Daniel over appraisingly and he returned their regard, seeing a man in his forties, slightly overweight and balding, and his female colleague, thirty-something, blonde and on the hard side of pretty.

'Are you staying in the village?' the woman asked. She wore her hair scraped back into a knot below her cap.

That was good. Jenny obviously hadn't mentioned the previous night's events.

'He's staying at the cottage in the woods – the one we call Forester's,' Jenny put in quickly.

Not that it was any of their business, Daniel thought sourly. Checking that he hadn't moved in with Jenny whilst her husband was out of the picture, no doubt. He'd have done the same in their place, but it felt different to be on the receiving end of such probing. If he *had* moved in, he'd probably have been added to the suspect list for Gavin's assault. Always supposing they had any suspects, he thought cynically.

The female officer's attention had transferred to his car.

'Had a spot of bother?' she asked, indicating the headlights.

'Yeah, kids, I think. Too much time on their hands.'

'When did that happen?'

'Last night.' If he lied, they'd want to know why he hadn't got the lights repaired yet.

'Out at the cottage? That's a long way to go for mischief.'

'Yeah, nicely remote,' Daniel said pointedly. 'Not much chance of being seen.'

'*Did* you see them?'

'It was dark. Time I got outside, they were long gone,' Daniel said.

'And er . . . ?' She indicated her own cheekbone, eyebrows raised.

'Tripped over the dog on the way out,' he explained blandly.

'Mm, well, you'll need to get those lights sorted before you drive that again,' she stated.

'Yeah, lucky it's a private road between here and the cottage, isn't it?'

The blonde head nodded to concede the point, and moved towards the Range Rover with her partner following. Even though she was outranked by her male colleague, she was clearly the dynamic one of the pair. She would go far, Daniel mused, glad he was out of the career advancement rat race.

'Do you have any theories about the missing pet problem in this area?' he asked, as they opened the Range Rover's doors. Both paused and looked at him.

'*Is* there a problem?' Predictably, it was the blonde who spoke.

'You must know there is,' Daniel replied. 'I've only been here a few days and even *I've* noticed all the posters and the notices in the local rag. There was even an article. What's the official take on it?'

'Well, yes, of course we're aware that a number of pets have been reported missing, but what often happens is that they stray for a day or two and then, when they turn up, their owners forget – or just plain don't bother – to take the notices down. It gives a rather misleading sense of the state of affairs.'

'So you're not overly worried about it?'

'We take all such reports seriously – but, as I said, many of them turn out to be false alarms. We simply don't have the time and the manpower to look into every lost pet claim, I'm afraid, much as we sympathize—'

'You're not concerned that it might be connected with something else, then?'

'Such as?'

'Well, dog fighting, perhaps?'

Now he had her interest. Her gaze sharpened.

'That's something of a leap, isn't it, Mr – er, I don't believe I caught your second name.'

'Whelan.' He supplied. 'And yours?'

'Paige. WPS Paige.'

'Well, not such a leap, really. It's a widespread problem, isn't it?'

Paige's male counterpart stepped forward, apparently feeling he should take some part in the conversation.

'And what's your interest in dog fighting, Mr Whelan?'

'As a dog owner, it disgusts me,' Daniel replied, transferring his gaze to the man. 'As it would anyone who had a spark of decency about them. And as a concerned citizen, I just wanted to know what was being done about it.'

'As I said, it's something we take very seriously,' Paige stepped in once more. 'And if we did have a problem in this area, we would be aware of it, I can assure you.'

'I thought I might have a word with the local dog warden . . .'

Paige's expression became positively glacial.

'Mr Whelan, we appreciate your concern, but it's something much best left to the relevant authorities.'

'Absolutely,' Daniel said obediently, his expression bland. 'Just as long as the relevant authorities have the time and the manpower to spare.'

Paige clearly didn't like having her own words used against her but struggled to find an answer. She favoured him with a look of sharp dislike and, with a nod to her colleague, took her leave of Jenny and got into the Range Rover.

'She didn't like me,' Daniel observed placidly, as he and Jenny watched the vehicle climb the hill toward the wood.

'Well, you did wind her up a bit,' Jenny pointed out, squinting against the sun as she turned to him. 'What was that all about? The dog fighting stuff, I mean. Where did that come from?'

Daniel told her about the missing pets posters and his research at the *DVG* offices, including the article about Maisie Cooper.

'Apparently she was convinced there were fighting dogs in the area. It made me think. We had a similar case when I was a rookie in Bristol.'

'I remember Maisie.' Jenny turned to go back into the house.

'She was a good soul but a bit of a drama queen. Nobody took her very seriously, I don't think. Poor old thing. She got knocked down by a car in Back Lane. There was a huge turnout at the funeral.'

'It seems someone took her seriously,' Daniel mused, almost to himself.

'What do you mean?'

'Nothing really. Just thinking aloud. Ignore me.'

Jenny gave him narrow look but apparently decided not to pursue it.

'So what was the visit for? Any news?' Daniel asked.

'No. Someone turns up every now and then just to let me know they're still working on Gavin's case. Don't know why they don't just phone. Anyway, how's Taz?'

'Oh, nothing too worrying. Antibiotics and a dressing. Your Mr Symmonds is a nice chap.'

'Isn't he?' Jenny responded warmly.

'What's the story with his son?'

'How did you know there was a story?'

'Oh, I don't know. Something in his body language. It seems odd that they don't run the practice together, seeing as it's called Symmonds and Son and he's obviously run ragged, in spite of having locums.'

'Yes, well, they did for a while. Philip moved around for a bit for a year or two after qualifying – to gain some experience, you know – but then his mother – Ivor's wife – died, and Philip came home and set up shop with his dad. It all seemed to be going OK at first, but rumour has it they had a terrific row and Philip walked out. I don't know the details – perhaps they found they just couldn't work together. It happens, although no one saw it coming – not even Hayley, his receptionist, who I know quite well. I don't suppose we'll ever know what went on for sure, but it has upset Ivor very badly.'

'When did this happen – the row, I mean?'

Jenny shrugged. 'Oh, I don't know. End of last year, I suppose it must have been. Before Christmas, because I remember we were all a bit worried about him over the holiday, having lost Enid as well.' She paused on the doorstep. 'Are you staying for supper? The kids are at Mum's.'

Daniel hesitated. 'Well, actually, I had thought of taking Piper out . . .'

'Do you feel up to it?' Jenny looked doubtful.

'Well, Taz is spoiling for a run and, to be honest, I think I'd sooner ride than walk. I won't go very far.'

'OK.' Jenny's face brightened. 'Would you mind if I came too? It seems like forever since I last rode purely for pleasure.'

'You're asking *me*? They're *your* horses. Anyway, I was hoping you might be able to come. I wondered if you could show me where old Woodsmoke holes up, if it's not too far. I'd like to thank him again for last night.'

'It's a deal. Two shakes, I'll just run and change.'

NINE

The evening ride was successful inasmuch as Jenny showed Daniel where Woodsmoke lived in a heather-thatched wooden building on a triangular piece of wasteland on the edge of the woods. However, Daniel was thwarted in his aim to try and extract more information from the poacher on the mysterious Butcher Boys, because he wasn't at home.

After a lazy Sunday at the cottage, during which he repaired the fence, restored the battered flower borders to some kind of order and spent a couple of hours exploring the surrounding woods with Taz, Daniel turned up for work on the Monday morning feeling eighty-five per cent fit.

Visually, there was very little damage to show for the events of Friday night, and the knowledge that, even after the considerable violence of the confrontation, he was able to meet Boyd and MacAllister pretty much as if he'd shrugged it all off gave Daniel confidence and a large measure of satisfaction. He was interested to see how Boyd played it.

In the event, more immediate matters were occupying Taylor Boyd's attention when Daniel walked into the drivers' room that morning.

Boyd had his back to the door, and facing him stood the diminutive figure of Reg Parsons, Summer Haulage's oldest driver, with his Jack Russell terrier, Skip, tucked under his arm.

Reg and his dog wore identical expressions of dislike, but while

Reg's language was tempered by social etiquette, Skip had no such inhibitions; he was exhibiting a neat set of small white teeth and growling at Boyd in one long, continuous grizzle.

Watching from one side, with every appearance of enjoyment, was Dek Edwards. Could he have been the mysterious third man responsible for netting Taz? It seemed unlikely. Whoever had spared the dog had done so in direct defiance of Boyd's wishes, and Dek had never given any indication of being an animal lover, and every sign of hanging on Taylor's sleeve whenever possible.

The big man, Macca, occupied the sofa, but he was reading a paper and didn't look especially interested in the dispute. A quick glance round the room found no sign of the youngster, Dean.

'What's going on?' Daniel enquired.

'His bloody dog bit me, that's what!' Boyd said hotly, without turning his head.

'Only because you nearly sat on him!' Reg retorted.

'He shouldn't be on the fucking chair!'

'He wasn't doing any harm. You didn't have to kick him, you bloody thug!'

'All right, gentlemen, that's enough!' Daniel said, unconsciously slipping back into the quietly authoritarian mode that had been habitual in his policing days. Surprisingly, even without the uniform, it worked. Recent history apparently momentarily forgotten, the aggrieved parties turned towards him, ready to put their side of the story forward, but he forestalled them with a hand held up.

'What's the injury?'

Boyd held up his hand, which bore two bleeding puncture wounds near the base of the thumb. Daniel glanced at it and then at the man's face, where an angry-looking cut lip confirmed his identity as Daniel's attacker, if any confirmation had been needed.

Reg snorted at the evidence. 'Hardly life-threatening!'

'That's not the point,' Boyd retorted. 'It's a dangerous dog and needs putting down. I can do it for you right now, if you like?'

'Enough!' Daniel cut in sharply. 'If the dog bit you and you kicked it back, then in my book you've had your revenge. Incident over.'

Reg clearly wasn't happy, but after muttering under his breath and looking from Daniel to Boyd and back again, he subsided into silence and turned away. With his bushy eyebrows and grizzled hair, he bore more than a passing resemblance to his feisty little dog, Daniel thought.

'If he fuckin' does it again, he'll get more than a kick!' Boyd promised, stabbing the air with his forefinger. Then, transferring his gaze to Daniel, demanded, 'Who asked you, anyway?'

He was saved the trouble of replying by the appearance of Jenny in the doorway. Something of the atmosphere must have struck her, or perhaps she heard Boyd's last comment, because she hesitated.

'Is everything all right?'

'Fine,' Daniel answered before anyone else could.

Jenny looked at her watch. 'It's gone half past . . .'

'I was just going to fetch the rosters from the office,' Boyd said defensively.

'No need, I've brought them over.'

'Deano's not here yet.'

'No, and he won't be coming. I've just had a phone call. He's quit.' Jenny ran a hand through her fringe. She looked near the end of her tether.

'He can't do that!' Boyd protested. 'What about his notice? He's supposed to give you two weeks.'

'He has, but he says he's ill.'

'And you believed him?' Boyd's voice was loaded with scorn.

'Whether I did or not is immaterial. I can't force him to come in. Anyway, I just came over to let you know you'll need to reallocate his drops. Sorry, but it's going to mean more work for you guys till we can find someone to replace him.'

Boyd began to protest again, but Daniel cut through him. 'It shouldn't be a problem between the five of us. Dean only drove the van, after all. I don't mind sorting out the schedules, if you're not up to it.'

'You bloody won't!' Boyd said, pushing past Jenny and heading for the office.

Daniel allowed himself a secret smile. He'd guessed that would get Boyd moving.

By working through his lunch break, Daniel was able to get his day's driving done in time to call in at the salvage yard again before it closed. This time, the Rottweilers were in view, tethered by stout chains in the shade of the main Portakabin. As Daniel jumped down from the cab of his lorry, they leapt to their feet, ran to the limit of their chains and set up a frenzy of barking, their jowls spattering the gravel with gobs of drool.

Left sitting on the front seat of the truck, Taz was inclined to join in until a word from Daniel set him straight.

A movement in the shadowy doorway of the reception building heralded the emergence of Ricky Boyd, wearing low-slung baggy jeans and an oil-stained, once-white vest. He carried a beer can in his hand, but it was presumably empty or virtually so, because after shouting at the dogs to no avail, he shied it at them. The Rottweilers dodged and retreated, still watching Daniel balefully.

Ricky hesitated a fraction as he saw who was waiting, looking right and left as if hoping for back up. None was forthcoming and he came reluctantly forward into the sunlight to ask Daniel what he wanted.

'Need a replacement pair of headlights for my car, if you've got 'em. Some tosser took a baseball bat to them the other night.'

For a fleeting moment, Ricky's facial muscles tightened involuntarily, and this reaction to his statement led Daniel to believe that Ricky knew of the night-time attack led by his older brother. Daniel imagined he would have been furious to be left out of such an excursion but felt that, in Taylor's place, he would probably have done the same.

'Erm, what sort of car is it?' Ricky asked then. He looked happier now, and Daniel could imagine his joy at repeating the "tosser" comment to his brother.

'Surprised you need to ask that.'

'What d'you mean?' All of a sudden the wariness was back.

'Well, you had a good look at it when I came into the garage that day. Don't you remember?' Daniel asked with wonderful innocence.

'Yeah. Of course.' Ricky's relief was comical. 'Mercedes-Benz C class. What year?'

He noted the details down on a grubby notepad he took from his pocket and, telling Daniel to wait, moved away towards the closest of the Nissen huts.

Left to kick his heels beside the Summer Haulage lorry, Daniel leaned back against the cab door and surveyed the mountains of metal that surrounded him. Vehicles of all kinds lay in a tangle with guttering, old baths, lengths of chain-link fence, kitchen appliances, oil drums and other unidentifiable items of twisted metal: some shiny, some painted, many rusting forlornly.

What was to happen to it? Daniel wondered. Was it all destined for the smelter? Some piles were already so big that there was no way of knowing what was underneath the surface layer. It seemed to him a very inefficient use of space. Away across the acres of scrap, he could see the towering arm of a crane-like vehicle, and beyond it again a big metal container with what looked like a hydraulic piston arm angled into the top. A metal compactor, he guessed. So, Boyd's Salvage Spares did the complete works, it seemed.

'Got nothing in stock,' Ricky said, striding back across the gravel. He seemed pleased with the information.

'Well, could you perhaps order them?' Daniel suggested.

Ricky grudgingly supposed they could.

'OK. Do that, then. When will they be in?'

'Dunno. Not sure. Tomorrow, maybe?'

'That'll do. And you'll fit them?'

'Can do. Not sure when.'

'Well, suppose you go and take a look in the diary,' Daniel suggested, at which point Ricky said it shouldn't be a problem as they weren't too busy.

Daniel paid a deposit and was just about to climb back into the lorry when an old-style VW Beetle swept into the yard. It had been converted into a soft-top, which was currently folded down, affording a view of a young woman with deeply bronzed skin, a platinum-blonde ponytail and a pink baseball cap. She turned the VW with a flourish and came to a halt in front of the Portakabin, where the dogs began to bark again, this time in welcome.

The girl's eyes were on Daniel as she climbed out of the car, revealing a cropped vest top and micro denim shorts above long brown legs that culminated in flip-flops sparkling with bling. She took off a pair of designer sunglasses and looked him up and down with every appearance of appreciation from beneath impossibly long black lashes.

From the passenger seat emerged a woman some thirty years older and a good six inches shorter. Blonde curls framed a face that wore too much make-up, to disguise a skin that had seen too much sun. A leathery décolletage hadn't stopped her donning a low-cut sun-top, but she had drawn the line at shorts, wearing instead a flounced, gypsy-style skirt.

Norman Boyd's wife and daughter, Daniel supposed. He wondered if the younger woman ever recognized her future self in the elder one, but didn't imagine she did. Even though she wasn't his cup of tea, it wasn't hard to see why Dek might have fallen for her.

'Hey, Melody. Did you get my smokes?' Ricky asked.

'Of course,' she replied, without taking her eyes off Daniel. 'You owe me twenty-five quid, and you don't get the fags till I get the money.'

Daniel climbed into the cab and started the engine. As he glanced out of the open window, Melody favoured him with a long, slow wink.

Dek Edwards was the only occupant of the drivers' lounge when Daniel got back to the farm. He had a newspaper open on his knee and had been sucking the top of a biro, but now he folded the paper and returned the pen to his shirt pocket.

'Don't stop on my account,' Daniel said dispassionately, going on into the kitchen area. Taz slunk across the room and flopped down in the coolest spot, eyeing Dek watchfully.

'Stop what?'

'Doing the puzzles.'

'Nah, I was just bored. Doodling, you know.'

'Oh, OK. I was just getting a coffee; want one?' Without Boyd around, Dek seemed more approachable, and he wondered if he might get him to open up a little.

'OK, thanks,' Dek said, sounding surprised.

'Just seen a friend of yours,' Daniel said casually. 'Melody Boyd. Nice-looking girl.'

Dek got to his feet and followed Daniel into the kitchenette. At once, Taz also stood up, with the suspicion of a rumble under his breath. It seemed his recent experience had made him regard everyone with suspicion.

'You saw Melody?' Dek asked.

'Yeah. At the scrapyard. I dropped in to see if they'd got any headlights for my car.'

'Oh, right. Look, second thoughts, I'll take a rain check on the coffee. Just remembered something I've got to do. Cheers, all the same.'

Daniel smiled a wry smile as he made his own coffee, hearing the door shut behind Edwards and, presently, his car driving away. Taking his mug, he went to sit in one of the armchairs, leaning back with a weary sigh. His muscles were still tender.

'Made a pig's ear of that, didn't I, Taz?' he commented, and the dog came to lie at his feet, panting. 'Wrong subject altogether.'

After a moment, Daniel picked up the newspaper and began to leaf through it with scant interest. It was a sensationalist rag and carried far too many stories about so-called celebrities for his liking. He saw evidence of Dek's doodling, several of the photographs having had moustaches and spectacles added. Thinking he might try the puzzles himself, he located the page and folded the paper down to a more manageable size. Then, ballpoint poised, he paused, eyes narrowing.

'Well, well . . .' he murmured, but his thoughts were interrupted by the ringing of his mobile.

'Daniel? Is that you?' The words were enunciated in the slightly over-perfect fashion of a foreigner.

'Hi, Joey. Thanks for ringing back. How are you, mate? And how's my little Bella?'

'I'm fine and so is Bella. She's a good little dog; I was lucky to get her. Did I ever thank you for that?'

'Bastard!' Daniel said, without heat. 'You know it wasn't by choice. Broke me up, losing her.'

'Your loss – my gain,' Jo-Ji observed cheerfully. 'Bella, she's very happy with me. She knows when she's got a good partner. Anyhow, I got your message – you say you want to know about the Butcher Boys.'

'That's right. Have you managed to find out anything?'

'Enough to know you don't want to be getting involved with them,' Jo-Ji stated grimly.

'I think it might be a bit late for that,' Daniel replied. 'I'm guessing we're talking dog fighting, here. Would I be right?'

'That's right. Have you looked them up on the net?'

'Haven't had a chance yet. No phone line where I'm staying.'

'Jesus, man! Where are you? Alaska?'

'No, just Wiltshire, but the cottage has been empty for a while and there isn't a library for miles.' He had been going to ask Jenny if he could use her PC that evening.

'Well, there's not actually a lot to find through Google. A couple of mentions on US pit bull forums and an advert for a Butcher-bred stud dog over there, too. They appear to be very shy of publicity, which isn't unusual with organizations of this kind, but what is surprising is the fact that they seem to be successful in keeping their details to themselves. It argues a tightly run ship and strong-arm reinforcement. Hard to get in, I'd say, and even harder to get out in one piece.'

'Is there anything on the PNC?'

'A little, but nothing very helpful. I *can* tell you that Wiltshire are very interested in them – and very cagey, too. I'm guessing an ongoing op, but no one would confirm it. If I were you, Dan, I'd take a step back and let them get on with it.'

'Happy to, as long as they've got it covered.'

'So, what's your connection?'

'A guy I'm working with – a real charmer, name of Taylor Boyd – is connected with them, if what I hear is true. It wouldn't surprise me. The father has a couple of dogs – at least two, maybe more – that he only brings out after hours, and if they're not pit bulls, then Taz is a Pekinese! Tried to tell me they were Lab–boxer cross. Had papers, he said. Now why would cross-breeds have papers unless they were imported? And why would you go to the expense of importing mongrels when the rescues are stuffed with them? Doesn't make sense.'

'You're not wrong. Lab-cross-boxer is the usual cover for a travelling pit bull, I believe. Give me those names again, and I'll see what I can dig up. May not be for a day or two, though, cos Bella's got an assessment tomorrow, but I'll do what I can.'

As Jo-Ji was speaking, Daniel heard the outer door bang and realized with a shock that although he'd heard the other lorries return, he'd been so engrossed in the conversation that he hadn't absorbed their significance.

'Got company!' he said in low tones. 'I'll text you those. So how's Tamiko?'

'Tami is well, thank you,' Jo-Ji said, following his lead without a pause. 'I'm planning to make an honest woman of her in the autumn.'

As Daniel offered his congratulations, the inner door opened to admit Boyd and Macca. They both ignored Daniel, but Taz lifted his head and rumbled audibly as they crossed to the kitchen area.

'Saw your ex the other day at a forces' social,' Jo-Ji continued at the other end of the phone.

'Amanda? What was *she* doing there?'

'Well, someone must have invited her, and there have been rumours linking her name with Paxton's.'

'You're kidding!' Daniel was genuinely shocked. 'Paxton? But he's old enough to be her father!'

'Almost. But it *is* only a rumour as far as I know. Perhaps I shouldn't have told you . . .'

'No, that's OK. Just took me by surprise. Look, I must go now. Speak soon.'

As he pocketed his phone, Daniel's thoughts were whirling. Amanda and DCI Paxton? Just what was she up to? The last time he'd heard, she'd been seeing someone called Darren. If there were rumours linking her to Daniel's old nemesis, you could be sure she'd planned it that way. The only thing he wasn't sure of was why? Paxton was in his late forties, Amanda twenty-nine. Although even Daniel couldn't claim the man was ugly, neither was he love's young dream, and he was already beginning to put on weight. Was it the attraction of power? Surely even *she* wouldn't go to such lengths just to get back at Daniel?

'Reg not back yet, then?' Boyd's enquiry cut through his thoughts.

'Er, no. I haven't seen him.'

'Late again.'

'Perhaps something's wrong. You could ring him,' Daniel suggested.

'*You* ring the old duffer. I'm not his friggin' keeper!' Boyd glared at him, took two cans of lager from the fridge and tossed one to Macca. Jenny wouldn't be happy to see alcohol on the premises – as professional drivers, they couldn't afford to take any chances – but Daniel kept quiet. Boyd was clearly in a confrontational mood and he had no intention of playing his game.

Moments later, they all heard Reg's lorry coming down the drive to the farm.

'There's Grandad,' Boyd said, stepping over the back of the sofa with the lager in his hand and sliding down to sprawl on its cushions. Macca came round the end of the chair to join him.

In due course, Reg came in, looking thoroughly fed up.

'You OK?' Daniel asked.

'No. Some joker let my bloody tyres down when I took Skip for a walk, lunchtime. I ask you – what's the point in that? I'd probably still be there if a breakdown truck hadn't come by. Luckily he came from a nearby garage and he nipped back to fetch a compressor. Still made me nearly an hour late.'

Daniel had been covertly watching the other two men while Reg spoke and would have been willing to bet that Boyd had known all about the flat tyres. His expression was just a little too carefully disinterested.

'Sit down, mate. I'll make you a cuppa,' Daniel told the older man. As he waited for the kettle to boil up again, his phone sounded and the display showed Amanda's name. He pressed the button to void the call. He did want to speak to her, especially in the light of what Joey had told him, but he didn't relish holding that particular conversation with three interested pairs of ears listening. She would keep.

'You look a bit stiff, mate. You all right?' Boyd asked, watching Daniel bring Reg's coffee to him.

'Yeah, fine. Been doing a bit of gardening. Gets your back when you're not used to it.'

'Quite the little homebody. You don't want to get too comfortable in your little cottage,' Boyd advised.

'And why would that be?'

'Well, I mean, you don't know how long you'll be staying, do you? Temporary drivers – here today, gone tomorrow. You know how it is.'

'Yeah, but now Deano's quit, we'll be shorter than ever,' Daniel pointed out. 'Can't see me going anywhere just for a while. Even to please you.'

Boyd shrugged. ''S'all the same to me.'

Daniel was the last to leave the drivers' lounge, hanging on so as to hide the fact that he wasn't going straight back to the cottage. Reg, perhaps seeing his reluctance to leave as loneliness, kindly suggested that Daniel might like to join him for a meal at The Fox and Duck in the village. Daniel thanked him but declined. He had plans to take Piper out again.

Passing the farmhouse on his way down to the yard, Daniel paused to admire the sleek lines of a black Porsche 911 Cabriolet with the current year's plates. It seemed that Jenny had a wealthy visitor. He wondered who it was.

Even as he hesitated beside the gleaming car, the door of the farmhouse opened and a man with pale blue eyes and a shadow of razor-cut gingery hair came out, turned to say goodbye to Jenny and then headed towards him.

'Just admiring your car,' Daniel announced, feeling he had to say something.

'Thanks. She's a beaut, isn't she?' The man was a Scouser, in his mid to late twenties. He wore expensive-looking clothes and had about him an air of assurance – a slight swagger even – that suggested he considered himself important.

Daniel wondered who he was. He stepped back as the man slid into the driving seat, donned a pair of designer shades and started the engine.

When the car had pulled away with a rather unnecessary amount of engine revving and wheelspin, Daniel turned to see Jenny standing on the doorstep.

'Jumped-up prick!' she said, with a look of contempt.

Daniel was surprised. The comment was out of character.

'So, who was he?'

'Liam Sellyoak.'

'The footballer? The one who owns next door? What did he want? Not that it's any of my business,' he added as an afterthought.

'He made me an offer for the farm,' Jenny said. 'A surprisingly good one, considering the state of the market.'

'Are you considering it?'

'No, of course not! At least – I don't think so. Do you think I should?'

'Is it yours to sell?' Daniel asked.

'Yes, it is. Gavin and I made a prenuptial agreement. The farm stays in my name.' She looked anxiously at Daniel. 'Are you shocked by that? Some people are.'

He shook his head. 'Surprised maybe, but no – not shocked. It's a sensible precaution when you've got so much to lose.'

'He was quite persistent – Liam, I mean.'

'So, why's he so keen to have it? Hasn't he got enough land with that huge house next door?'

'Actually, there's not all that much with the manor. Nothing like there used to be. The last owner sold it off piecemeal to try to keep his head above water. When Liam bought it, there wasn't much more than fifteen acres left with the house.'

'Enough, I would have thought,' Daniel mused. 'Considering he's probably hardly ever there. What does he want more for?'

Jenny shrugged. 'He says he fancies farming, though I doubt that would last. Anyway, I told him I had no plans to sell. The farm's been in my family for three generations, you see, and I always thought that Harry might . . . But of course, he's way too young to know what he wants. It's just that sometimes, after what happened to Gavin and with all the stress about the business, I just feel I'd like to walk away from it all and live a *normal* life.'

'Don't let him bully you into it,' Daniel advised. 'And don't rush into anything. You're tired at the moment; you don't want to make a decision you'll regret later. A lot can change in a very short time.'

'Don't I know it,' Jenny agreed. 'Are you taking Piper out? Have a nice ride.'

'I will, and, Jenny . . . normal's seriously overrated, you know.'

She responded with a wistful smile. 'You're probably right.'

TEN

D aniel was to remember his words, a few days later, with a strong sense of irony, when events in his own life had taken an unexpected and tricky turn.

All in all, things had seemed to be settling into a fairly steady routine after the violent events of the weekend. Summer Haulage was managing to meet its targets in spite of its reduced workforce, Taylor Boyd had pulled his head in and made no further attempts to confront or intimidate Daniel, and Daniel had got his car fixed.

The first interruption to the status quo was the sad disappearance of Reg's Jack Russell, Skip, while on his early morning walk in the woods behind their home. Reg suspected the little dog might have gone to ground after a rabbit and become stuck, and took a day off to search for him with no success. In the evening, Daniel offered the services of Taz, to try and track him, but although the German shepherd started eagerly enough, all at once he seemed to lose the trail and cast about randomly in a vain attempt to pick it up again. As dusk fell, they had to admit defeat, Reg disconsolate at the loss of his companion.

Daniel tried to offer words of hope and comfort, but felt hypocritical doing so, with the knowledge of the many other missing pets uppermost in his mind. If Woodsmoke was right, he feared that Skip might well have signed his own death warrant when he chose to bite Taylor Boyd. The way the little dog's trail had suddenly petered out suggested to him that Skip might well have been picked up at that point, and memories of the net used on Taz gave a clue to how it might have been accomplished. He very much feared that Skip wouldn't be found alive.

The next ripple on the pool of life came in the form of news from the hospital.

Arriving for work on the Thursday morning, Daniel found the drivers' room abuzz with speculation.

'Mrs Summers has been called in to the hospital,' Boyd told him. 'Looks like the boss might be waking up. Get him back at the helm and we'll start to see things done properly. Haulage is no business for a woman.'

Daniel was surprised to find Boyd so enthusiastic at the prospect of Gavin Summers' possible return. After all, it would surely put a crimp in his extracurricular activities.

'Even if he is coming out of the coma, it might be a long time before he's fit for work again,' he pointed out.

'On the other hand, he might just wake up and be right as rain. Happened with the son of a friend of mine,' Boyd replied. 'That lad who got knocked out in the ring – you remember, Macca? You trained him.'

Macca replied with a nod and a grunt, not bothering to lift his eyes from his dog-eared copy of *Amateur Boxing* magazine. Across in the armchair, Reg sat with a cooling cup of tea cupped between his hands, taking no interest in the conversation. He looked as though he hadn't slept.

'Be interesting to hear what he has to say about the assault or whatever it was that put him there,' Daniel mused. He watched Boyd as he spoke, but the other man appeared unmoved by the prospect.

'Probably won't remember a thing,' he said dismissively.

'No doubt the police will be waiting by his bedside in case he does,' Daniel said.

'Nosy buggers!' was Boyd's surly response. 'Hope he tells 'em where to go.'

'Why would he do that? Surely he'd want them to catch whoever it was who clobbered him.'

Boyd appeared to find the idea amusing.

'OK. So, what's funny?' Daniel asked.

'Yeah, right. As if that lot could find a nun in a bloody convent!'

Daniel shook his head and went to make himself a coffee. In his pocket, his phone chimed twice. It was a text from Jo-Ji.

Can you talk?

He sent back a negative, promising to call back later, but before he'd finished making his drink another text came through. Amanda, this time. He remembered guiltily that he hadn't returned her call and was surprised, too – she wasn't known as an early riser.

You didn't answer my text so assume OK. Will be there 5.30. A.

'What?' Daniel exclaimed under his breath. 'I didn't get any bloody text!'

'You're popular this morning,' Dek commented. 'Chick trouble?'

'Hardly. Ex-wife, actually.'

'Didn't know you'd been married.'

'No reason you should.' Daniel wasn't in the mood for casual conversation. He was trying to figure out what Amanda could mean by *be there 5.30*. Be where? Surely not at the farm? And, if so, what reason could she have unless it was to hand Drew over to him. It was the only time they ever had contact these days.

A small worm of unease started turning in Daniel's mind as he recalled an unfinished conversation they'd had just before he had left for Wiltshire. She'd said something then about him having Drew for part of the holiday, and he'd told her he couldn't make any firm plans until he'd at least got to Maidstone Farm. Predictably, she'd protested, there had been heated words and the issue had remained unresolved. Or so he'd thought.

Taking his coffee with him, Daniel went outside to try to ring her back.

Frustratingly, his call went straight to the answering service and a call to her landline produced no better results. He left a message for her to ring him as soon as possible and went back inside. One way or another, whatever her plans, she must be made to see that it was impossible for him to have Drew at the moment; it just wasn't safe – even if he hadn't had to work all day. She wouldn't be happy – that was a given – but she'd understandably be a great deal more annoyed if she made the journey from Bristol to Great Ditton before she found out.

As the day wore on, Daniel began to suspect that Amanda was actively avoiding contact. All he could get on her house phone or mobile was an answering machine message. After lunch, with visions of her and Drew setting out, he tried calling Drew's mobile, but he had no joy there, either. It looked as though he was powerless to stop them coming, if indeed that was the plan.

In a dark corner of Daniel's mind there lingered a tiny spark of hope that he'd got the wrong end of the stick and his nine-year-old son wasn't on his way to stay with him, but it wasn't much more than a faintly glowing ember and it was effectively snuffed out by the sight of a silver sports coupé parked in front of Jenny's house when he returned at the end of the day.

'There's no one in,' were Amanda's first words as he stopped the lorry and jumped down from the cab. She was standing beside the car, dressed in skinny, pale pink jeans and a lace-trimmed vest, sunglasses perched on her short, pixie-cut blonde hair. Drew stood on his side of the car, looking a little sulky. Daniel guessed the journey hadn't been wholly harmonious.

'There wouldn't be,' he told her. 'Jenny's been at the hospital all day, and I imagine the kids are with her mother. Hi, Drew. How're you doing?'

Drew shrugged and tilted his head in a non-committal way and said nothing, but his mother had picked up on one particular word.

'Jenny?' Her eyes narrowed suspiciously.

'Jenny Summers, my boss. Her husband's been in a coma for weeks and he's finally showing signs of waking up. That's why I'm here to help out, remember?'

'Meanwhile, you've been keeping her company here?' She fixed Daniel with a gimlet gaze.

He looked at her immaculate make-up and the perfect bone structure of her sharp face and wondered, not for the first time, how he'd ever found her attractive. Talk about double standards – she'd not gone short of company since the break-up, from what he'd heard.

'Meanwhile, I've been living in an empty cottage in the woods on the other side of the farm,' he countered calmly.

'Cool! Is that where I'll be staying?' Drew put in, showing his first sign of interest. A slight boy, with his mother's bone structure and his father's generous mouth, hazel eyes and wavy brown hair, he had an intense, sensitive nature, and his parents' break-up had affected him deeply.

'Look, Drew . . .' Daniel began, hating to disappoint him.

'I imagine so, darling,' Amanda cut in, going round to the back of the car to retrieve a sports bag and a rucksack. 'Sounds deadly to me, but no doubt it'll be right up your street.'

'Amanda, can I have a word?' Daniel asked, quietly fuming.

'Only if you're quick,' she said, dumping Drew's luggage by the car's front wheel and looking pointedly at her watch. 'I've got a plane to catch.'

'A plane?' He felt control slipping away.

'Yes, that's right. You know – big red and white thing with wings.'

Daniel ignored her flippancy.

'Where are you going?'

'The Maldives,' she said, adding defiantly, 'For two weeks.'

'Who with?'

She raised an eyebrow. 'I don't see that's any of your business.'

'Not Paxton?'

That shocked her; she stared. 'How the . . . ? No. With Yvonne and Paul, actually.'

Paul 'Jono' Johnson was one of Daniel's colleagues from his policing days at the Bristol Met, and Yvonne, his wife. They and Amanda were welcome to each other, he thought. Like Daniel's ex-wife, Jono had proved to be less than loyal when he had needed support, and his wife was a plump, painted doll who cared only for money and status.

'When was this all organized?' he demanded. 'And why didn't I know?'

'You did know!' she retorted. 'I told you, weeks ago, that I was thinking of going and you said you'd be happy to have Drew.'

'In principle, yes, but always depending on commitments. You knew that. We never talked specific dates, never settled it. It was only ever a possibility, as far as I remember, and I didn't know what the situation would be here at that point.'

'Oh, that'd be right. You don't want me, either,' Drew said, leaning on the roof of the car and looking sulky.

'No, it's not that, Drew. It's just that it's taken me by surprise and it's really not the right moment.'

'It's never the right moment,' Drew complained, turning away and scuffing the gravel with his trainers.

'I emailed you on Saturday,' Amanda stated.

'But I haven't got the internet. There's no landline at the cottage,' Daniel told her. 'Didn't you wonder why I didn't reply?'

'How was I to know you'd hidden yourself away in the back-woods?' she snapped. 'I thought you'd have soon told me if it wasn't all right, so I assumed it was.'

'No internet?' Drew turned round. 'What do you do all evening?'

'You'll find something to do,' Amanda said impatiently. 'Go out looking for your bloody owls, or something. Look, this is pointless. I have to be at the airport at eight thirty. If I don't go now, I'll miss my flight.' She walked over to Drew and gave him a quick hug and a peck on the cheek. 'You'll be fine. See you in a fortnight. Bye, darling!'

Before Daniel could think of anything else to say in protest, she was settling back into the driver's seat of the silver car. Starting the powerful engine, she lowered the window.

'I'll text you in a day or two,' she called, as she put the car in reverse and backed out, and Daniel wasn't sure if she was talking to Drew or to him. A wave of a small, neatly manicured hand and the car swept out of the yard and away up the hill.

Drew continued to scuff his toe in the stones, but after a moment he looked up under his brows at his father, saying nothing.

Feeling sorry for him, Daniel swallowed his frustration with Amanda and smiled.

'Well, it was a bit of a surprise, but a nice one. It's good to see you, Drew,' he said warmly.

'You don't mean that.'

'Of course I do. I'm not mad at you – it's your mother. She always winds me up. I tried to ring you earlier, but you didn't answer . . .'

'Mum took my phone away. I was playing games on it and she said the noise was giving her a headache,' Drew said, pulling a face. 'So what *do* you do in the evenings?'

'Well, actually, the last few evenings I've borrowed a horse from Jenny and gone riding,' Daniel told him. 'You could come with me if you like . . .'

Drew's answer was to purse his lips and shrug his shoulders once more, and Daniel didn't pursue the subject. He knew Drew liked riding but guessed he wasn't in the mood to be overly enthusiastic about anything just at the moment. He couldn't blame the boy; he must have felt that neither of his parents wanted to be bothered with him.

'OK, well, let's put your bags in my car and then you can come and help me hose the lorry down,' Daniel suggested. 'Taz'll be pleased to see you. See, he's looking out the window.'

Knowing there was little food at the cottage, Daniel treated Drew to a pub meal. Remembering that Boyd and his cronies frequented The Fox and Duck, he decided in favour of The Crown, at the opposite end of Great Ditton. Taylor Boyd would find out about Drew's arrival soon enough, even if the village grapevine hadn't already alerted him, but Daniel wanted to delay the inevitable meeting until he had at least had a chance to speak to Drew.

A part of him still hoped he could come up with an alternative and safer solution to the problem of what to do with Drew for the next couple of weeks. In the meantime, however, he needed to impart a few carefully chosen words of caution on the subject of the Boyds – enough to make the lad wary, without scaring him.

Their meal was interrupted by two phone calls: the first was from Jenny at the hospital. She sounded exhausted and said that Gavin's condition seemed to have stabilized once more and that the doctors were unsure whether the increased brain activity he had briefly shown was the harbinger of changes to come or just a blip.

'It's the not knowing,' she told Daniel. 'You feel you could cope if you just had something definite to focus on, but this uncertainty drains you. I'm longing to come home and be with the kids, and yet I feel I have to be here just in case he does wake up.'

There was little Daniel could offer in the way of comfort. All he could do was promise to keep an eye on things at the farm while she was at the hospital.

The second call was from Jo-Ji Matsuki.

'Hi, Joey – sorry, Jo-Ji.'

'Joey's OK. I'm used to it,' Jo-Ji said with deep resignation.

'I tried to ring you earlier but no answer. What've you got for me?'

'Well, I did some digging on your Boyd family, and I find they are very well known to our lads in your neck of the woods. Farm theft, aggravated assault, possession of firearms, receiving of stolen goods, suspected arson, harassment and threatening behaviour, to name but a few things they've been had up for. In fact, it would be quicker to list the charges they haven't faced. The family has been linked to a number of robberies at stately homes in the area, and the younger son, Ricky, currently has an ASBO served on him.'

'That doesn't surprise me in the least. And they're all still walking about scot-free because . . . ?'

'There's never enough evidence to make the charges stick,' Jo-Ji said disgustedly. 'The family you know is only a small part of a Boyd dynasty that covers most of the south-west. Some of them are travellers; some, like your little lot, have put down roots and settled. No one messes with them – or if they do, they don't do it a second time. Their names come up again and again, but when push comes to shove, witnesses change their stories, evidence disappears and alibis are cast iron, whenever called for. Most of the cases never get to court. Are you getting the picture?'

'Clear as day,' Daniel replied. 'And have you found anything to link the Boyds to the Butcher Boys?' He lowered his voice as he said it, casting a quick glance round at the clientele of The Crown, but it was, as Sue had suggested, an eatery more than a traditional local, and most of the diners were chattering family groups or loved-up couples.

'Now, that's the interesting thing,' Jo-Ji said. 'I haven't found anything as such, but take a guess what Lynda Boyd's name was before she married your friend Norman.'

'Aha, not Butcher, by any chance?'

'Got it in one. And the Butchers – as a family – are right up there with the Boyds at the top of the local police's Most Wanted list.'

'Well, well,' Daniel mused. 'I suppose the name could be a coincidence . . .'

'Not when you take into account that three members of the Butcher family were had up for illegally owning fighting dog breeds – as recently as last year.'

'Convicted?' It was said with little optimism.

'Pleaded ignorance. Looking after the dogs for a friend,' Jo-Ji replied. 'Judge let them off with a caution. No actual mention of the Butcher Boys, as such, during the trial, but, interestingly, the dogs in question mysteriously disappeared from the holding kennels before the ink was dry on the charge sheet.'

'So, well organized and possibly well connected, too,' Daniel said. 'What now?'

'I suggest you keep your eyes and ears open and your head down. And if you discover anything at all, you report it to your local nick.

You're not a copper now, remember? You get mixed up with those guys and you'd have no back-up. It's not worth the risk.'

'I know, but it's so bloody frustrating not to be able to do anything,' Daniel complained. 'Anyway, thanks for that, Joey. You're a star.'

As he returned the phone to his pocket, the waitress appeared with their desserts. When she'd gone again, Daniel found Drew watching him with a strange expression on his face.

'What's wrong?'

'Who were you talking to?'

'Someone I used to work with.'

'When you were a cop?'

'That's right. He had my drugs dog when I left the dog unit.'

'So what were you talking about? Police stuff?'

'Kind of . . .' Daniel hesitated. How much to tell him? His son was mature beyond his years,and sometimes he had to remind himself that the boy was only nine. 'Listen, Drew, how are you with secrets?'

'I would *never* tell!' Drew declared, bristling with indignation that it should be doubted.

'Well, I haven't told anyone here that I used to be a copper. Do you think you can remember not to give me away?'

'Is that all?' Drew asked, disappointment evident on his serious young face. 'That's *easy!*'

'But it's important,' Daniel assured him.

'Are you undercover?'

Daniel hesitated. He supposed he was, inasmuch as he had come, unheralded, as a sort of minor troubleshooter.

'Kind of, but only to help Jenny sort out her business.'

'Who are the Butcher Boys?'

'They are a criminal gang, and that's something else you mustn't mention. OK? Don't even mention the name.'

'Why? Are they violent?'

'Very.' Daniel was searching his memory for any other compromising snippets the boy might have overheard during his phone conversation. 'And there's another family, called the Boyds, that you want to be a bit careful around. One of them works at Summer Haulage with me. His name is Taylor.'

'If he's a criminal, why does he work at Summer Haulage?' Drew went straight to the point, as only a child can.

'Because Jenny's husband isn't from round here and he didn't know the family's reputation,' Daniel told him, wishing for Jenny's sake that he could be sure it was the truth.

'He's the one in hospital.' Drew tucked into a large portion of sticky toffee pudding.

'That's right. They think he might have been attacked, but he hasn't woken up yet, so they don't know for sure what happened.'

'Did the Butcher Boys do it?'

Daniel was about to say no but he stopped short. After all, wasn't it a possibility? He already suspected that, as a thrill-seeker, Gavin Summers might have been tempted towards the dog-fighting world, and if that was the case, it was entirely possible the connection had proven a dangerous one for him. Hadn't Jo-Ji said the gang would be hard to get into, but even harder to get out of in one piece? Maybe Summers had discovered that to his cost.

'I don't know, Drew,' he said truthfully. 'It's possible.'

'Are you going to find out?'

'Maybe. If I can. But—'

'I know, I mustn't tell anybody,' Drew said, rolling his eyes heavenwards. 'Yada yada yada . . .'

Daniel made a mock swipe at him across the table.

'Cheeky little Herbert!'

ELEVEN

With Jenny still at the hospital, and the children staying with her mother, Daniel had no option other than to have Drew with him in the cab all day on Friday. However, if he'd thought it would be any hardship to the lad, he'd have been wrong; Drew loved every minute of it. In turn, Daniel found his enthusiasm infectious and his chatter helped pass the time.

Back at Maidstone Farm at the end of the day, Daniel saw Jenny's Land Rover parked outside the house, and after hosing the truck down, he told Drew to wait for him and went to see if she was about.

The door was open, so he rapped on it and leaned into the cool kitchen. Jenny was standing at the sink with her back to him, apparently staring into space. She jumped when Daniel spoke her name, and turned round quickly.

'How is he?' Daniel asked. She had wet hair and wore no make-up, the dark shadows beneath her eyes accentuating the natural paleness of her skin. He thought she looked exhausted.

She shrugged. 'I don't know – *they* don't know, really. It's a case of wait and see. I've just come home for a bath and a change of clothes. I was beginning to feel dirty. But now I'm here . . .'

'You don't want to go back,' Daniel supplied.

'Is that dreadful? It's so peaceful here, and I just want to go upstairs, open the windows wide, pull the curtains and sleep for hours and hours.'

'Then do it. You can't spend your life at the hospital. Gavin's been there for a couple of months already; he might be there for another two – you just don't know. Nobody will blame you for taking some time out. They'll call you if there's any change.'

'It's those bloody monitors bleeping. I sit and stare at them for hours and watch the squiggly lines and the readings going up and down, but I don't even know what most of them are for. Every now and then someone'll come in and check the drip, or read his notes, and then just go away again. I sit, I watch, I drink tea, I worry, and occasionally I fall asleep. And the monitors just go on bleeping.'

'Go on,' Daniel said firmly. 'Go upstairs and get some rest. Go back in the morning.'

Jenny sighed. 'I don't know . . .'

'Do it.'

'OK.' Halfway to the door she paused. 'By the way, why are you soaking wet?'

'Ah. Drew was helping me hose the lorry down and things got a little out of hand.'

'Drew? Of course,' she said remembering. 'Look, if I stay, will you have dinner with me? You and Drew, I mean? Mum's taking the kids to the pictures and they'll be staying at hers.'

Daniel hesitated, an image of Amanda's suspicious face in his mind's eye. Something else to warn Drew not to talk about. Yada yada yada . . .

'It'd only be salad and stuff, but I'd like the company,' Jenny said. 'Or maybe you had something planned?'

'Only a ride – if Sue can find something suitable for Drew.'

Daniel came to a decision. 'Thanks. We'd love to come. Now go and get your head down. We'll come about eight.'

There was no sign of Drew and Taz when Daniel emerged into the sunlight again, but he found them in the drivers' room, in company with Dek Edwards. Edwards was sitting on the worktop in the kitchen area, a can of beer in his hand, whilst Drew was on the sofa, drinking a glass of juice, with Taz on the floor at his feet. The dog had his chin on the boy's knee and Drew was rubbing him behind his ears.

As soon as Daniel arrived, Dek swallowed the last of his beer, crushed the can and left the room, nodding to Daniel and raising a hand to the boy as he went.

Daniel stepped aside to let him pass, then looked at his son in surprise.

'What was that all about?'

'Oh, nothing. We were just talking. He's quite nice.'

'Dek is?' Daniel struggled to keep the disbelief from his voice. 'What did you talk about?'

'Oh, just stuff. He was asking me where I live – normally, I mean – and he wanted to know about you, what you did before you came here and stuff. Yeah, yeah, I know. I didn't tell him anything. I just said you'd been driving lorries in Devon.'

'What else?'

Drew shrugged. 'I don't know. Nothing important. Wasn't I supposed to talk to him? You didn't say.'

'No, you're OK. I just wondered. He doesn't usually talk much, that's all. Now – what d'you say we go down to the stables and see if Sue can find you something to ride?'

'OK, cool. Can Taz come?'

'Absolutely. You just try stopping him!'

Used to riding the moorland ponies belonging to Daniel's friend on Dartmoor, Drew was tickled pink to be given what he termed a 'real horse' to ride, and one, moreover, that was taller than the horse Daniel himself was riding.

Sue had come up trumps for Drew with Alfie, a piebald cob of some fifteen hands and three inches, which, she assured Daniel, was as safe as houses. In a very short time, they were both mounted and heading out along the track that led to the ridge.

Daniel had been using his evening rides to get a feel for the land, exploring a new area each time. On this occasion, when he topped the ridge, he rode straight over and down the other side, enjoying the low golden sunlight, the movement of the horse beneath him and the company of his son.

Above them, a family group of five buzzards was circling, calling with their distinctive mewing cry, trying to scare their prey into revealing movement. Daniel pointed them out to Drew, who was developing a great interest in birds of prey, although owls were his favourites.

Taz circled the horses at a distance of a few yards, sometimes following, sometimes alongside, apparently convinced that he was in charge of keeping them together.

Topping the brow of another rise, Daniel was about to suggest that they follow the track right-handed along the ridge when Drew pointed to a large building at the other end of the field they were facing.

'Do you think there might be barn owls in that barn?' he asked eagerly.

'It's possible, I guess.'

'Could we go and look? Please?'

Daniel hesitated, consulting his watch. 'OK. But then we must turn back. I told Jenny we'd be with her about eight.' He looked at the grassy headland. 'Fancy a canter?'

Drew nodded and within moments they were galloping, Piper keeping up effortlessly with Alfie's more laboured, ground-thumping action, but, for Drew, the cob could do no wrong and when they pulled up in the barnyard, his eyes were shining with pride for his mount.

'He can really go, can't he, Dad?' he demanded, patting the cob's sweaty black-and-white neck.

'Like the wind,' Daniel agreed. 'And your riding is coming on in leaps and bounds.'

Drew didn't reply, but his glowing smile was reward enough.

Daniel turned his attention to the building ahead of them. It was a huge structure, metal-framed, with breeze-block walls and a roof of corrugated sheeting. The big sliding doors were closed but not padlocked, and after they had tied the horses to a rail beside a water trough, Daniel and Drew went to investigate.

Daniel laid his hands on one of the heavy iron doors and, with surprisingly little effort, rolled it back a couple of feet. Drew immediately stepped through the gap, eyes darting to the shadowy heights of the inside. Daniel followed more slowly, noting the well-greased rollers at the top and base of the door.

'I can't actually see any owls yet,' Drew reported from his position a third of the way down the building. 'But you have to look out for droppings and pellets. That's how you can tell if they've been there.'

In the cool gloom of the interior, Daniel could see that, under a layer of dirt and hayseed, the barn had a concrete floor and had at one time been used for storing hay and straw. Now it was less than a quarter full, and what bales remained looked and smelled musty and were stacked in tiers against the walls to each side of the building, producing an effect something like stage seating. The space in between was littered with farm rubbish – plastic sacks, corrugated sheeting, quantities of fencing posts, rolls of wire and a rusty wheelbarrow, amongst other not instantly identifiable detritus.

'Have you found any owl pellets?' Daniel asked his son, who was by this time diligently scanning the ground beneath the lofty metal cross-beams. Taz, uninterested in owls, was quartering the hay-strewn floor, snuffling excitedly as he hunted for rats.

'Not . . . as . . . such,' Drew said in the slow way he had when he was playing for more time. 'But it's just the kind of place where you'd expect to find them. Pellets are what they regurgitate when they've finished eating, you know.'

Daniel was pleased that the boy had such an interest in nature. In his own youth, he had run wild in the countryside of Dorset, spending long hours in the company of a local gamekeeper. He was thankful that Drew had taken after him rather than his trend-obsessed mother.

Unwilling to spoil his fun by hurrying him, Daniel stepped on to the first line of bales and sat on the second, noticing thoughtfully that the surface of the hay was soiled and gritty. Below him, Taz was pushing eagerly at the piled-up rubbish with his nose, his tail up and waving. Daniel recognized the signs.

'You found something, Taz?'

The dog stopped his rummaging and looked up.

'Whatcha got, lad?'

With a whine of excitement, Taz pawed at a sheet of corrugated iron. Afraid that he might hurt himself on the sharp edges, Daniel went down to help.

To move the iron sheet, he first had to clear its surface of much of the rubbish piled on top, and, as he did so, it occurred to him that the arrangement wasn't as random as it had initially appeared. The roofing panels sounded hollow as he stepped on them, and the reason for this was that they had been laid on several lengths of four-by-two timber to cover a void below.

Just as interested now as the shepherd, Daniel heaved one of them aside to reveal the corner of a concrete-lined pit some four feet deep. Taz immediately dropped down into the hole and disappeared under the remaining sheeting.

'Taz, no!' Daniel said sharply, and after a moment the dog reappeared, sniffing his way along the edge of the pit. 'Come on, out,' he commanded, and Taz stood back and then leapt upwards. A helping hand in his collar and the shepherd was safely at ground level again.

'What've you found?' Drew came over to have a look, watching with interest while Daniel slid the remaining iron sheets aside to reveal the whole of the sunken area. 'What is it? Aw, that's gross!'

It wasn't difficult to see what had prompted the boy's reaction. The pit was some fifteen feet square and its concrete base was littered with the carcasses of what looked like upwards of twenty brown rats.

Drew stepped closer, drawn by a kind of horrified fascination – what Daniel and his colleagues had called 'car crash syndrome'.

'How did they die? Did they fall in?'

'No. I imagine they were killed by dogs,' Daniel replied, putting an arm round the boy's shoulders. Drew had seen the evidence – he wasn't about to lie to him. If he looked more closely, he would see the walls of the pit were smeared and spattered with blood. He glanced down at Drew to make sure the boy wasn't too upset, but he seemed instead to be full of morbid curiosity.

'Did someone *put* them in there?'

'I'm afraid so.'

'Wow! Where would anyone find that many rats?'

'I don't know, Drew.' Daniel took his mobile phone from his pocket and activated the camera facility, taking several shots of the pit and the inside of the barn.

'Are you going to report it?'

'I shall certainly tell someone.'

'Is it illegal to kill rats, then?'

'Not as such,' Daniel told him. 'But when it's done like this it's usually for gambling, and then it is illegal.'

'And it's cruel to the rats, isn't it?' Drew said, and Daniel remembered a time when the boy had yearned for a pet rat. Amanda, predictably, had refused point blank.

'It could be cruel to the dogs, too, in a pit like this. Rats are vicious when they're cornered – and who can blame them? Terriers are incredibly quick, but that many rats could pose a threat to a dog if they turned on it. I've seen a terrier blinded by a single rat bite.'

'Did you arrest the owner?'

'No, he was a farmer. The dog was ratting in his barn,' Daniel told him. 'Rats are vermin and have to be controlled, otherwise they'll overrun a place. Ratting with terriers is kinder than poison and much safer if there are other animals around, but this is different.'

Putting the phone away, he started to pull the roofing sheets back over the pit, and after a moment Drew joined in. When they left the barn, it looked much as they had found it.

'Did you find any pellets, after all?' Daniel asked as he pulled the sliding door shut behind them.

'No. I don't think it's the kind of barn owls like much,' Drew stated with resignation.

Drew and Jenny hit it off straight away, and before long the boy had regaled her with the gory details of their discovery in the barn.

'That sounds like the big breeze-block barn on Colt's Hill,' Jenny said, reaching into the oven with a gloved hand to give the jacket potatoes a squeeze. 'I haven't been out there for ages. It's mainly used for storing farm machinery and hay. There should be around a thousand bales in there from last year. It was a mild winter, and I didn't use as much as sometimes. If it's still good, I ought to sell it.'

Daniel raised an eyebrow. 'I think you might find someone has helped themselves. There's only a few hundred left, I'd say. I didn't see any farm machinery, either.'

Jenny straightened up, frowning.

'Well, there wasn't a lot, because we sold a fair bit when we got rid of the stock, but there should be an old tractor and trailer, and – if I remember rightly – a muck spreader.'

Daniel shook his head. 'Didn't see anything like that, I'm afraid. Closest thing was a wheelbarrow, and that was rusty.'

'Oh no!' Jenny moaned. 'I thought it was remote enough to be safe, right out there.'

'Not these days, with aerial views of practically the whole world available for all to see on the internet,' Daniel said sadly.

'It was padlocked, but I suppose if they want to get in, they just take a crowbar to it.'

'Yeah, there was no sign of a padlock. What was the pit used for? It looked too shallow to be an inspection pit.'

'I don't remember a pit,' Jenny replied helplessly. 'Unless Gavin had it put in for some reason. He was doing some work on one of the barns earlier this year – I remember him saying – but I'm afraid I didn't take much notice.'

'Well, you should report the missing machinery, and it wouldn't do any harm to mention the pit and the rats. Not that they'll do a lot, I imagine, but at least it'll be on record.'

'I suppose so,' she said, looking depressed.

'I didn't find any owls,' Drew told her. 'I think the barn may have been too big. Owls like low, dark places.'

'Then you should look in the one at the top of Coppice Field. That's old and dark and practically falling down; I should think it must be absolutely stuffed with owls!' Jenny told him.

Drew chuckled and began chattering animatedly about the solitary hunting habits of barn owls. Daniel watched him fondly, grateful for the change of subject. Jenny's remark about her husband had set his thoughts on an unwelcome tack, and one that he had far rather not discuss with her at this juncture.

Later, when the meal was over and Drew was playing happily with a computer game belonging to Jenny's son, Harry, Daniel asked if he might use the office computer the next morning.

'Of course.' Jenny looked enquiringly at him over the rim of her coffee cup. 'Are you looking for something specific?'

'Not really. Discrepancies, I suppose. I thought it would be a good opportunity, as Boyd isn't working tomorrow. I see Reg is doing his shift.'

'Yes, Taylor's away. Gone off to Ireland for the weekend. God knows why. Dek's gone, too. Blokey bonding or something. I assume they'll get plastered, though why they have to go to Ireland to do that, I don't know. It was Holland last time. I must be paying them too much!'

'Holland?' Daniel's ears pricked up. 'Are you sure?'

'Yes, I think so. Yes, I'm certain because Taylor was talking about getting the ferry from Harwich to the Hook. Why? Does it mean something to you?'

'It might. Or it might be pure coincidence. I'll let you know when I find out.'

'Normally, I wouldn't let you get away with that, but just at the moment I'm too tired even to be curious,' Jenny said. 'Drew's a nice lad,' she added softly, nodding in the direction of the boy, who was totally absorbed in his computer game on the other side of the room. 'It's a shame he's here now, when my lot are with Mum. Any other time you could have left him with me while you were working. It would have been good for Harry to have some company for a change.'

'Yeah, that would've been nice, although Drew was as happy as Larry in the lorry with me today. He said he'd like to drive a truck himself when he grows up. Good job the novelty will soon wear off, or I'd be even more in the doghouse with Amanda!'

'So, why did she bring him all the way here, when she knew you were working?' Jenny asked curiously. 'Not that I mind, but couldn't he have gone to another relative?'

Daniel shook his head. 'Amanda's an only child. Her father's dead and her mother lives in the south of France. Besides, she likes to make things difficult for me, if she can, to prove that I'm not fit to look after him.'

'Well, what about your family? Your mother? Couldn't she have asked her?'

'No, she wouldn't do that. The thing is, my mother's never actually met Amanda.' Although he knew it was odd, saying it out loud made it seem extraordinary. From the look on her face, Jenny plainly thought so too.

'Let me get this straight. Your mother has never met your wife? That's unbelievable! Didn't you invite her to the wedding?'

'Yes, of course I did, but she didn't come.'

'But why?'

'Because most of my friends were cops – even Amanda was working at HQ, in a civilian capacity – and my mother hates anything to do with the police because of my father. You see, he left us when I was eight. Just walked out one day, after fifteen years of marriage, and went back to his first love – the police force. Mum never forgave him – never even spoke his name again, in my hearing anyway; he became "that man" whenever anyone mentioned him. And then, when I told her I was joining up, too, we had an almighty row and she more or less told me to get out and not come back.'

'But she didn't *mean* it,' Jenny said. 'It was just a spur-of-the-moment thing, I'm sure. We all say things we don't mean when we're upset.'

Daniel shrugged. 'I don't know. I didn't wait around to find out. I was mad, too. I packed my bags that night and left the next day.'

'How old were you?'

'Eighteen.'

'But you've been back since, surely?'

'Oh yes, of course, but it's always – well, difficult. There's an atmosphere.'

'And what about Drew? Please tell me she's met her grandson?'

'Of course. A couple of times. Not for a year or two, though. To be honest, I don't often go down there. It upsets her too much.'

'Says who?'

'Penny. My sister. She still lives in the village.'

Jenny made an exasperated sound.

'*What*?' Daniel demanded.

'Phone her,' she told him. 'Your mum, I mean. Take it from me – whatever she may say, she's a mother and she wants to hear from you. I mean, what if something happened to her? How would you feel? You have to sort this out, Daniel. Life's too short. I mean, look at me and Gavin.'

'Mm. I know.'

'Well, do it. There,' she said with a half-embarrassed smile. 'I've done my bossy bit. Another coffee?'

TWELVE

Daniel's session on the office computer that Saturday morning gave him plenty to think about.

Reg and Macca, as the drivers rostered on, had taken the lorries out earlier that morning, Jenny had returned to her vigil at the hospital, and Sue had very kindly offered to keep Drew amused at the stables, so he had the yard to himself with no likelihood of being interrupted.

The first thing he did was open and read the computer personnel files on all the drivers past and present. As he suspected, Reg had been with the company the longest, and his reference was simply that he had worked for Jenny's family before. Macca had been taken on on the strength of a reference from a fuel delivery firm who had previously employed him, and Dean Stevens had come straight from driver training and a shelf-filling job in an out-of-town supermarket.

It appeared that Taylor Boyd hadn't needed a reference at all, a fact that made Daniel raise an eyebrow, and the most recent employee, Dek Edwards, had arrived with a commendable report of his character written on headed notepaper. The company wasn't one Daniel had heard of, but an inked circle round the contact number indicated that the reference had been followed up to Gavin Summers' satisfaction.

Daniel noted down the address of the most recent deserter, Dean Stevens, with the idea of paying him a visit in due course, and – on a whim – also made a copy of Dek's reference on the office photocopier.

Next, he spent a laborious hour and a half cross-referencing orders, invoices and delivery records against one another, noting, as he did so, that much of Taylor Boyd's so-called 'overtime' was not logged. It seemed that Dek was not above earning a little extra pocket money, either, which, considering the proposition Daniel had been offered at the end of his first day's driving, didn't surprise him overmuch. What did surprise him was the extent of Boyd's activities. Daniel estimated that barely ten per cent of his after-hours work was legitimate, and, with the facts and figures at hand, he could see that it was costing Summer Haulage dear.

He supposed that Boyd was banking on the assumption that, with spending so much time at the hospital, Jenny wouldn't be able to keep tabs on exactly which of her vehicles were out and when. He probably felt that as long as he logged *some* extra hours, she wouldn't look too closely at the detail, and the premise had obviously worked. Daniel printed off several pages and the notes he took down filled two A4 sheets and made damning reading.

Finally, satisfied that he'd learned all he was going to from the office records, Daniel made himself a mug of coffee, logged on to the internet and brought up Google Earth. Zooming in on an aerial view of the farm, he tried to follow the route he and Drew had taken on their ride the previous evening.

After a couple of false starts, he found the barn they had visited and worked his way back along its access track in the direction of the village. For what he judged was the best part of a mile, the track was of chalk and ran in a fairly straight line towards the dark mass of trees in which Forester's stood. There it joined the tarmac road that had obviously once serviced the old disused timber yard and which ran through the trees, past Daniel's cottage, to join the main farm drive and, ultimately, the road to Great Ditton.

Daniel sat and gazed thoughtfully at the screen for a long while, his coffee cooling at his elbow. The barn had only the one access road and Forester's Cottage was on it. If the barn was being used for ratting and/or dog fighting, would that be reason enough for Boyd to want the cottage empty? It was impossible to cross silently over the cattle grid, and any occupant of the cottage would inevitably be suspicious of a large number of vehicles passing during the evening or night.

Gavin had had a plan for the cottage, Jenny had told him when he first moved in, but she didn't know what. Daniel would have given a lot to know just what that had been.

Driven by curiosity, he panned the aerial view on down the road to the village and along the main street. He was interested to see just how big the Boyd's salvage yard was.

The answer was – huge. The layout had changed somewhat since the aerial image had been taken, and in the interim it seemed Norman Boyd and his family had accumulated a great deal more scrap metal. Daniel could see the reception unit and its accompanying sheds, and away behind these, standing incongruously in their own patch of garden amidst the metal jungle, were two large mobile homes. Chez Boyd, Daniel guessed, though an attempt to zoom closer only resulted in revealing the poor definition of the satellite imagery.

Panning across the rest of the site, he could make out the roofs of two other long, narrow buildings. Daniel sat back, thoughtfully, reaching for his coffee mug. He didn't remember those. Reducing the zoom, he tried to calculate where they would have been in relation to where he'd stood to wait for Ricky the day he'd been to see him about the headlights. All he remembered seeing were the mountains of scrap, but, then, if the buildings were single-storey, they would probably have been hidden from view. For some reason, he found himself very curious to discover what those buildings were.

Sipping his coffee, Daniel wrinkled his nose. It was stone cold.

He got up to make himself another, glancing back at the screen. Remembering the barking he had heard, could the buildings be kennels to house Norman Boyd's pit bull terriers? If it weren't for Drew, he would have been tempted to pay Boyd's Salvage Spares another visit that afternoon.

As it turned out, Drew wasn't a problem. Over a lunch of fish and chips, eaten al fresco, Daniel enquired what he fancied doing that afternoon, and Drew asked if it would be OK if he spent the rest of the day at the stables.

'Sue said she'd teach me to ride Western-style,' the boy said. 'On Piper, cos he's the only one really trained for it.'

'Oh, I see,' Daniel replied, putting spurious disappointment into his tone.

'You don't mind, do you?'

'Of course not. I suppose you're getting too old to want to spend time with your father . . .'

'Dad!' Drew rolled his eyes exaggeratedly.

Daniel laughed at the boy's expression. 'It's OK. I'm only teasing. You'll love riding Piper – he's amazing.'

An hour or so later, with Drew safely back in Sue's care, Daniel turned the nose of the Merc towards Ditton Cheney, the village where he'd found Mal and Sally Fletcher, and where, it seemed, Dean Stevens also lived, with his father.

It was clear by the noise emanating from the open window of number nine, Church Cottages, that a football match was being watched on the TV, and Daniel guessed his interruption would not be welcome, but that couldn't be helped.

His firm push on the doorbell button evoked no response, and he had to press it twice more before he heard the sound of heavy footfalls approaching. The door was yanked open by an unshaven, pot-bellied, middle-aged man wearing knee-length shorts and a Manchester United shirt.

'It's ten minutes to half time; couldn't you have waited?' he demanded.

'Who's winning?' Daniel asked, not even knowing who was playing.

'We are, of course,' the man said, apparently apportioning himself some credit for the fact. 'Which you'd have known if you'd stayed in and watched the match, instead of banging on people's doors in the middle of it. What d'you want, anyway? Who are you?'

'I'm looking for Dean. Is he here?'

'Who wants to know?'

'My name's Daniel. I used to work with Dean.'

The man sniffed noisily, screwing his face sideways as he did so. 'You're the one with the dog,' he said, which was no great feat of deduction, as Taz's head could be clearly seen leaning out of the open window of the car.

'That's right.'

'Well, he don't want to talk to no one.'

'Could you please just ask him?'

'He's not 'ere.'

'All right.' Daniel had heard the sound of wood being chopped at the back of the end-of-terrace property and had his own suspicions about that. 'I'll let you get back to your match. Will you tell him I called?'

The man sniffed again. 'No point,' he said, stepped back and closed the door in his visitor's face with more vigour than was strictly necessary.

'Charming.' Daniel shook his head slightly at this overt rudeness and, retracing his steps to the car, let Taz out. Whistling him to heel, he then followed the hedge of number nine round the corner into the adjoining road. Here, he found his luck was in. A full-height wooden plank gate was let into the clipped hawthorn and the catch lifted under the pressure of his thumb.

The gate opened on to a small back garden which was half rough grass and half vegetable plot, where summer vegetables flourished in neat rows. The orderliness seemed at odds with the character and appearance of the man he had just met.

Beyond the stately rows of beans, Daniel could see a slight figure in jeans and a T-shirt, wielding a small firewood axe. Hoping it was indeed Dean, he went in, quietly closing the gate behind him.

In circumnavigating the vegetable plot, Daniel's route took him within a few feet of what was obviously the sitting-room window, but the curtains were drawn and, from the sound of it, half-time had not yet been reached.

The noise from the TV also served to drown out Daniel's approach and he was consequently quite close when he said in a normal voice, 'Hello, Dean.'

At the sound of his voice, Dean whipped round, axe in hand and eyes darting from left to right as if expecting other intruders to materialize.

'Stay back!' he said agitatedly, focusing on Daniel.

'OK, no problem,' Daniel said matter-of-factly, coming to a halt and putting a restraining hand through Taz's collar as he made to pass. The dog whined and barked in frustration, and Daniel had to speak sharply to him.

'What do you want? I'm not coming back.'

'Mrs Summers said you were ill.'

Dean looked discomfited. 'Yes, well, I've not been feeling so good lately.'

'You know that's bullshit,' Daniel said mildly. 'You didn't want to face Boyd again.'

'No! That's not true. It's got nothing to do with him. I've been getting pain – in my back. The doctor said the lifting's making it worse, so I didn't have a choice . . .'

'So he prescribed chopping wood as a cure? Come on, Dean, I wasn't born yesterday! Tell me the real reason.'

Dean shook his head vigorously. 'I can't. He said they'd smash my knees if I talked, and they'd do it too – they'd cripple me. You don't know what he's like.'

'Who said that? Boyd?'

Dean looked round desperately, as if searching for a way out.

'Who said it, Dean? Come on, you've told me this much. I want to help you.'

'How can you help? You don't know them – they're evil.'

'Was it Boyd?'

'Him and that psycho buddy of his.'

'Macca?'

'No. Dek.'

'Dek threatened you?' Daniel was remembering him talking to Drew and Drew's comment that he was 'quite nice'. A man of contrasts, it seemed.

'They both did.'

Daniel hazarded a guess. 'Because of what happened with Taz? Is that why they were angry?'

Dean's face would have been answer enough; he clearly had no idea what Daniel was alluding to.

'What d'you mean?'

'That night at the cottage. In the storm.'

'No! I had nothing to do with that. I overheard them talking, that was all, I swear!'

'You weren't there?'

'No. I swear I wasn't.'

Daniel was puzzled but inclined to believe him.

'So you overheard them talking. Boyd and Dek, was it? What were they saying?'

Dean shook his head and almost sobbed. 'No, I can't tell you. They'll do what they said and then I'll never be a professional.'

'Professional?'

'Golfer. I told you, I play golf. But I can't play if I'm a cripple, can I?'

Daniel did indeed recall Dean telling him he was to play in a tournament, but he hadn't realized the youngster was so serious about the game. Boyd clearly had known. Boyd had a mean streak a mile wide and a gift for homing in on a person's vulnerability.

'Look, I need you to trust me—' he began, but Dean interrupted.

'Why should I? I don't know you. You could be in with them. Why should I listen to you?'

Why indeed? For a fleeting moment, Daniel toyed with the idea of revealing his past in an attempt to persuade Dean to trust him, but he dismissed the idea. The youngster was too scared and the risk was too great. If Boyd were to find out, the cat would be amongst the proverbial pigeons.

He decided on one last stab in the dark.

'You overheard Boyd and Dek talking about coming out to the cottage and giving me a working over – is that it?'

'They didn't do it, though? Did they?'

'In a manner of speaking,' Daniel said dryly. 'But I don't think it went entirely to plan.'

'I wanted to warn you,' Dean's face beseeched him to believe it. 'But they said, if I did . . .'

'. . . they'd smash your knees.'

'Yes. I'm sorry.' Dean hung his head miserably, the axe hanging by his side. Behind the closed curtains a whistle blew to signify half-time, and shortly after Stevens senior bellowed out, 'Dean? Put the kettle on, eh?'

Dean raised his head.

'My dad,' he said.

'Yeah, we've already met. He did his best to get rid of me.'

'He's all right, my dad,' Dean stated loyally, then raised his voice and shouted, 'Just coming.'

'Who does the garden – the veg?' Daniel asked.

'Me, mostly,' Dean said, relaxing into justifiable pride.

'It looks great. So, what did they say – Boyd and Dek? What did you overhear?'

The guarded look returned in a flash and Daniel sighed.

'Come on, Dean. You've told me most of it already. Both of them are away for the weekend, so there's no one to know I've been here, and I promise I won't say a word.'

Dean groaned. 'Oh, all right. I was in the back of the van, see, and they were walking past. Boyd says, "We need to get Whelan out of there before much longer, and anyway I think he could be trouble. Far better get shot of him." Then Dek says, "So, when do we do it?" and Boyd, he says, "No time like the present. We'll go tonight, late, and give him a night he'll remember. I'll give Macca a shout and see if he's up for it." Then Dek says, "What about the dog?" I tried to move closer to the side of the van so I could hear what Boyd said next, but I tripped over the pallet and they heard me. I'll never forget Boyd's face when he opened that back door. I thought I was dead, there and then!'

Before Daniel could say anything more, the French windows of the house slid back and Dean's father appeared in the aperture.

'What the hell? What are you doing here?' he roared, his face turning red with fury.

'It's all right, Dad,' Dean called.

'I told him you weren't here.'

'And yet here he is,' Daniel couldn't resist pointing out, and Stevens senior turned puce.

'You'd better go,' Dean suggested diplomatically. 'And please – you won't tell Boyd? You promised.'

'I won't tell him,' Daniel said, and, whistling to Taz, he left the way he had come in, favouring the youngster's father with a cheery wave.

With time on his hands before meeting up with Drew again, Daniel called in on Boyd's Salvage Spares on his way back to the farm. Rather than go straight to the business end of things, he drove slowly round the navigable alleyways, trying to locate the spot where the aerial photos had shown the buildings to be.

Barely five minutes into his search, however, when he had got out of the car for a closer look, he was confronted by Ricky Boyd on a quad bike, demanding to know what he was up to.

'Promised I'd repair something for Mrs Summers and was just looking for the right bit of metal,' Daniel lied.

'Well, you need to come to reception and ask,' Ricky told him. 'Can't just go rummaging around on your own; it's too dangerous. Health and safety and all that. Didn't you see the notices?' He gestured at the closest one: crudely fashioned, red painted letters on scraps of hardboard, requesting visitors to stay in their cars and ask for assistance at reception.

'Evidently not,' Daniel said pleasantly.

'What exactly were you looking for?'

'Ah, well, it's a bit difficult to explain but I shall know it when I see it.'

Ricky looked understandably sceptical. It was the first time Daniel had seen him without his shades, and, up close, the weak eyes under their puffy brows were reason enough for his preference for sunglasses.

'What are you trying to repair, then?'

Daniel walked back to his car and opened the driver's door.

'It's something for the stables. Tell you what, I'll come back when I know more what I'm looking for. Thanks for your help.'

Ricky scowled and moved his quad bike further into the path of the car, but if he thought this would discommode Daniel, he was to be disappointed. Putting the Mercedes into reverse, he backed at speed down the alleyway between the towering walls of scrap until he could turn, and then, with a wave of his hand, headed for the exit.

It had been Daniel's intention to drive straight past Maidstone Farmhouse and on to the stables to meet Drew, but as he drove down the drive, he saw Liam Sellyoak's black Porsche parked untidily in the yard and the man himself standing by the front door with the air of someone who is waiting for a response.

As Daniel slowed up, the footballer turned away from the house and came to meet him, sunglasses perched on his shaved head.

'Saw you here before, didn't I?' Sellyoak said by way of a greeting.

'Mrs Summers isn't here. She's at the hospital with her husband.'

'I thought that might be it. Any news?'

'Not that I know of,' Daniel said. 'Can I give her a message?'

'No, you're all right. I'll call back another time.' He angled towards his car, but Daniel's next words turned him.

'You want to buy the farm, I understand.'

A flicker of annoyance touched Sellyoak's face. 'I think that's between Mrs Summers and me.'

'I'm a friend. She told me. She also said she's not ready to make a decision just yet, so I think you should lay off the pressure. Especially while her husband is so sick.'

'I'm a busy man, Mr – er, I don't think I caught your name . . .'

'Whelan.'

'Well, Mr Whelan, as I said, I'm a busy man. Got the new season coming up. I don't want to upset her – of course I don't. I just want to get this sorted. If you was a real friend, you'd tell her to accept my offer. She won't get a better one, and this place is too much for a woman on her own.'

'I'll tell her you called,' Daniel said flatly, and watched while Sellyoak departed with bad grace.

THIRTEEN

Contrary to Daniel's expectations, Drew wasn't kicking his heels, waiting for his arrival. He was in the feedstore, helping Sue measure coarse mix into buckets for the horses' teas, a fact that hadn't escaped the notice of the yard's occupants who were variously moving about restlessly, whinnying or banging impatiently on their doors.

'Hello, Sprout,' Daniel said, ruffling the boy's hair. 'Had a good day?'

'Brilliant!' Drew said. 'Piper was amazing.'

'You weren't so shabby yourself,' Sue put in from the other side of the feedstore. 'You've got a natural on your hands, there, Daniel. I reckon he could be a top rider, given the chance.'

'Mum would never let me have a horse,' Drew said despondently. 'She thinks they're dirty and smelly.'

'She might have a point,' Daniel said, tugging the hem of Drew's rather less than pristine T-shirt. 'But, seriously, we'll have to put our heads together and see if we can come up with something, if you're really keen.'

'Really?' The boy's shining eyes told their own tale.

'Yep. Now, when you've got these hungry critters fed, we'll go find something ourselves, and then I thought we might go on an owl hunt.'

'Excellent! This holiday is turning out to be hist–oric!'

It might have been expected that after a day of outdoor activity, a city boy would be out for the count by ten o'clock that night, but when Daniel followed him upstairs to bed at eleven thirty, a glance into his room found him sitting up in bed, wide awake.

'Can't you sleep?' he asked.

'There's a mega conversation going on between two tawny owls in the wood,' Drew replied. 'Did you know that one owl goes t'wit and another one goes t'woo. It's not one bird.'

'Actually, I did know that.'

'I suppose we couldn't go over into the wood with a torch now, could we?'

'No, we couldn't. Maybe another night.' Even Daniel, who considered himself a fairly keen nature lover, had about had his fill of owls for one day.

'But they might not be there another night,' he observed wistfully.

'They nearly always are,' Daniel told him. 'Sleep now.'

Whether Drew did sleep or not, he wasn't sure, but about an hour later Daniel was woken by the scraping of Taz's claws on the wooden floor, a noise that he was particularly tuned in to. The dog made his way over to the open bedroom door and on to the landing.

'No, Taz! Go back to Dad! Go on!' Drew said in a stage whisper.

An owl hooted loudly in the woods opposite, and Daniel raised his voice to say resignedly, 'The front door key's on the hook. You can open it, but don't go out, OK?'

'Oh, Da–ad.'

'Promise.'

'OK.'

'And make sure you lock it again afterwards.'

'OK.'

Daniel smiled to himself and rolled over, punching the pillow to get comfortable. He was aware that he'd probably taken the edge off the boy's enjoyment of his midnight escapade, but safety had to come first, especially in the light of recent events.

In spite of having a number of things on his mind, Daniel slipped back into sleep almost immediately, and when he was woken by the revving of car engines and the squeal of tyres, he had no idea how much time had passed.

He sat bolt upright, his heart rate accelerating into the hundreds, as his mind tried to surface through the layers of sleep and sort out what was happening. Taz started barking frantically, his claws scrabbling on the boards as he left the room and charged downstairs.

In a kind of reflex action, Daniel shouted for the dog even as he swung his legs over the side of the bed and grabbed a pair of jeans from the chair. Whatever the emergency, he wasn't prepared to face it wearing only a pair of thin cotton sleeping shorts.

As he pulled up his zip, he heard two sounds in quick succession that drove all other thoughts from his head: the crunch and tinkle of breaking glass and a terrified shout from Drew.

'Dad!'

In an instant, Daniel was across the room and out on to the landing.

'Drew!'

'Dad! Quickly!'

Daniel started down the stairs even as Drew began to race up, leaving Taz barking furiously just inside the front door.

'Go up and lock yourself in,' Daniel said urgently as he passed his son halfway down, but Drew grabbed his arm and wouldn't let go.

'It's all right. Go on up.'

'No! Dad! It's on fire! The house is burning!' Drew cried, shaking Daniel's arm, and in the same instant Daniel saw a flickering orange glow in the open doorway of the sitting room.

'Right. Then we get out. Now!'

He turned Drew round and started down, but before they reached the hall, a river of orange flame seeped under the door and across the tiles, tongues of fire licking up the flowered wallpaper as it reached the edge. With a startled yelp, Taz turned tail and leapt for the stairs just inches ahead of the deadly tide.

'Petrol!' Daniel gasped. He turned Drew round once more and half threw him back up the stairway. 'Into your room, quick! Open the window and stand by it.'

As they reached the tiny landing, Daniel dodged into his own bedroom, pausing just long enough to gather up his jacket, the pockets of which held his wallet, mobile phone and car keys. Already the floor felt hot under the bare soles of his feet, and smoke was beginning to seep insidiously through the old boards. Putting the jacket on as he hurried after Drew, he found the landing smoke-filled and was glad to see the dog had followed the boy into the back bedroom. Quickly, he shut the door, gathered a blanket from the bed and stuffed it as hard as he could into the gap along the bottom.

'They threw them through the windows!' Drew shouted over the growing roar of the blaze. 'Bottles that just exploded!'

Daniel went across to where the boy could be dimly seen, standing obediently by the window.

'We have to get out,' he said, raising his voice to be heard. 'No one will come because no one will know. Get the sheets off your bed, quickly!'

As the boy hurried to do so, Daniel opened the window and leaned out. Fuelled by the petrol, the fire had spread with terrifying speed. Directly below, the window of the kitchen glowed orange, glass as yet intact, but he was grimly aware that it could shatter at any time, sending a whoosh of flame up the side of the building and engulfing anyone who was unlucky enough to be suspended above.

There were, however, no other options, and speed was of the essence. As Drew reappeared at his side, holding out the sheets with shaking hands, he took them and knotted the two together, tugging them savagely to ensure the join would hold.

'Wrap this round one hand a couple of times and hold it tight with the other hand, too,' he instructed, coughing a little as the acrid fumes began to filter through from below. He lifted Drew on to the window sill and looked into his face, speaking slowly and clearly. 'I'm going to have to let you down fast. When you touch down, let go and run right to the end of the garden, OK?'

'OK.' Drew nodded, terror in the tight muscles of his face. 'What about you?'

'I'll be right behind you. Now hold tight!'

The floorboards were becoming almost unbearably hot as Daniel lifted his precious cargo over the sill and paid out the length of material as fast and smoothly as was possible. From the rooms below, he could hear the staccato pops and bangs of mini explosions as the fabric of the house succumbed to the blaze.

Down the boy went, spinning a little and bumping against the brickwork. Daniel stopped. He couldn't afford for Drew to swing towards the window with the orange squares of glass an incendiary about to go off. Readjusting his position, he leaned out as far as he could, the window catch pressing painfully into his midriff, and let the sheets run through his fingers.

Moments later, the cotton rope went slack as Drew dropped to the ground, staggered and then, freeing his hand, turned and ran away from the burning building as fast as he could.

The relief was so great that for a moment Daniel almost forgot that there was still himself and Taz to save, but a sharp crack as the kitchen window succumbed to the heat brought him instantly to his senses, and he reeled back from the upstairs window as the first furious rush of flames surged upwards, engulfing the length of cotton sheet. Hastily unwinding it from about his own hand, Daniel let the burning material fall to the ground, knowing as he did so that he had lost his lifeline.

Daniel turned round to find Taz beside him, standing up at the window, panting and whining. The rush, roar and popping of the flames tearing through the doomed cottage was deafening and the air was heavy with smoke.

There could only be seconds to spare. They would have to jump, but he wanted something to break their fall.

Daniel's fingers found his pocket-sized LED torch in his jacket, switched it on and shone it briefly round the room. Visibility was extremely poor but he could see enough to judge the positions of the twin beds. Mattresses. They might make the difference between bruises and broken bones.

Flashing the beam in the direction of the door, he saw the cream paint blistering and running, the whole thing blackening around the edges. Praying that the floorboards weren't about to crumble from under him, he took a lungful of air from the open window and then, in two quick strides, ran to the beds, snatched the mattresses and dragged them back, trailing bedclothes.

The mattresses were too wide to fit through the tiny cottage windows and resisted his efforts to bend them.

'Come *on*, for fuck's sake!' Daniel groaned, struggling with the unwieldy things. At last he managed to fold them just enough to push them, one after the other, through the frame and drop them to the ground below.

Telling the frantic dog to wait, he leaned out to see where they had landed. The downstairs window was no longer belching flame, just a billowing plume of black spark-filled smoke, but, with a sinking heart, Daniel saw that one mattress had fallen some feet away from the wall and the other had come to rest on its end, leaning against the brickwork.

'Shit!'

There was no plan B. Taz was dancing beside him, his feet no doubt as uncomfortably hot as his own were. Daniel folded the bedspread that was trailing over the window sill, looped it under the dog's belly and chest and lifted him into the opening.

'Sorry mate,' he gasped, choking in earnest now as the fumes threatened to overwhelm him, and lowered the dog to the full extent of his arms, grateful that the dog's helicopter winch training was keeping him calm.

It wasn't until the moment of release that he realized the two mattresses were now perfectly positioned at the foot of the wall, one atop the other. Sending thanks for a son with courage and initiative, he watched the German shepherd drop the last six feet or so and bounce harmlessly on the improvised landing mat before regaining his feet and jumping to the ground.

Swinging his own legs over the sill, he sat for a moment, perched on the wooden frame, heart pounding and a familiar panic freezing his limbs.

The skin on his back felt as though it was already blistering and burning, but even so he hesitated.

The pale rectangle of the mattresses waited below.

If the dog could do it . . .

'Come on, you stupid bastard!' he told himself angrily.

Suddenly, behind him, there was a whoosh as the bedroom door finally failed, a glance over his shoulder showing him a tide of rolling orange flame curling at high speed across the ceiling.

Better jump than burn! The words echoed in his head as he launched himself from the window sill. There was a brief rush and whistle of air past his ears and almost at once he hit the cushioning bulk of the mattresses and the hard ground beneath, rattling his bones and driving the air from his lungs.

All at once, Taz was all over him, licking his face in an ecstasy of joy, and he had to push the dog out of the way in order to roll off the mattresses and scramble clear of the danger zone.

As Daniel got to his feet, he was taken by a fit of coughing and bent double, feeling as though the fire was actually burning in his lungs.

Immediately, Drew was there, frightened eyes reflecting the glow of the fire. 'Dad? Are you OK?'

'I will be – thanks to you,' Daniel croaked, eyes watering. He took the boy's arm and hurried him further away from the cottage. Then, together, they turned and gazed at the furnace it had become, the fierce orange glow showing through every chink. Smoke was pouring thickly from all over the roof, and tiles began to come free and slide down the slope of the roof in cascades, tinkling like demented wind chimes and shattering on the baked earth below.

Even as they stood there in the first thrall of horrified fascination, part of the roof fell in, leaving a skeleton of burning rafters outlined against the sky. Drew jumped, clinging more tightly to his father's arm, and Daniel could feel the boy trembling. He folded him into an embrace.

'That was my bedroom,' Drew said through chattering teeth. 'We were in there just a minute ago!'

'I know, but don't think about it. We're safe now.' Easy enough to say, but he himself was deeply shocked by how close to tragedy they had come.

Still coughing spasmodically, Daniel took his mobile from his pocket and keyed in 999. His own network was useless here, but the emergency number would try all available networks in an attempt to find a signal.

There was none.

A shower of sparks tore upwards through the smoke as the chimney and another section of the roof collapsed, some of the burning debris sliding down the remaining tiles to land in the garden. Even from where they stood, they could feel the intense heat tightening their skin, and the trees all around the garden boundary were bathed in an orange glow. On the cottage, only the row of ornamental ridge tiles remained, outlined against the flames.

'What about your car?' Drew asked suddenly, looking up at his father. 'Will it be all right?'

Daniel stifled an oath. 'I don't know. I've got the keys. Let's see if we can get round the front.'

They made it, by dint of forcing a way through the side hedge and making their way through the wood to reach the lane. Once there, Daniel could see that his car was as yet undamaged. It was out of the range of the falling tiles, and what wind there was had blown the flames the other way.

He judged it was fairly safe to retrieve it and, telling Drew to stay put, ran forward, operating the remote locking system as he did so. The car's bodywork felt warm on the side furthest from the house but not overly so. The inside was like an oven, and the leather seats and the steering wheel were hot to the touch, but thankfully the trusty engine started first time, and, putting it in gear, he drove it to safety some fifty feet up the lane. He supposed the smart thing to do would be to drive on until he picked up a mobile signal, but he'd have to take Drew and the dog with him.

As soon as he opened the car door, he was met by Taz who'd been running in its wake. Drew wasn't far behind, breathlessly calling.

'Dad! Dad! Listen!'

'What is it?'

'Sirens – listen!'

Sure enough, over the spit, roar and crackle of the conflagration, the urgent double note of an approaching fire engine could be heard. Even supposing someone had spotted the glow of the fire almost straight away, they had been extremely quick. It was a shame the cottage was already beyond saving.

Blue flashing lights hove into view between the trees, and within moments two units had drawn up in front of the burning building. Uniformed men spilled out in all directions and went to work deploying their hoses, whilst one spotted Daniel and the boy and strode towards them.

'D'you know if there's anyone inside?' he shouted.

'No. It was just us,' Daniel replied, indicating the three of them, and the man raised a hand, turned on his heel and went back to the

others, the bright fluorescent strips on his sandy-brown uniform
appearing to dance independently in the light from the vehicle.

'Can we go back and watch?' Drew asked.

'I expect so, but we mustn't get in the way. Stay close to me,
OK?'

They moved closer. There was no novelty in the spectacle for
Daniel, who had attended many fires during his time on the force,
but for Drew, who watched all the activity with round eyes, gripping
his father's hand tightly, it clearly held a scary magnetism. He was
shaking with a mixture of fear and excitement, but Daniel suspected
that wild horses wouldn't have dragged him away.

The firefighters went about their business with brisk efficiency,
and soon two jets of water were cascading through the roof cavity
of the doomed cottage, causing the smoke to turn thick and grey,
before it was gradually replaced with hissing steam.

When it was clear that the battle was a fair way to being won,
the officer in charge came over to talk to Daniel.

'You the owner, sir?'

'No. It's owned by Mrs Summers of Maidstone Farm. We were
staying here.' As soon as Daniel started to speak, he began to cough
again.

'Are you all right?'

He nodded. 'I will be.'

'There's an ambulance on the way. They'll check you over,' he
said. 'Do you have any idea how this started?'

'According to my son, someone drove by and lobbed a couple
of petrol bombs through the downstairs windows.'

The officer looked down at Drew, who looked somehow smaller
and younger than normal in the odd mixture of pyjamas trousers,
a jumper and training shoes.

'It's rather late for a youngster to be up, isn't it?'

'I was listening to owls,' Drew answered, as if that were the most
natural thing in the world for a nine-year-old to be doing in the
early hours of the morning.

'I certainly heard the cars and someone shouting,' Daniel added.
'I imagine you'll find evidence of accelerants.'

'We'll be conducting a thorough investigation in due course, sir,'
the officer promised, in the tone of one who wasn't keen on being
told how to do his job. 'If accelerants were used, we'll soon find
out.'

'Oh, and they sloshed petrol against the front door. It was coming underneath,' Daniel said remembering. 'I saw that myself.'

The firefighter's eyes narrowed.

'Sounds as though they intended to make a thorough job of it, then.'

'It seems so.'

'And you were both in the building when this happened?'

'Yes, we got out of the back bedroom window, but it was a close-run thing,' Daniel told him.

'I understand from one of my colleagues that this cottage has been empty for some months. I suppose it's quite possible that the persons responsible assumed that it still was?'

'My car was parked out here on the lane,' Daniel pointed out. 'I moved it just before you came.'

'Ah,' the officer said grimly. 'That puts a different slant on it. I imagine the police will be keen to speak to you in due course.'

As if on cue, more blue lights were seen approaching, and a police car came to a halt behind the second fire engine, closely followed by a paramedic car. Four more uniforms spilled out into the crowded lane and, after speaking to the pump crew, headed en masse for where Daniel, Drew and the fire officer stood.

Daniel sighed inwardly, Taz leaped and plunged against the hand in his collar, excited by the sight of the uniforms, and Drew watched the oncoming tide of authority with wide eyes reflecting the barrage of flashing blue lights.

A wearisome hour followed, during which Daniel answered the same questions over and over again, to a seemingly endless stream of officers of one kind or another. The two paramedics in the fast response car were rather keen that Daniel should visit A&E to monitor the effects of his smoke inhalation. This manifested itself in an annoying cough that set in every time he started to talk, but nevertheless he declined. He had seen enough of A&E departments on a Saturday night into Sunday morning to last him a lifetime, and he had no intention of spending the night in one when what he really needed was a chance to get his head down and sleep.

Eventually, they gave in, dressed a burn on his hand and checked Drew over before climbing back in their car and disappearing along the lane towards the village.

One or two sensation-seeking locals had driven up since the fire engines' arrival, most taking pictures on their mobiles before going away, disappointed, Daniel suspected, at the lack of ongoing drama. Because of this no one took much notice of the appearance of a Land Rover, until its driver got out and ducked under the blue and white tape stretched across the lane and demanded to know where Daniel was.

'I'm sorry, miss,' a burly firefighter said, standing in her way. 'You must stay back.'

'Not until I've seen Daniel.' She raised her voice, trying to see round the man. 'Daniel?'

'It's all right. That's Mrs Summers – the owner,' Daniel called out. 'Jenny, I'm over here!'

'Oh, thank God!' She ducked under the firefighter's outspread arm and hurried towards him. 'Are you OK?'

'Fine.'

'And Drew? Where's Drew?' She glanced round anxiously.

'He's fine, too,' Daniel assured her. 'It all got too much for him and he's asleep on the back seat of one of the police cars.'

The police officer who had been questioning Daniel now cleared his throat and turned his attention to Jenny.

'Mrs Summers? I'm afraid we shall need to ask you one or two questions . . .'

She ignored him.

'I don't understand. How did this happen?' she asked Daniel. 'It wasn't the chimney, was it? I've been meaning to get that swept for ages.'

'No, it wasn't that. I'm afraid it was deliberate. Someone threw a firebomb through the window.'

'No!' she gasped, putting a hand to her mouth. 'Oh, my God! Why?'

Daniel wasn't prepared to discuss that in front of the policeman, so he just shrugged and shook his head helplessly.

It was another twenty minutes before they were free to leave the scene of the fire, and a glance at his watch showed Daniel that it was nearly four in the morning. The crew of one fire engine were stowing away their equipment in preparation to leave, whilst the other would be remaining to carry on damping down the smouldering cottage, the officer in charge told Jenny before he left in his own car.

The police patrol cars had gone, and Drew walked sleepily beside Daniel, holding his hand, as they followed Jenny towards her Land Rover, the Merc being the wrong side of the fire tenders in the narrow lane.

'So, how come you're here and not at the hospital?' Daniel asked as he slid into the passenger seat. 'Did someone phone you?'

'No.' Jenny glanced over her shoulder to where Drew was already asleep once more, belted into the back seat. She continued in a lower tone. 'Actually, um . . . there was nothing to stay for. Gavin passed away just after one o'clock this morning.'

FOURTEEN

'Oh, Christ! I'm sorry, Jenny,' Daniel said, putting his hand on her arm. 'And now this. What a bloody awful night for you!'

Jenny took a deep breath.

'I've had better,' she acknowledged, with just a hint of unsteadiness.

'Would you like me to drive?'

'Thanks, but actually I'm better when I'm doing something. Just don't be sympathetic, all right?'

'OK.' Daniel understood.

There was a hint of rosy grey in the east as they drove clear of the trees and over the last rise before the dip to the farm. Jenny slowed up and stopped. Below them, the patchwork of fields and hedges spread out in the first milky light of dawn, surrounding the old farmhouse and its outbuildings and looking much as it had probably done for centuries past.

'It's beautiful, isn't it?' Jenny said, drinking in the scene.

'It is.'

'I've always loved this farm, this land,' she said wistfully. 'I've loved the thought that so many generations of my family have lived and worked here over the years. I was proud to think that I was carrying on the work they started – somehow it gave everything a meaning, made sense of life. I thought – I hoped – that maybe one of the children would want to take it on after me. Harry's always loved the outdoor life. But now I don't know what I'll do. Nothing seems to make sense any more, and I don't know if I've got the energy to go on alone.'

'Maybe – when this is over – you should get away for a bit. Take the kids and go somewhere with no memories, where you can just relax and recharge your batteries. I find sometimes you need to distance yourself from something to see how important it really is.'

Jenny turned her head to look at Daniel in the muted light of the Land Rover cab.

'But is it going to be over? At the moment it just seems to be getting worse. I feel like everything's out of control and it scares me. I mean, look at tonight. You could have been killed. You *and* Drew. And for what? What's going on, Daniel? Do you know?'

'I know a little, and I've got a pretty good idea about the rest. What I need now is some proof, and I will get it, so hang in there for a bit longer, eh?'

Jenny watched him for a few seconds, then sighed. 'OK. But whatever you find out, I'd like to know. I mean, I've wondered sometimes, lately, if Gavin was mixed up in something. It wouldn't surprise me. I suppose I've known for a long time that he was bored with his life here – with me too, I think. You can tell me. I won't be shocked.'

'If I knew, I'd tell you,' Daniel said simply. 'But I don't.'

'Fair enough.' She put the car in gear and they moved forward once more.

When they reached the farmhouse, Daniel carried the sleepy Drew inside and followed Jenny upstairs to Harry's bedroom, where he laid the boy on the bed, eased his trainers off and gently pulled the quilt over his sleeping form, clothes and all.

As if aware of being watched, Drew stirred, shifted on to his side and pulled the quilt high over his face until only a glimpse of a lean cheekbone with its sweep of dark lashes remained. Daniel half smiled, remembering how the boy had always slept like that, even when he was very small. Amanda had worried that he would suffocate himself.

Amanda.

What would she say if she ever learned of this night's events? And she *would* learn of them; that was a certainty. Daniel would have to tell her himself, even if it had her divorce solicitor rubbing his hands in glee. The inevitable accusations of being an unfit parent would be bad enough, without the added crime of an attempted cover-up.

He looked down at the boy once again. So innocent, so entirely dependent on him for protection and guidance. The fact hit him again with a jolt. His son had almost been killed because of him. Perhaps Amanda was right; perhaps he wasn't fit to take care of a child.

No. He gave himself a severe mental shaking. That was exhaustion talking.

'Is he still asleep?' Jenny was in the doorway.

'Yes. He didn't wake at all.'

'Do you want to get straight to bed, or would you like a cup of tea?'

'Tea,' Daniel said decisively. 'My throat's horribly dry and sore.'

Daniel slept in late the next morning, glad that it was a Sunday. He woke to the smell of frying bacon wafting up the stairs and made good time showering and getting dressed. With practical foresight, Jenny had left a T-shirt out for him: one of Gavin's, he supposed. A glance into Drew's room revealed nothing but a tumbled bed and half-drawn curtains, and when Daniel reached the kitchen, he found the boy already there and tucking into a full English breakfast.

'Just in time,' Jenny said, carrying two more laden plates to the table. 'I was about to call you.'

'Wow! You've been busy!' A swift scrutiny noted slightly swollen eyelids and skin paler than usual, but, all in all, he thought she looked as though she was holding up quite well.

'Cooked breakfast on a Sunday is a Maidstone Farm tradition,' she told him. 'Help yourself to coffee. I'll run you over to pick up your car later on.'

Conversation, as they ate, was restricted to everyday matters, Daniel reluctant to dwell on the subject of the fire with Drew present and Jenny apparently equally keen to avoid talking about her loss. However, when Jenny rose from the table to make another pot of coffee, Drew spoke up of his own volition for the first time, and it was obvious where his thoughts had been.

'Why did they do it, Dad? They must have known we were inside because of the car – that's what you told the fireman.'

'I don't suppose they knew you were there. And, anyway, I expect they thought we'd wake up and get out in time.'

'But we almost didn't . . .'

Daniel's wish to save his son from harsh reality led him to search for a mitigating answer.

'A lot of people don't realize quite how quickly a fire can take hold,' he said, conveniently disregarding the fact that these particular people had made quite sure of a rapid spread by using petrol bombs. Although he didn't think his death had been the primary aim, he didn't kid himself that the reported discovery of his charred remains would have occasioned too much grief in the Boyds.

'It might even have been bored teenagers,' he added, tearing a piece of toast with which to mop up his egg yolk.

'Who called the fire brigade?' Jenny asked.

'Someone from the village. The officer said they were already out on a shout when they took the call about Forester's, but it turned out to be a false alarm – some drunks setting fire to a dustbin or something. That's why they were so quick.'

'Not quick enough,' she said gloomily.

'Good job I was downstairs,' Drew observed, and Daniel agreed. No need to frighten the boy with how close he had been to disaster. If he had been in either of the front rooms when the firebombs had come through the windows . . .

'You didn't see what kind of cars they were?' Jenny asked the boy.

Drew shook his head sadly. 'No, only the lights. One of the cars had loads of lights on top. I told the policeman that.'

The look Jenny flashed across at Daniel held a wealth of meaning. The significance of the lights clearly wasn't lost on her.

'So, what now?' she asked after a moment.

'We let the police and the fire investigators do their thing, I suppose. And Drew and I go shopping for some clothes.'

'Dad, I've got a pair of Harry's trousers on,' Drew piped up. 'They're a bit short.'

'You're taller than he is,' Jenny told him, before turning back to Daniel. 'Yes, but what will you do? Where will you stay? You know you're welcome to stop here – there's plenty of room. The children will be back later, and it'd be nice for Harry to have someone of his own age around.'

'Can we, Dad? Harry's got some ace games on his Nintendo!'

Daniel hesitated. It was a difficult line of discussion to pursue in front of Drew. It was tempting to say yes, but with Gavin not twenty-four hours dead, he felt that he would be laying Jenny open to the kind of gossip that could be extremely hurtful. And there was no way that it wouldn't become common knowledge with Taylor Boyd on the case.

Jenny saved him the awkward explanation.

'If you're thinking about what people will say – I don't really care. I'm past worrying about that. It's none of their business.'

'*You* don't care, but what about your kids? Other kids can be cruel.'

Jenny's face fell. 'Oh. I see what you mean. But it seems so stupid, you paying for a room in the village when there are rooms to spare in this old house.'

Daniel shrugged. 'That's life.'

Drew had been following this exchange and now looked disappointed.

'Oh, can't we, Dad? Please?'

'Well, I suppose there's no reason why *you* can't . . .' he said slowly. 'If Jenny doesn't mind?'

'Of course I don't. We'd love to have him,' she said promptly.

Drew's eyes shone. 'Hist–oric!' he exclaimed. He pushed back his chair and stood up. 'I've finished. Can I get down now?'

'Of course,' Jenny said, and when he had disappeared up the stairs to his borrowed bedroom, she added to Daniel, 'Maybe he'll pass on some of his lovely manners to my lot.'

'He's not always quite so polite,' Daniel said ruefully. 'I warn you, it may wear off. But – you, Jenny. How are you doing? Truthfully.'

'Oh, I'm OK. Tired and a bit fragile, but OK. I always knew it might come to this and I think I've done most of my grieving over the last few weeks.'

'All the same – when they were saying he might wake up, you must have hoped . . .'

'Yes, it was a bit of a shock.'

'And the children? How will they take it, do you think?'

'To be honest, Lucy and Harry have never been especially close to Gavin,' she admitted. 'He was kind enough to them, but I don't think there was ever any real warmth. Izzy is a different matter, but, like me, she's already done her grieving. Lately, she's stopped asking me when he's coming home. She'll be upset, but she'll mend. I think having Drew around will be good for all of them.'

Although Daniel didn't tell her so, Jenny's offer to have Drew to stay suited him in more ways than one. With Drew to cater for, Daniel would have been forced to stay in one of the B&B pubs in the village, which would have put a decided crimp in some of the half-formed plans he had. There was no way he would have gone out at night and left the boy alone in his room. Now that he was certain Drew would be safe, Daniel had free rein to do as he pleased, and no one would be any the wiser.

The news of Gavin Summers' death was received with varying degrees of shocked surprise by the drivers on the Monday morning.

Until Jenny appeared, the hot topic of conversation in the drivers' room had been the fire at Forester's, and although Taylor made no pretence of sorrow over the incident, he was too clever to give away any detail that might reveal a closer knowledge of the crime.

Now, watching the reaction to Jenny's news over the rim of his coffee mug, Daniel saw Reg and Macca's initial shock turn to thoughtfulness, as they no doubt considered the possible consequences for their ongoing employment. Boyd and Dek were not so easy to read. Dek was directly opposite Daniel when Jenny told them and showed not the slightest flicker of surprise. If Daniel hadn't known that he'd only just got back from Ireland, he would have said that somehow the man already knew about Gavin Summers' death. Boyd, on the other hand, was clearly taken aback by the announcement, though Daniel found it difficult to gauge with what emotion he received the information.

After mumbled expressions of sympathy had been offered and accepted, Jenny addressed the unspoken question that was fairly buzzing in the ether.

'Naturally, you'll all be wondering what this means for you, and all I can say is that, for the moment, everything will go on as normal. If, in future, I see the need for change, I promise you'll be the first to know. OK?'

The assurance was one that countless employers had made before her, and Daniel could see that at least three of those listening gave it no credit whatsoever.

Jenny had much to occupy her in dealing with the formalities that inevitably follow a death, so her mother was to look after the children, and Drew had elected to spend the day with them on the farm while Daniel worked.

Sitting in a lay-by, sipping an over-hot cappuccino from a

polystyrene cup, Daniel decided to ring the company that had supplied Derek Edwards' reference. The call was answered after barely four trills by a cautious-sounding female voice that merely said, 'Hello?'

'Ah, good morning. Is that Lampard's Logistics?' Daniel asked.

'Er . . . yes. Excuse me, can you hold the line for a moment?'

'Of course.' Daniel listened to the agitation at the other end with a raised eyebrow. For perhaps half a minute, all he could hear were the sounds of a busy office-like environment, and then in the distance he clearly heard someone say, 'What does he want?'

The reply was an impatient, '*I* don't know, I didn't ask! I just came to find you.'

Seconds later, the handset was picked up and a male voice asked, 'What can I do for you, Mr . . . er?'

Daniel ignored the invitation.

'Is that Lampard's Logistics?' he repeated.

'I'm afraid Lampard's has ceased trading,' the man replied. 'May I ask where you got this number?'

Daniel thought fast. 'I work for Summer Haulage and I was just following up a reference,' he said.

'Well, I'm sorry I can't help. I've taken over the office but I have no knowledge of former employees. Goodbye.' The man spoke pleasantly enough, but there was no mistaking the message implied by the abrupt severance of the connection.

Daniel returned his mobile to his pocket and picked up his coffee once more, wishing it tasted more like a genuine cappuccino and less like the contents of a sachet mixed with hot water.

The call had been interesting. If he had learned only one thing, it was that the office to which that particular phone number was assigned had never been occupied by Lampard's Logistics – if indeed such a company ever existed.

In the evening, Daniel, Jenny and the three older children went for a ride, while Jenny's mother looked after Izzy. With Jenny leading the way, they crossed Barn Field and made their way along a wooded ride to come out eventually in the lane just a few hundred yards along from Forester's.

The hooves of the five horses and ponies clattered impressively on the tarmac as they rode along the lane, and the kids chattered happily about everything and nothing.

For a moment or two, the family scene beguiled Daniel, and he found himself dreaming of his childhood home in Dorset and a different life that might have been. Even though he'd worked in a city for the last ten years, he'd always felt the pull of the country, and while he understood what had prompted Jenny's disillusionment, after living on the farm all her life he couldn't imagine how she would ever be happy anywhere else.

Before the cottage even came into view, they could smell the acrid tang of smoke and charred wood on the air, and the horses began to flare their nostrils and snort uneasily as the odour tickled their sensitive noses.

Although he had known what to expect, the sight of the cottage was still a shock to Daniel. It had a sobering effect on the children, too. After an awestruck 'Whoa!' from Harry and a gasp from Lucy, they fell silent as they approached the blackened shell of the building. One or two roof struts remained, standing up like burnt ribs above the brick walls, but the front door and all the windows had gone, and inky puddles lay on the path. In the front garden, the steel-sprung remnants of beds and chairs lay in the boot-churned mud.

The horses and ponies drew up in a line in front of the blue-and-white tape that stretched across the lane and stood staring curiously at the devastation beyond, seeming to sense that something was amiss.

A Wiltshire Fire and Rescue van was parked in the shadow of the trees on the far side of the taped-off area, and the horses' heads rose sharply as a black Labrador suddenly appeared in the doorway of the cottage. The dog stopped short, looking back at them.

'Monty!' Harry exclaimed, turning to look at Jenny. 'It's Monty!'

'No, darling, it isn't,' she said. 'It's just a dog that looks a bit like him.'

'It *is* Monty,' he persisted stubbornly.

'It's not Monty – Monty's dead,' Lucy stated impatiently, and Daniel saw Harry's eyes start to fill with tears.

'That's actually a fire investigation dog,' he put in hastily to divert the boy's thoughts. 'See his little boots? That's so he doesn't burn his feet or cut them on broken glass.'

'What does he do?' Harry's attention was successfully caught, and Jenny flashed a look of gratitude in Daniel's direction.

'He's been trained so that he can smell accelerants – that means things like petrol that people might have used to start a fire – and show his handler exactly where the fire started.'

Harry wrinkled his nose. 'I don't like the smell of petrol.'

'But when there's been a fire, there's hardly any petrol smell left, which is why you need a dog to sniff it out,' Daniel explained.

'Why does he do it?' Lucy wanted to know. 'Does he like the smell?'

'No. He does it because to him it's a game. When he finds what he's looking for, his handler throws a ball for him to play with as a reward. That's all he wants – a game.'

The conversation was interrupted by the appearance of the dog's handler in the doorway.

'Good evening!' Jenny called out. 'Did you find anything, or are you not allowed to say? I own the cottage, by the way. Or what's left of it.'

The man clipped his dog on a lead and came towards them, taking off his hard hat to reveal short brown hair. As he drew closer, he opened his eyes wide and a smile lit his strong-boned face.

'Well I never! Jenny Maidstone! Or – no, not Maidstone – you got married. What is it now? We went to school together,' he added for the benefit of Daniel and the others.

'It's Jenny Summers, and it was Barton before that,' she told him.

'Well, you have been busy!'

'And you, too. Look at you,' she retorted, indicating his fire investigator's jacket. 'Is this the Paul McCreesh who used to sit behind me and put things down my neck?'

He laughed. 'I have moved on a bit.'

'You were always going to be a pilot,' she quizzed him.

'Mm. Changed my mind.'

'So,' Jenny said, 'can you tell me about the fire?'

McCreesh's face took on a more serious expression. 'Nothing you don't already know, I gather. The dog has confirmed the use of accelerants and that the seat of the fire was threefold – that is to say, in both downstairs front rooms and the hallway. It was definitely arson.'

The children had been sitting quietly on their ponies, but now Harry spoke up.

'What's your dog called?'

'Roscoe,' McCreesh said, and the dog immediately looked up at him and wagged its tail.

'We had a dog just like that. His name was Monty but he died,' Harry said.

'I'm sorry to hear that. Would you like to come and talk to Roscoe? He loves children.'

Both Harry and Lucy scrambled off their mounts and went to greet the dog, who wriggled ecstatically, his tail doing overtime. After a moment, Drew followed. Daniel smiled inwardly. Reserved by nature, he never normally put himself forward in this kind of situation. Being with Jenny's children was already doing him good.

'It was funny, seeing Paul again, after all these years,' Jenny said as they turned the horses towards home. 'I remember I used to have a crush on him at school.'

'Seems like a nice guy,' Daniel said, more for something to say than anything.

'Mm, quite pleasant,' she agreed. 'So, anyway, where did you stay last night?'

'In the village,' Daniel replied evasively.

'The Fox and Duck?'

'No, they were full. Weekend ramblers.'

'I'm surprised they had room at The Crown, then; they're usually busier.'

'They didn't,' Daniel admitted reluctantly. 'I slept in the car with Taz.'

Jenny rounded on him.

'You promised to come back if you couldn't find a place!'

'I did find a place. In my car. It's quite comfortable. I've often slept there. Besides, it was late.'

'Well, what about tonight?'

'It's not the weekend, now. They won't be so busy.'

'Well, have you booked?'

'Not as such . . .'

Jenny rolled her eyes heavenwards and Daniel laughed.

'It's all right, you know. I can take care of myself – I'm almost grown-up.'

'If you ask me, men never grow up,' she said in a blighting tone.

'Ouch!' Daniel responded in a small voice.

FIFTEEN

When Daniel left Maidstone Farm after dinner that evening, the children were already in bed and the sky was darkening into night.

Before he had driven a hundred yards, his mobile trilled.

'William,' he said, recognizing the number of the *DVG* office. 'Not working at this time of night, surely? You won't have any friends, you know!'

'Not working, exactly,' he said. 'But I've found something I think you might be interested in.'

'Oh? What's that?'

'Come and have a look,' William suggested. 'Unless you're too busy with your own dazzling social life.'

Daniel laughed. 'Touché!'

When he arrived at the *DVG* office, Daniel found the door at the bottom of the stairs ajar. As he let himself in, he noticed that there was a light on at the vet's. Presumably Ivor Symmonds with an emergency on his hands. Upstairs, William was sitting at his computer, his skinny frame clothed in jeans, a collarless white shirt and a black waistcoat, his mop of hair as unruly as ever.

'Pull up a pew,' he invited. The screen in front of him was showing an aerial view of an area of countryside, overlaid with a map.

'So where's that?' Daniel said, leaning forward to peer at it. Taz flopped to the floor beneath his chair.

'Actually, that's where I used to live as a child, a couple of miles down the road. I was just surfing while I waited for you. By the way – hard luck about your cottage. That's a bit of a bummer.'

'I might have known you'd be on to that.'

'Not just on to it – you're on the front page of today's paper,' William told him, picking up a copy of the *Gazette* from a pile and handing it across. 'Didn't you see it?'

'Yes. Taylor showed it to me.' William had done the story proud with a photo of the blackened ruin of Forester's taking up more than half the first page, under the headline 'Forest Cottage Gutted by Fire'.

'Yeah, well, luck didn't come into it,' Daniel said grimly. 'Some bastard lobbed a couple of petrol bombs through the windows.'

William swivelled his chair round to get a better look at his visitor. 'You're kidding!'

'I'm not, though.'

'Any idea who?'

'I have, but I'm not going to tell you because I don't want it splashed across the front of next week's paper. A court case I can well do without.'

'Strictly off the record . . .'

'Oh, come on, you're a journalist! It would be positively cruel to tell you something you couldn't publish. So, what was it you wanted to show me?'

'At this point I could offer to strike a bargain with you,' William observed slyly.

'Except that you're too decent a bloke to stoop so low,' Daniel stated.

William grinned good-humouredly. 'Bastard. OK, take a look at this.'

Clicking on the monitor screen, he changed the aerial view to another one, centred it and zoomed in.

Daniel obediently leaned forward.

'That's the salvage yard, isn't it? I Googled it myself.'

'Yes, except this isn't Google; it's an aerial photo taken earlier this year. The Google one is a couple of years old now. Look right in the middle where that digger is working.'

'I'm looking,' Daniel said. He could see the JCB William had pointed to and, beside it, a circular hole in the ground ringed by two concentric circles. 'What are those? Walls? Foundations?'

'I presume so,' William said. 'But whatever it is, my point is: where is it now? I've flown over the village several times this summer. I have a microlight,' he explained. 'Anyway, there's no sign of any structure there now, just piles of scrap. So, where is it?'

'Buried under the scrap?'

'That's the only answer I could come up with. But why go to the trouble of building something and then burying it?'

'Why indeed?' Daniel agreed. 'Only if you didn't want anyone to know it was there. Those are quite sizeable footings, if that's what they are. One wonders if our friend Norman had planning permission for his little project . . .'

'He didn't,' William said. 'There's no record of any application.'

Daniel raised his eyebrows, impressed by the editor's initiative. 'And that's not the only disappearing building on that site. When the Google photos were taken, they had a couple of long buildings, but I can't find them on the ground.'

'No, they're still there – look, next to that crane-like thing but tucked well away.' William pointed.

Daniel leaned in closer.

'You're right. You know, with a bit of imagination you might almost say that circular feature of yours had the makings of a dog-fighting pit with a viewing area around it. They wouldn't have the nerve, would they? Right in their back yard.'

'I wouldn't put it past them,' William said. 'But it seems a lot of effort and expense to go to just to set up a dog fight.'

'Peanuts!' Daniel said. 'Organized dog fighting is big business. People will come from all over the world to a big fight. Massive amounts of money change hands.' He sat back in his chair. 'So, what got you looking at these photos? Why the sudden interest in Boyd's Salvage?'

'It was after your visit the other day. I got to thinking that if anyone in this area was involved in dog fighting, I'd put money on it being our friends the Boyds, so I did a little digging.'

'And what else did you find out, I wonder?'

'Not a lot that I didn't already know. The family has been in the news quite a bit but mostly for minor stuff – disputes with neighbours, untaxed vehicles, etcetera. They're suspected of a whole lot more but they're slippery customers and mostly seem to get away with it.'

'So I gather. I've done some digging of my own – or at least got a friend to do it,' Daniel said. He filled William in on some of what Jo-Ji had told him about Lynda Boyd's connection with the Butcher family and how they'd been had up for owning fighting dogs.

'No convictions, because the dogs in question were stolen from the holding kennels by persons unknown before the case actually came to trial.'

'Yeah, right! Persons unknown,' William snorted.

'Exactly. I'm pleased to say they're a bit more careful these days. They don't tell the suspects where they're taking their dogs.'

'I can't believe they ever would have,' William said incredulously.

'Bit of a no-brainer, isn't it? Anyway, this aerial photo is a real find. You've done well.'

'Thank you.' William inclined his head. 'So, what do we do now?'

'*We*?'

'Well, I think I've earned the right to be involved, don't you?'

'Maybe, but why would you *want* to be? These are not nice people.'

'I get that. It's just – I spend all my working time reporting on life's events. Sometimes I feel I want to be out there taking part in them.'

'You're bored,' Daniel said bluntly.

'Well, OK. Yes,' he admitted.

Daniel regarded him for a long moment and then said, 'Well, actually, I'm not sure what to do next – or, at least, I know what I'd like to do, but I can't see how to do it at the moment. I'd like to go and have another poke round the salvage yard, but with their bloody CCTV you only get about five minutes before someone comes to ask you what you're up to.'

'Perhaps I could distract them,' William ventured hopefully.

'And how do you plan to do that?' Daniel asked, amused. 'Do a striptease or something?'

'I could go and be an awkward customer. Complain very loudly – ask to see the manager. That sort of thing.'

Daniel pulled a face. 'It'd never work. You're too well known round here. What I'd like to do is find the entrance to this secret building – if it really does exist – and plant a little spy camera of my own.'

'Have you got one?' William was clearly impressed.

'No, but they're easy enough to get hold of. Pretty cheap, too.'

'Well, we'll have to think of something else, that's all.'

'Fine. Let me know what you come up with,' Daniel said. 'Right now, I'd better go and see if I can find a bed for the night.'

'Um . . . You can always stay here, if you want. I do sometimes, when I've worked really late and I can't be bothered to go home. It's only a camp bed, but it's OK, and there's a loo and a shower and a kitchen and everything. It used to be a bedsit, you see. But you probably have other plans . . .' he tailed off.

'Only the pub,' Daniel admitted.

'The Fox'll cost you seventy quid a night and The Crown is even more,' William said promptly.

'And what do *you* charge?'

'Don't be daft! It makes no difference to me. It's yours as long as you want it.'

'You're very trusting. I might make off with the safe!'

'You're welcome to it. It's only got some photographic negatives and stuff in it. I can't imagine they'd interest you. Besides, if you can't trust an ex-copper, who can you trust?'

'Ah. So you've been checking me out. I might have guessed you would.'

'I was curious. It's in my nature.' William looked slightly uncomfortable. 'I couldn't work out why you were getting so involved, so I Googled you and came up with some newspaper stuff from Bristol. It doesn't change anything. And I won't tell, if you don't want me to.'

'I'd appreciate that. And about the room, thanks – I'll take it.' Daniel was genuinely grateful. 'I imagine I'll be gone long before you get here in the morning.'

'I imagine you will,' William said with a grin. 'I don't generally get here before midday, though Amy's here by ten. Or so she tells me,' he added thoughtfully. 'By the way, there's no food, but the baker's up the road is open at half seven and they do a mean breakfast. I can vouch for that.'

William was right. The baker's did do a good breakfast, and Daniel was just swallowing the last of his coffee when he was surprised to see William himself come in, looking even more unkempt than usual.

'Good God! Either I'm very late, or you're inordinately early,' Daniel exclaimed, glancing at his watch.

'I'm horribly early,' William said with a shudder, slipping into the vacant seat opposite him. 'But I had to show you this.' He deposited a printed sheet of paper in front of Daniel.

Daniel scanned it briefly. It was from the local electricity supplier, giving notice of work to be carried out in the high street later that week.

'And . . . ?'

'Well, they're doing maintenance work,' he explained in the tone one would use for a small child. 'That means the power has to be turned off – look, it even says so. We apologize for any inconvenience, blah blah . . . interruption to the power supply at any time between nine thirty and three thirty on Thursday for a period of not

more than two hours. And if there's no power, there's no CCTV at
the salvage yard, am I right?'

'Ah, I'm with you. Good thinking, Mr Faulkner! And all before
eight o'clock in the morning. I'm impressed.'

William caught the eye of the woman behind the counter.

'Black coffee, please, Brenda, and one of your breakfast baps
with all the trimmings,' he said with a winning smile.

'You'll get fat,' Daniel joked, eyeing his companion's lean frame.

'I wish. Anyway, as it's only two days away, I thought you'd
want to know about the power being off straight away, so you can
get hold of what you need.'

'Right-oh, thanks.' Daniel drained his mug and stood up. 'I'm
going to have to leave you. Work calls. Tell me, are you still thinking
of coming along on this jaunt?'

'Absolutely.'

Daniel shook his head, looked heavenwards and left with Taz at
his heels.

Thursday morning found Daniel's lorry parked up in the disused
timber yard beyond Forester's Cottage. From there, William picked
him up just before nine thirty in a small white hatchback that had
seen better days. Taz was spending the day with Jenny and the
kids.

Daniel had been at the yard a quarter of an hour and had used
the time to effect a minor transformation to his appearance with the
aid of some instant tan, a beanie and a pair of black-rimmed spectacles. Thankfully, the day wasn't too hot and a baseball jacket
completed the look. William's face, when he leaned across to push
open the passenger door of the car, was a picture.

'My God! I nearly didn't stop,' he exclaimed. 'If I hadn't expected
you to be here, I'd never have recognized you.'

'Objective accomplished, then,' Daniel observed. 'I've got a
couple of bits here for you. It's just in case we get caught on camera.
I don't intend to, but it never hurts to be prepared.'

'Is that really a false moustache?' William asked gleefully. 'Crazy!
Can I wear that?'

'You can – it's your colour. Now get that hair tied back out the
way, it's a dead giveaway.'

Five minutes later, in a baseball cap and a denim waistcoat,
Daniel judged William to be sufficiently disguised to fool a casual

glance, which was all that was needed. He had no intention of subjecting either of them to close scrutiny by the enemy, if he could help it.

As William drove them towards the village, he was practically buzzing with excitement, and for the first two hours that they sat in the car in the lane that ran behind Boyd's Salvage Spares, he continuously fidgeted and checked his mobile phone.

'It's not going to ring any sooner for you looking at it,' Daniel observed with amusement. William had asked his assistant, Amy, to let him know as soon as the power went off.

'But they said between half nine and half three, and it's nearly twelve already.'

'So, it might not go off until two – or even not at all. Be patient.'

'How can you just sit there and do those damn things?'

Daniel raised his eyes from a book of Sudoku puzzles.

'Cos it's better than doing nothing.'

'But the waiting's driving me mad!'

'If you'd spent as many hours on obs as I have, you'd have learned patience. Many's the time I've sat in a car or an empty building for days, and at the end of it all nothing has happened. All part of the job.'

'Have you got the camera?'

Daniel slapped his forehead dramatically. 'Gee, no! I knew there was something I meant to bring . . . Of course I've got it. Now, stop stressing, will you?'

Procuring the camera had been as easy as Daniel had predicted. After wading through an endless list of surveillance equipment on eBay, he chose a medium-priced outfit and contacted the seller, who was willing to send his order with next-day delivery. Within an hour the deal was done.

Another few minutes passed, during which William fiddled with the car's ancient stereo system and failed to find decent reception. When the long-anticipated call finally did come, he jumped as if he'd been given an electric shock. Fumbling with shaking fingers, he put the phone to his ear.

'OK, thanks, Amy,' he said almost immediately, before ending the call and looking at Daniel with a mixture of excitement and trepidation. 'The power's just gone off.'

'OK. Let's get to it, then,' Daniel said. 'We don't know how long we've got.'

He was out of the car as he spoke, pulling a small rucksack after him. Beside the lane, the corrugated iron fence stood a good eight feet tall, with two strands of barbed wire above that.

William came to stand beside Daniel, looking up.

'So, tell me again how we get in?'

'I put my hands together, you step in them and I boost you up. You should clear the top, easy.'

William gave him a sideways look. 'You are kidding, right?'

'Of course I am. Just along here there's a panel that's loose at the bottom. It's come away from the next one just enough to let a person slide through. Here it is.' He caught hold of the iron sheeting at its bottom corner and, with an effort, pulled it away from its neighbour, bending it up a little.

'That's handy. I wonder how that happened . . .' William said with another sideways look.

Daniel shrugged. 'Can't imagine. Lucky for us, though, eh?' He had spent an industrious half-hour after dark the previous evening, removing the rivets. 'Now, are you going first or am I?'

William stood back. 'Be my guest,' he offered.

'Chicken!' Daniel murmured.

A couple of minutes later, they both stood inside the perimeter fence, surveying the mountains of scrap before them. Daniel removed a copy of the aerial photo from his pocket and oriented it so that their current position was closest to him. They were at the furthest side of the premises from the gate, and their target area was only a few yards away as the crow flew.

'Let's just hope they haven't changed the layout since this was taken,' he said, low-voiced, and then pointed down a scrap-formed alleyway to their left. 'Should be down there and to the right.'

He swung the backpack into position and then set off, with William on his heels. As they turned the first corner, William grabbed Daniel's arm and pointed upwards to where the unblinking eye of a CCTV camera stared down at them.

Daniel disengaged himself.

'They're off, remember? That's why we're here,' he said softly.

'Are you sure? They might have a generator or something.'

'If they have, we'll soon find out,' Daniel told him.

'How?' William looked up at the camera.

'Because somebody will come looking for us. Now you've given them a close-up of your mug, let's keep going, shall we?'

A couple of paces on, Daniel paused, looking at a torn black bin bag that had snagged on the handle of a rusting garden roller.

'Actually . . . If I lifted you up, do you think you could drape that artistically over the camera? Try and make it look as though it's blown there. Just as a precaution for the return journey.'

'Now you're talking. Artistic is my forte,' William said grandly. 'Lift away.'

With the lens safely out of commission, it took only a couple of minutes to bring them to the spot where, according to William's aerial photo, the circular feature was situated, and, as they expected, there was no sign of any structure at all. The mound of scrap metal that confronted them was just a continuation of the piles that adjoined it, although Daniel noticed a preponderance of decommissioned white goods: washing machines, cookers, dishwashers and tumble dryers. He pointed this out to William.

'That's clever,' he said.

'Because people are less likely to be interested in those, you mean? So there's less danger of anyone moving them.'

'Exactly. Old cars, sheet metal, wire and oil drums, people could conceivably want parts of, but old ovens? No good to anyone. I reckon we've found our spot.'

'Now we just need to find how to get in.'

William looked at the pile of rusting metal helplessly.

'Is that all?'

'It's not quite as hopeless as it seems,' Daniel replied. 'They're not going to want to shift a load of junk every time they need to get into their den, so we look for something large that's still fairly movable.'

'Like the shell of a transit van?'

Daniel followed his gaze. '*Just* like the shell of a van.'

'But it's got no wheels . . .'

'No. Well spotted,' Daniel said, gazing thoughtfully at the wreck, which had a massive dent in the front corner of its roof and a previous owner's business name imperfectly concealed by a coat of white paint. Items from the overflowing scrap pile had spilled on to the roof. 'I wonder . . .'

Moving to the back of it, he inspected the area around the handle and lock. 'Bingo!' he said softly.

'What?' William was at his shoulder. 'What are you looking at?'

'See here?' Daniel pointed. 'This door has been reinforced. Most doors can be opened in a few seconds by someone with a screwdriver and a couple of brain cells, but not this one. The lock has steel plating round it.'

'But couldn't that have been done *before* it was scrapped?'

'It could,' Daniel agreed. 'And it might well have been. Either way, it's ideal for their purposes. I'm betting, if we could see inside, we'd find they've modified the sidewall to make a way through.'

'What? You mean, this is the entrance to their building? They actually walk through the van to get to it?'

'That's what I'm thinking. Clever, isn't it?'

'So, what now? Can you pick the lock?'

'Possibly, given long enough, but if they've gone to this much trouble, I'm thinking there's every possibility it's alarmed. No. As this is the only real candidate, we'll stick to our original plan and set up our own little spy camera.'

'Will it take long?' William was looking distinctly uneasy.

'Not too long. Nerves bothering you, Mr Faulkner?'

'It's all right for you. I'm not used to this sort of thing.'

'Wishing you'd stayed at home?' Daniel asked, removing the tiny camera and its fittings from his backpack.

'Not at all,' William replied stoutly. 'What kind of a range has that thing got?'

Daniel pursed his lips. 'They say fifty metres tops, but I'd say that's probably pushing it. If I can get it high enough, we should get a signal outside in the lane.'

'You mean you've got to sit in the lane every evening just on the off chance that someone uses the entrance – even supposing it *is* the entrance,' he added pessimistically.

'What I'm really interested in is an actual fight, and that's more likely to be a Friday or Saturday night,' Daniel said, noting that William hadn't included himself in the proposed watch. The thirst for involvement was apparently wearing off.

Positioning the camera securely took several minutes, and William's nerves didn't improve. More than once he took his mobile from his pocket and checked the display. From other parts of the premises there came vehicle noise and the occasional sounds of voices. When Daniel finally pronounced himself satisfied and clambered back to ground level, William was clearly in a fever to be off.

'Is that it?'

'Well, I thought while we're here, I might have a quick look for those other buildings we saw on the aerial shots.'

'You *are* kidding, right?'

'You're welcome to go back, if you want,' Daniel said mildly.

'No, no. In for a penny . . .' William said. 'Which way?'

'I've highlighted them on this photo,' Daniel said, taking his A4 printout once more, 'And I reckon they should be just the other side of this lot.' He indicated the wall of scrap curving away from beyond the transit van.

'Isn't that getting a bit close to Boyd Central?' William asked, peering at the picture over Daniel's arm.

'We'll just have to be extra quiet, won't we?' he replied with a wink.

It seemed that luck was with them. As they rounded the end of the sloping bank of metal, they were confronted by a compound bounded by a multi-strand barbed-wire fence on which hung notices, every few feet, warning of the danger of moving machinery inside. Inside the fence were stacked rolls of wire netting and sheets of corrugated iron, forming an effective screen, and, some way beyond those, the bulk of the metal compactor.

'If you held the wire apart, I might just slip through,' he suggested to William.

'Do you think that's a good idea? What if someone comes?'

'That's all right. I've got you as a lookout.'

'I don't know . . .'

'I'll be quick,' Daniel promised. 'I just want to see what's behind those convenient piles of fencing material. According to our photo, it should be the missing buildings.'

Moments later, his assumptions were confirmed. The two single-storey prefab buildings stood parallel to each other, about twelve feet wide and some thirty feet long. Each had a door at one end, and the only windows were narrow elongated panes, high under the eaves. Unable to see in, even on tiptoe, Daniel took a small camera from his backpack and holding it near the glass of each window, pressed the shutter, fervently hoping that his hunch as to the buildings' purpose was correct and there would be no humans inside.

As he put the camera away, Daniel heard a low whistle and became aware of the sound of an approaching engine.

A quad bike. Ricky.

Cursing under his breath, he dropped down to crouch behind the concealing wall of stacked iron sheets, hoping William had kept his head and also found somewhere to hide. Had they been seen somehow, or was it just a precautionary tour of the site?

A scrabbling noise to his left made him whip round, ready for action, and he came face to face with William, on hands and knees, looking dusty and dishevelled.

They both waited, listening, as the quad bike came bucketing along the rutted dirt track towards the compound, circled round the fence and away down another alleyway.

As its engine noise receded, Daniel straightened up and held out a helping hand towards William.

'You look a little ruffled, my friend,' he observed, as he hauled him to his feet. 'How did you get through the fence?'

'I went under,' William said. 'I find there are some advantages to being the shape of an anorexic stick insect, after all!'

Daniel laughed.

'Shall we go home?'

'*Please*. I've decided I quite like being a looker-on, after all.'

On their way out, they paused long enough to uncover the Boyds' CCTV camera once more, before slipping out through the gap in the fence and into the lane.

'Job done,' Daniel stated, throwing his backpack into the car and getting in after it. 'Now I just need to see if it works.'

It did. The image on his laptop screen was clearer than he had hoped for, although for the moment it showed nothing more than the closed rear door of the transit and part of the scrap pile.

William leaned over to see.

'What happens if it's after dark?' he wanted to know.

'That's when the night vision function kicks in. Won't be a great picture, but hopefully enough to identify faces.'

Taking his camera from the backpack, he took the flashcard out and slid it into a dock on the side of the computer. A few taps on the touchpad later, several rather dark thumbnail images appeared on the screen. Choosing the least obscure, he brought it up to full-screen size. The flash had reflected on the window glass, but it was just possible to make out one or two details.

'What's that? It looks a bit like a gym?' William said, head on one side.

'It is, in a way,' Daniel said grimly. 'A gym for dogs. A treadmill for endurance training. A hanging tyre to improve jaw strength and grip. I can't make out what that other thing is. but it's a copybook set-up for training fighting dogs.'

'So, we were right.'

'Unfortunately, yes.' Daniel snapped the laptop shut. 'Shall we go?'

William already had the engine going.

When Daniel got out of his camp bed just after midnight to get a drink of water, he glanced out of the window of William's bedsit and looked down at the moonlit courtyard below. There were only two parking spaces in the quadrangle, both reserved by day for veterinary emergencies, but now they were both filled. Even from above, Daniel recognized Ivor Symmonds' estate car in one, while the other was filled by the rectangular roof of a dark-coloured van.

He was about to turn away when the courtyard was flooded with light from a security lamp, and two men emerged from the doorway immediately below his window. Without further ado, they got into the van, backed and turned it and drove away.

Daniel waited. A minute or two later, a silver-haired man appeared, turned to lock the door and then got into the car.

As its red tail lights disappeared out towards the road, Daniel looked down at Taz, who was lying watching him from a blanket at the foot of the camp bed.

'Well, well. What business do you think our friend Ivor could possibly have had with Norman and Taylor Boyd so late at night, eh, lad?'

Taz lifted his head and fixed him with an intent gaze.

'Yup, I think you're right,' Daniel agreed, ruffling the fur on the dog's head. 'I have my suspicions, but, whatever it was, it's a fair bet they were up to no good.'

SIXTEEN

'This belong to anyone?' Dek held out a small leather collar upon which several ominous dark stains could be seen.

Across the room, Reg looked up from his paper and the colour left his face.

Dek had arrived late in the drivers' room that Friday morning, with the aim, Daniel instantly suspected, of making just such an impressive entrance.

'Looks like it belongs to a small dog,' Boyd suggested, clearly enjoying the moment. 'Say – a Jack Russell, or something. Didn't you used to have a Jack Russell, Reg? Whatever happened to it? Ah, yes, I remember. You lost it. Very careless, I always thought.'

Dek laughed with Boyd, but Macca had the grace to look a little uncomfortable.

'That's enough!' Daniel said sharply as Reg threw the paper aside and surged out of his chair, a tortured expression on his face. He snatched the collar from Dek and turned it over in his hands.

'Where did you get it?'

'Found it. Lying beside the road. Like you do,' he added airily.

Reg squared up to him, his lower jaw thrust forward like a bulldog. At fully six inches shorter than the younger driver, it would have been comical if the circumstances hadn't been so tragic.

'What have you done with him, you bastard?' he growled.

Dek backed away, holding his hands up in mock fear.

'Steady on, old man. You'll have a heart attack or something. I thought you'd be pleased to have his little collar back again.'

'Yeah, you should be thanking him,' Boyd put in. 'Save you buying another one for the next pooch, unless you decide to get a proper dog.'

Reg cast them both a look of loathing, pushed past Dek and left the room.

'Give you a kick, did it?' Daniel asked mildly. 'Upsetting an old man. Make you feel good?'

'Ah, shut up!' Boyd answered. 'You can go and hold the silly old fart's hand if you want.'

Daniel got to his feet.

'Well, I certainly prefer his company to yours,' he commented on his way to rinse his coffee cup.

He found Reg in the depot yard, leaning on the gate, waiting for the warehouseman to finish loading his lorry.

'You all right, mate?'

Reg didn't turn his head.

'I shouldn't let them get to me, I know, but I couldn't help it. They caught me on the hop.'

'As they meant to.'

Reg sighed. 'What makes people like that? So needlessly unpleasant.'

'Something missing in their little lives,' Daniel said. 'That's what I've always thought. Trying to prove themselves. I'm sorry about Skip.'

'Thanks. It's been a week. I didn't really think I'd ever see him again – but a part of you keeps hoping, doesn't it?'

Daniel put a hand on the older man's shoulder briefly, then moved away.

When Daniel finished work on the Friday evening, he found a note from Woodsmoke tucked under the windscreen wiper of his car. It had been written with a none too sharp pencil and said simply, *Need to see you, urjent. Will wait at the stables. W.*

There was no suggested time, but doubtless Woodsmoke knew what time the lorries normally returned, so Daniel turned round and headed straight for the stableyard.

When he reached the yard, Sue was coming out of one of the boxes.

'He's round there,' she said, jerking her head in the direction of Barn Field.

Daniel carried on through past the stables and found Woodsmoke leaning on the field gate, still attired in his long coat and hat, in spite of the heat of the afternoon.

'Hi. What's the problem?' he asked.

'No problem,' Woodsmoke grunted. 'Just heard something I reckon you'd be innerested in.'

'OK?' Daniel waited.

'Can't say for sure that it's true, cos you never in general get to hear of these things, but I thought it was worth telling you.'

'Right.'

'Word is there's a meeting on tonight.'

'*Is* there so?' Daniel was suddenly very interested. 'And where did you hear this word?'

'I wuz in The Fox at lunchtime, an' I reckon they thought I wuz asleep. I might even have led them to think I wuz, come to that,' he said with the suspicion of a twinkle under the brim of the hat. 'It were that Boyd nipper. He told this other fella he had a mind to try his dog out. The other one, he said to count him in and he knew a few others who'd come along, iffen he wanted.'

'Did you catch where and when?'

'Reckon it wouldn't be much good telling you iffen I hadn't,' Woodsmoke observed.

Daniel couldn't argue with that. He waited.

It seemed almost as if the old poacher was reluctant to give up this last bit of information; he was enjoying the moment too much. But eventually he did so. 'Nine o'clock. Radpole's Barn.'

Daniel frowned, taken aback. He'd been hoping Woodsmoke would name the salvage yard. 'So, where's that?'

'Way out yonder,' the older man said, waving an arm towards the fields on the horizon. 'You'd never find it in a month of Sundays, I reckon. Course, I could show you, iffen you wanted.'

'I expect I could find it on a map. No need for you to get involved.'

'Happen you could find it, but then what? You can't go barrellin' up there in your car. They'll be watchin' the track, sure as anything. You need to come at 'em unexpected, across the fields.'

'OK. Where shall I meet you, then?'

'I reckon you know the barn on Colt's Hill.'

That had been the one where Daniel and Drew had found the rats in the pit. He nodded.

'Meet you there, half eight, if you like. Will you come on the liddle pony?'

'If Jenny agrees.'

Daniel's conversation with Woodsmoke left him with a great deal of food for thought. Even though instinct urged him trust the old poacher, he couldn't completely banish the suspicion that Woodsmoke had been allowed to overhear the arrangements being discussed in The Fox and Duck. Dog-fighting rings were customarily obsessive about security. The whereabouts of meets were not normally disclosed, even amongst the supporters' network, until perhaps half an hour before the event, when a text message would go out to selected members of the group, to spread the word to the waiting punters. In extreme cases, those attending would be collected and taken to the venue in minibuses. To think that Taylor Boyd would have been so careless stretched credibility.

On the other hand, thinking back, Woodsmoke had described the man he'd overheard as 'that Boyd nipper'. Did that mean it had been Ricky, rather than Taylor, who had let the information slip? That would certainly be more believable, and the very fact that he had access to that privileged knowledge meant that the Boyds must indeed be key players in the Butcher Boys fighting ring. Why tell Ricky, though? In their shoes, there was no way Daniel would have trusted the hot-headed youngster with such potentially dangerous information.

Was it possible that the Butcher Boys somehow suspected Daniel was interested in their activities and were laying a trap? If so, that would also presuppose that they knew of his friendship – if such it could be termed – with Woodsmoke. There were a lot of ifs, but one way or another Daniel couldn't feel easy with what he'd learned.

Whatever his misgivings, if there was any chance the information was kosher, he couldn't risk passing up such an opportunity. He would meet Woodsmoke, but, knowing how these gangs operated, he would take absolutely no chances.

Eager to show off his blossoming riding skills, Drew took no trouble to hide his disappointment that Daniel proposed to go out without him that evening, and for a few minutes it seemed that a full-on strop might be in the offing. Jenny stepped into the breach, however, with the suggestion that she take all the children to the local bowling alley for the evening, a manoeuvre that earned her Daniel's heartfelt gratitude.

'Thanks,' he said, out of Drew's hearing. 'I owe you.' He had told her the purpose of his excursion.

'Indeed you do,' she said. 'And I'll collect, believe me. But, Daniel – be careful, won't you? I don't think I could handle another tragedy just now.'

'Don't worry. I'll listen to my inner coward, I promise.'

Twenty past eight found Daniel stepping down from Piper's saddle in the lee of the barn on Colt's Hill. After a day of hot sun and blue skies, the evening had become overcast and a blustery wind sprung up. He'd left Taz at the farmhouse. The dog had been just as disappointed as Drew but had accepted his fate more philosophically, merely watching Daniel's exit with lowered ears and reproachful eyes.

'You're here, then.' Woodsmoke's sonorous tones broke in on Daniel's thoughts. 'Wasn't sure you'd come.'

As Daniel turned, the poacher looked momentarily taken aback but recovered quickly. 'Iffen you're thinking of going in amongst 'em, reckon you'd do well to think again,' he suggested.

'I've no plans as such but I like to be prepared,' Daniel said. He'd used a change of clothes and his box of tricks to subtly alter his appearance, topping the effect off by tucking his hair under a beanie. He'd been fairly pleased with the result and Woodsmoke's reaction confirmed his success.

'You said it was the Boyd nipper you overheard. Did you mean Ricky?'

'Arh. The young un.'

'I'm surprised they'd trust him with that kind of information.'

Woodsmoke nodded. 'Thought on that. Reckon it's his shooting match.'

'You think Ricky organized it himself?'

'Thass what I said.'

'So how far is this barn from here?' Jenny had thought Radpole's Barn was a good distance away, on the neighbouring farm, and had loaned him Alfie the cob for Woodsmoke to ride.

Daniel had been surprised. '*Can* he ride?'

'Oh, yes. He used to have a hairy little pony that he rode everywhere until it died about ten years ago,' she had told him.

'Take about half an hour,' the poacher said now, in answer to Daniel's query. 'A sight less iffen that black-and-white creature is for me.'

'It is.' Daniel held out the reins.

'A good girl, that Jenny,' Woodsmoke said approvingly.

'So where's Gypsy?' Daniel asked as the older man settled into the cob's saddle and arranged his long coat over the animal's back. With his wide-brimmed hat, he looked like a gaucho from the plains of Argentina.

'Left her back home. Reckon she's in the family way,' he grunted.

Woodsmoke looked quite at home on the horse, although he declined to go faster than a jog, claiming that he was 'too old to want to shake up his vitals'. Even so, they reached the barn in only a little over fifteen minutes, tethering the horses and continuing on foot when they were nearing their goal.

They approached to one side of the barn where the cover was thickest, Daniel following Woodsmoke without a word, bowing to his knowledge of the locality. The poacher moved through the dense woodland like a wraith, his feet in their soft-soled boots making no sound, even though the ground beneath the trees was littered with twigs. Daniel had spent a good deal of his childhood shadowing the gamekeeper on the estate that bordered his own home and as a youngster had thought himself something of a woodsman, but Woodsmoke put his efforts to shame. When they were close to the edge of the clearing, yet still hidden by a stand of bracken, they hunkered down and observed the scene.

Radpole's Barn was a structure that had seen better days. Built of timber that had gone silvery with age, topped off with a mossy tiled roof, it stood in a woodland clearing with nettles growing thickly against its walls. Nearby stood the remains of a second building that had fared even worse over the years and was in a state of dereliction, its tin roof caved in on one side.

There was no doubt that Woodsmoke's information had been correct. Their current position was level with the double doors at the front of the barn, with a good view of anyone entering or leaving. Parked untidily in front of the building were several vans, a minibus with darkened windows, and two or three pick-up trucks. A number of rough-looking individuals loitered nearby, smoking and talking in overloud voices. One even held a muzzled dog on a rope, which he kept pushing with his foot, laughing when it eventually whipped round at him. Daniel guessed a search of the vans might yield other potential fighting dogs.

In spite of Woodsmoke's warning, he hadn't come this far to watch tamely from the outside if there was any chance that he could get inside, but he knew he'd have to time his move well.

As they looked on from the sidelines, Ricky Boyd came to the door of the barn and stepped outside, looking away down the track and then at his watch. Another man appeared by his side and said something. Ricky shrugged and again looked down the track, before taking his phone from his pocket and making a call. It looked as though Woodsmoke had been right. The meeting was Ricky's baby, and Daniel doubted that his father and brother knew anything about it.

'He says five minutes. He's just down the road.' Through a lull in the general conversation level, Ricky's voice carried to the watching pair as he pocketed his mobile.

All of a sudden, two men pushed past them in the doorway, one holding the other in a kind of armlock. Half a dozen others followed and stood watching and cheering as a rough-and-tumble fight ensued.

'Did you invite all these people?' Ricky asked his companion uneasily, raising his voice to be heard over the noise. 'I didn't expect so many.'

'Most of them. Relax. It's cool.'

At this point, Daniel and Woodsmoke heard a vehicle approaching along the track, and a few seconds later a silver van with tinted windows roared into the clearing and pulled up in front of the barn, sliding impressively on the loose gravelly surface.

All at once, the fight was over, the protagonists slapping each other on the back as they got to their feet and everyone turning to look at the newcomer. A fat, unshaven man emerged from the silver van, hitching up a dirty pair of jeans and waving a hand at Ricky before opening a sliding side door and taking out a large carrying crate with a mesh door. There was a cheer from those assembled, and within moments everyone in the clearing was following him into the barn, Ricky and the fat man in the forefront.

Without a word, Daniel rose to his feet, stepped through the bracken screen and tagged on to the end of the shuffling queue. Behind him, he faintly heard a bitten-off exclamation from Woodsmoke.

Just inside the doorway stood a muscle-bound bruiser, and Daniel's heart skipped a beat or two until he realized that it wasn't Macca. Although the man was presumably there as a bouncer of sorts, he hardly spared a glance for Daniel, looking past him to see if there were any further punters before he closed the door.

Against all the odds, Daniel was inside and, for the moment, could breathe again.

The barn was not big, less than half the size of the one on Colt's Hill, with a mezzanine at the door end, which was probably a hayloft. In the centre of the ground floor was an enclosed area about twelve feet square with walls formed of laminated boards, screwed on to angle-iron stakes that had been driven into the earth floor, and rubber mats underfoot. This improvised pit was brightly lit by spotlights positioned around the eaves, and, by contrast, the viewing area around it was shadowy and dark, which suited Daniel very well.

There must have been forty or fifty men round the outside of the square, two on opposite sides obviously running books on the upcoming fights. They were doing a roaring trade, as most of those present seemed to be pushing forward, eager to place their bets.

Anxious not to stand out in any way, Daniel joined the crush, finally putting a bet on a dog called Reckless in the first bout.

The man immediately behind him in the queue snorted derisively.

'Like throwing your money away, do you?' he asked, but before Daniel could formulate a response, one of Reckless's supporters took up the dog's defence and much good-humoured heckling ensued.

Relieved to have the attention lifted from him, Daniel moved away and took up a position standing on a ring of hay bales that had been laid against the barn walls.

'Friend of Roy's, are you?' a voice enquired beside him.

Daniel stayed silent, hoping whoever it was hadn't been talking to him, but moments later an elbow nudged him and the question was repeated.

'Oh, sorry,' he said, glancing at the unsavoury-looking character beside him. 'No. A friend of Ricky's.'

'What do you think of that new dog of his, then? Have you seen it? Think it was the eighth wonder of the fucking world, the way he goes on about it, wouldn't you?'

'Haven't seen it yet,' Daniel admitted. 'I've been away for a week or two. Just got back.'

After another couple of comments about dogs that were due to fight that evening, Daniel's unwanted new acquaintance clearly decided he was poor value as a viewing companion and moved away to talk to someone else.

Another potentially sticky moment passed. Daniel breathed deeply and considered whether he might be getting soft. He'd done a fair bit of undercover work when he'd been at Bristol Met and, in a skewy way, enjoyed it. But then it was different when you had the full support of a police force behind you. Now he was on his own, unless you counted the old poacher waiting outside. At least, he hoped he was still waiting . . .

There was a stir of excitement, the crowd parted and the fat man with the crate pushed his way through. He stepped over the barrier and into the makeshift pit before putting the crate on the ground. Moments later another man followed with two rough-coated black terriers under his arm. It seemed the evening's entertainment was about to begin.

The fat man bent down with a wheezing effort to open the door of the crate, and a buzz of excitement went round the barn as what must have been at least two dozen brown rats spilled out into the pit, immediately scurrying round the edges, searching for a way out.

The two dogs became frantic in their efforts to escape their owner's clutches, as instinct kicked in and the urge to kill drove all other thought from their minds.

'Give you fifty to one on the rats!' someone called out.

'Fuck off!' came the reply from elsewhere. 'The dogs'll slaughter 'em. I'll put a pony on the Patterdales clearing up in two minutes.'

The challenge sparked a frenzy of betting on whether rats or dog would triumph, and how long it would take. Daniel listened, trying hard to keep his face impassive, when, in truth, the whole scenario disgusted him. He wondered if the fat man had caught the rats, or whether the poor things had been bred for this cruel end. Although he knew wild rats were the carriers of disease and were present in epidemic proportions across the country, it was no fault of theirs and didn't excuse using them in this way.

After what seemed an age, during which the terriers continued to wriggle and yap furiously, and the rats milled around and around in search of a way out, the last bets were laid and the contest got underway.

The man with the Patterdales bent over to hold them just above the ground, their legs paddling furiously, and on the signal of another man, who held a stopwatch, the dogs were released and the slaughter began.

The terriers needed no second bidding. They were ruthless and efficient killers, dispatching the rodents with a bite and a flick of the head that sent them flying through the air to land limp and broken, feet away. The dogs didn't have it all their own way, however. Several of the rats, finding themselves cornered, turned on their hunters and latched on to their faces, necks and paws, drawing blood that spattered the wooden walls as the Patterdales shook and broke the backs of yet more of their number.

Daniel knew from his research that, in times gone by, single dogs would be put in pits with so many rats that sometimes, by sheer force of numbers, the rats *did* prevail. He was glad that this wasn't part of the current evening's sport because, little as he relished seeing the rats slaughtered – it was at least quick – he doubted his ability to stand by and watch a dog gradually overcome and killed by a horde of rats, whilst men stood by waiting to time the moment of collapse.

The noise in the barn was deafening; the blood lust of the men as all-embracing as that of the terriers, and they crowded the barriers, urging the dogs on. Daniel hung back on the fringes and hoped they were too engrossed in the action to notice the swift and stealthy use of his mini camera.

Finally, the massacre came to an end and the two dogs circled the pit sniffing the rats' bodies for signs of life before standing panting in the centre of their scene of triumph, tongues lolling and blood seeping from numerous tiny bite wounds.

The man with the stopwatch announced the time taken, and all at once the focus was on collecting the money from bets placed.

'Awesome!' The man next to Daniel exclaimed enthusiastically. 'I'm going to get me some Patterdales.'

Daniel was saved the trouble of replying by the interruption of another man, who was adamant that a good Jack Russell would give the Patterdales a run for their money any day.

He wandered away to distance himself from the chatty man. The less he had to talk, the less likely it was that he would give himself away.

To one side of the pit, first aid was being administered to the terriers' wounds. Daniel watched from a distance for a moment, noting the extensive and professional-looking kit the handlers seemed to have at their disposal. He doubted that even a vet would have been better equipped.

The ring was cleared with a broom and shovel, and, in due course, two dogs were led in, already lunging at one another and snarling through their muzzles.

To Daniel's knowledgeable eye, the animals were classic pit bulls, their well-muscled frames clothed in jackets bearing their names, like boxers parading in the ring. The darker of the two dogs bore the name Reckless – the one Daniel had bet on.

The handlers let their dogs stand nose to nose for a minute or two, shaking their collars. The encouragement was completely superfluous. The dogs couldn't have been more hyped up, and the crowd wasn't far behind. At the pitside, the self-styled bookies took bet after bet, and then, when the buzz of anticipation had almost reached fever-pitch, the dogs' coats, collars and muzzles came off and the handlers held them on what Daniel guessed were some kind of quick-release leads.

Someone counted them down, the dogs were loosed and a battle of primeval, snarling ferocity commenced.

Daniel watched, sickened, as the two dogs fought. What disgusted him most was the bestial behaviour and appearance of those at the pitside. You couldn't blame the dogs for fighting. They were hapless pawns, bred and trained to enhance their natural aggressive instincts by men who got their kicks witnessing the suffering of another being. In his mind, it was the worst form of cowardice.

Hoping all eyes were on the battle in the pit, he palmed the key ring camera again and lifted his hand high to snap off a couple of pictures of the crowd.

The two dogs were well matched and fought each other to a standstill. Finally, with torn flesh and bloodstained fur, Reckless prevailed, catching the other dog in a vice-like grip around the throat and holding on until his opponent's legs buckled beneath him and he slumped to the ground.

The response from the crowd was a mixture of cheers and groans, and the dogs' handlers climbed into the pit to retrieve their animals. Reckless staggered with exhaustion as he was paraded round the pit by his crowing owner. The other dog lay where it had fallen until his handler picked up the limp body and made his way out.

Daniel had seen more than enough and would have been happy to leave, but he hadn't yet managed to get an incriminating photo of Ricky Boyd. If he could do that, he would at least have gained something worthwhile from the appalling episode he'd witnessed.

His luck was in. It seemed the next bout was the highlight of the evening: a match between Ricky's new dog and that of the man known as Roy. From the posturing and strutting, Daniel guessed this was a grudge match and was the whole reason for Ricky setting up the meet.

The proceedings followed the same format as before. The two dogs were paraded, goaded and then set upon one another. Ricky's dog, Razor, was the bigger of the two by some way, but Daniel thought he was carrying a little too much weight for peak condition, and he heard the same opinion voiced by others around the barn.

Sure enough, after an impressive start, Razor seemed to flag, and the smaller dog, which had been riding the storm with his chin tucked into his chest, began to show his mettle. As the minutes passed, Ricky's dog grew less and less able to defend itself, and its sleek pale fawn coat became streaked with blood from the many lacerations it had sustained. Hopelessly outclassed, and with desperation in its eyes, it tried to turn away from its relentless attacker, and several of the onlookers called to Ricky to withdraw it and let it fight another day.

'He's not fit, mate! Get him out,' one shouted, but many more jeered at Ricky's discomfort, and he became furious with rage and disappointment, leaning over the wooden barrier and yelling at his exhausted dog to get stuck in.

Razor couldn't do it. Head down and breath rasping through his throat, he finally collapsed in the corner of the pit, the smaller dog worrying at him and trying to pull him away from the protecting wall.

With an oath, Ricky leapt into the pit, but Daniel's momentary optimism that he was going to do the right thing and save his dog from further punishment was dashed as he set about the animal with his boots, screaming at it to get up and fight.

His actions produced a mixed response. The other dog's handler jumped in to drag his own fighter away; there were a few boos, and some onlookers laughed at Ricky's efforts.

'Always was a bad loser,' someone called out.

Daniel started to move forward through the crowd, aware that by intervening he risked discovery, but no longer able to stand the sight of such needless cruelty.

'Not so much of a Razor as a steak knife!' a man shouted as Daniel elbowed his way through the last row of spectators. With an almost manic expression on his face, Ricky took a flick knife from his pocket, released the blade and slit his dog's throat. Tossing the bloodstained body aside like an old coat, he wiped the blade on his jeans and pocketed it.

'That's a couple of grand down the drain,' someone commented. 'Wouldn't like to be him when Taylor finds out.'

'No point keeping a loser,' another voice replied.

'Too young. Shoulda waited,' was the opinion of a burly man at the pitside.

Daniel halted at the barrier, trying to stifle the urge to leap into the ring and plant his fist in Ricky's face. A couple of deep breaths restored reason. The dog was beyond his help now and, as satisfying as it would be, the action would undoubtedly draw down on him the kind of attention that would lead to his unmasking.

Ricky would have to wait.

As the dogs were removed and the excitement died down, Daniel made his way back to the obscurity of the darker fringes. He'd seen more than enough. It was time to go.

It seemed, however, that leaving wasn't going to be as easy as getting in had been.

At the rear of the crowd once more, he edged towards the barn door, trying not to make his intention obvious. He was still some feet away, however, when another man passed him and slouched towards the exit.

All at once the bouncer materialized and put out a hand to stop the man.

'And where might you be going, sunshine?' he asked.

'Just need to get some air.'

'Not with that, you don't,' the bouncer said and turned his hand over to make a beckoning gesture. 'Come on, you know the rules. You should have given that up before you got on the bus. How did you get it in?'

Sulkily, the slouching man handed over an expensive-looking, slimline mobile phone. 'Had it in the waistline of me boxers,' he said with a touch of cockiness.

'Pity. It looks a nice phone,' the bouncer commented, turning it over in his hand. The next moment he had dropped it on the floor and ground it into the dirt with his heel.

'You can't do that!' the slouching man exclaimed, red-faced.

'Done it. Run along now and, next time, do as you're told.'

The slouching man pushed past the bouncer in a childish show of rebellion, and the big man chuckled as he watched him go.

Daniel wasn't laughing, though. He not only had a phone on his person, he had the mini camera. If that were to be found, he would be in big trouble. Needing time to think, he edged away from the doorway and joined the fringe of the crowd once more.

When the hand descended on to his shoulder, he almost jumped out of his skin.

'What are *you* doing here?' a voice demanded in his ear.

SEVENTEEN

With no idea what to say, Daniel froze, turned slowly and came face to face with a complete stranger.

The man immediately held his hand up in a placating fashion. 'Oh, sorry, mate. Thought you was someone else. No worries.'

'No problem,' Daniel responded, his face calm, even though his heart rate had accelerated into the hundreds.

In the pit, two more dogs were being readied for combat. It was the last fight of the evening, but Daniel's full focus had shifted to the problem of how to get out of the barn. It was possible that if he remained until the end of the fight, he might be able to leave as he'd arrived, mingling with the other punters, but there was the possibility that some kind of social mingling might ensue, and that was something he wished to avoid at all costs. There was also the little matter of Woodsmoke waiting for him outside. He had been longer than he intended already and he didn't want the poacher to feel it was up to him to do something.

There were no side doors, as far as he could see – just the main double doors by which they had all entered – and, as one would expect of a barn, no windows.

While he pondered the problem, he became aware of the sensation of being watched, and turned slowly and casually to survey the area behind him. No one there except the bouncer and he was leaning against the inside wall, absorbed in fashioning a roll-up with his large and far from dextrous-looking fingers.

Daniel's eyes lifted to the hayloft. Was that a possibility? Searching his memory of the outside, he recalled a loft door in the apex of the roof. It would mean dropping down right outside the doors, but these were closed at present; he would just have to pray they remained that way. The first problem was working out how to access the loft from the inside.

He let his gaze travel round the dim interior of the rear portion of the barn and finally caught sight of a crude wooden ladder built flat against the back wall in the corner. All well and good, but just how was he to climb it without being seen? Facing the pit once again, he moved along the rear fringe of the crowd of onlookers as if searching for a better view of the upcoming fight. Now the ladder was a scant ten feet away and everyone's attention appeared to be fixed on what was happening in the pit, but Daniel wasn't deceived. He still had the eagle-eyed bouncer to contend with.

As the dogs were loosed and the buzz of anticipation became a roar of excitement, Daniel had to resign himself to the fact that the ladder was a non-starter. It looked as though he'd have to wait and take his chances at the end of the evening, after all.

Suddenly, he was startled by a voice, several decibels louder than the rest, yelling, 'Come on, my son! Come on, Tyson!'

Looking to his right, Daniel saw that the bouncer, driven by an overriding enthusiasm, had left his post by the door and was standing amongst the rearmost members of the crowd, shaking his fist in the air.

Tyson obviously held some special significance for him, Daniel decided, but there was no time to consider the matter if he was to take advantage of the man's momentary inattention.

Daniel moved swiftly to the rear of the barn, selfishly hoping that the two dogs would make a good long fight of it. Long enough, at least, to see him up the ladder and out of sight.

Standing by the ladder, he hesitated. He was painfully aware that as soon as he started to climb, he was burning his bridges as far as blending in with the other fight-goers was concerned. With one last glance at the bouncer's broad back, he turned and scrambled up the crude wooden rungs as fast as he could, expecting at any moment to hear a shout of discovery or feel a hand grabbing his ankle.

The ascent took only a matter of seconds and then Daniel was hauling himself through the hatchway and rolling over on to the hay-cushioned floor above, heart thudding.

An instant later, a half-seen flurry of movement brought him upright in a flash. He wasn't alone in the loft. Straining his eyes to see in the extremely low light, Daniel waited. Could it have been pigeons, or one of Drew's beloved owls? It was possible, but he thought not. The impression had been of something bigger.

The continuing clamour from below made speech redundant, but Daniel couldn't afford to wait until the fight was over because his chances of leaving the building without being detected were reliant on the bouncer still being occupied inside.

Suddenly, he remembered the mini torch in his pocket. He had nothing to lose by disclosing his own whereabouts – the watcher in the shadows was obviously well aware of his presence – so he took it out and switched it on.

In the furthest corner of the loft, a diminutive figure shrank back with wide, scared eyes. A boy, no more than six or seven years old. Directing the beam at his own face, Daniel put a finger to his lips and winked.

Moving closer, he said as loudly as he dared, 'It's all right. I won't tell. What are you doing up here?'

The boy shrugged. 'Me da told me to come up here outta the way. But I don't like seein' the doggies hurt each other anyway.'

'Neither do I,' Daniel agreed. He shone the little torch round the loft and located the double doors that formed the hatch to the outside. He turned back to the boy. 'I bet my mate I could get out of the barn without him seeing. If I go through that door, can you shut it for me, so he doesn't know which way I went?'

'Like a game?'

'That's right. It's a joke – but don't tell anyone, OK?'

The lad shook his head vigorously and followed as Daniel made his way over to the hatch.

The ring handle was so stiff to turn that, for one anxious moment, Daniel thought it might be padlocked on the outside, but then the latch lifted with a sound like a pistol shot and the door yielded creakily to his push.

No time to wonder if anyone had heard the noise; too late either way. Daniel crouched in the opening, feeling the cool night air fanning his face. Below was only blackness, the doors apparently still safely shut, and, without giving himself time to think, he pushed himself away from ledge, jumping out and down before the familiar panic could set in and freeze his muscles.

The ground leapt up to meet him, catching him off balance. His knees buckled and he stumbled sideways, putting out a hand to save himself and dropping the torch in the process. On his feet once more, he glanced back in time to see the faint oblong glow of light narrow and disappear as the boy closed the hatch. He had no idea if the lad would tell of their meeting or not, but it didn't really matter now. There wasn't much that anyone could glean from his tale.

Anxious to get away, Daniel nevertheless took a few moments

to photograph the number plates of all the vehicles parked outside the barn.

The roar from the barn rose to a crescendo and then broke up into cheers and groans. Another poor bugger had been beaten down, Daniel thought sadly as he turned and ran for the trees.

The ride back to the farm was a sober one. Woodsmoke had been waiting just inside the treeline with both horses. 'Reckoned you might want a quick getaway,' he explained to Daniel.

With clouds still covering the moon, visibility was poor and they held the horses to a walk, Daniel using the time to give the poacher an outline of what he'd seen in the barn.

'Not surprised about the Boyd nipper,' Woodsmoke grunted. 'Allus had a nasty streak, that one. There was a time, ten year or more ago, when cats were bein' shot with an airgun. Most of us knew who t'was, though no one ever seed 'im. Was only 'bout 'leven or twelve then, so I reckon t'was borned in 'im.'

Daniel and the poacher parted company at the barn where they'd met earlier that evening, Woodsmoke melting off silently into the darkness, while Daniel headed for the farm and stables on Piper and leading the cob.

At the stables, Daniel rubbed the horses down and released them into the paddock with a handful of grass nuts each, before turning his steps wearily towards the farmhouse in happy anticipation of a cup of tea.

Jenny was waiting at the door to meet him, her face drawn with anxiety.

'Thank God!' she said as he approached.

'What's the matter? Has something happened?' Daniel asked, his tiredness forgotten in an instant.

'No. I was just so glad to see you back,' Jenny said. 'You've been much longer than I thought. It reminded me of – well, you know, the night Gavin went out.'

Daniel glanced at his watch. It was half past eleven. 'I'm sorry. I should have called you when I was on my way back.'

'No, it's OK. I'm just being silly. Come in. I'll put the kettle on, and there are jacket potatoes in the oven.'

'Music to my ears!' Daniel exclaimed gratefully, fondling Taz who had pushed forward to greet him, tail waving happily.

Inside the house, he was surprised to see that Jenny's vigil hadn't been a lonely one. The children had gone to bed, but leaning against the range with a mug in his hand was the fire investigator they had encountered at the cottage earlier in the week.

Jenny saw his surprise.

'Paul's been back to the cottage and dropped in to see me,' she explained with a touch of self-consciousness. 'We've been chatting about old times.'

Paul McCreesh nodded to Daniel with no hint of embarrassment. 'I could see she was worried, so I offered to stay with her till you got back,' he said. 'But now I should probably be on my way. Eveything OK?'

'Yes, fine.' Daniel said, wondering how much Jenny had told him.

The fireman hesitated, as if expecting him to elaborate but, when he didn't, took his leave, kissing Jenny on the cheek as he left.

'I told Paul about the dog fighting,' Jenny said as the door closed behind her visitor. 'I had to say something – you don't mind, do you?'

'How much did you tell him?'

'Oh, no details, just that you were worried someone might be using one of my barns. I didn't say who or anything.'

'So what brought him over? Is there any more news on the investigation?'

'No. I think he was just being friendly. Someone had told him about Gavin and he came to offer his sympathy.'

And get his toe in the door, Daniel thought cynically, but he didn't say so.

'So, what happened? Was Woodsmoke right about the barn?'

'He was.' Daniel gave her a highly edited account of what he'd discovered, sparing her the unpleasant details.

'What will you do now? Tell the police?'

Daniel shook his head. 'The time to do that would have been while they were all still inside the barn. I think they'll have gone by now. The trouble is I'm pretty sure this was Ricky's idea. There were certainly some hardcore characters there, but not Norman or Taylor, and it's them I want to see rounded up.'

'But if they caught Ricky . . .'

'I don't know. Would they stand by him, or deny all knowledge? They're slippery bastards. If we don't catch them red-handed or at least provide cast-iron proof, I'm afraid they'll find a way to wriggle out of it again.'

It was well past midnight when Daniel left the farmhouse, feeling much better for two jacket potatoes and a mug of tea, and when he approached his temporary digs, he was surprised to see a light on in the office. The door was unlocked, and he opened it with caution. It was possible the light had been left on by mistake, but he wasn't going to take any chances.

There *was* someone waiting for him, but not with any sinister purpose in mind. Slumped in the armchair in the corner of the room he found William, fast asleep and lightly snoring.

Daniel gently shook the journalist's shoulder.

'Sweet of you to wait up for me, but you shouldn't have,' he commented.

William opened his eyes and stretched like a cat.

'I didn't intend waiting for you. I fell asleep.'

'Any news?' He'd managed to coerce William into monitoring the remote camera at the salvage yard, just in case Woodsmoke's tip turned out to have been a decoy after all.

'No, damn you! I spent three hours sitting in my bloody car and for what? Absolutely zilch! Nada! Diddly squat!'

'Nothing, then?' Daniel enquired. 'Welcome to the world of observation work.'

'Yes, well, you can count me out another time. I had a numb backside, got bitten to death by midges and was dying for a pee. I didn't dare desert my post, because sod's law says that would be the exact moment something happened. Only it didn't. I stayed there till eleven o'clock,' he finished, with the air of one who expected to be praised for his efforts.

'Excellent work. Take the day off tomorrow,' Daniel offered.

'Thanks a bundle!' William unfolded his long limbs and stood up. 'You never thought anything was going to happen tonight, did you?'

'Well, not really. But it might have. As it happened, the tip-off I had was genuine, so I got all the action.' He proceeded to give the William a summary of the events at the barn.

William was greatly impressed by Daniel's adventure, but sickened by what he heard – especially the savagery of Ricky Boyd.

'I know there've been rumours about him in the past, but you don't know what to believe, do you? I mean, we went to the same school,' he said, as if that should preclude him from doing anything immoral.

'Even murderers have childhoods,' Daniel observed dryly.

'Yes, I know, but . . . Oh, well, I'm going home to bed,' William said. 'I'm too tired to spar with you.'

As the door closed behind him, Daniel woke up one of the computers from its hibernation and plugged the camera in to upload his film and stills. The quality of the resulting images varied but was generally passable. Faces were fairly clear, on the whole, and the fragmented footage of the fight reawakened all the disgust he'd felt at the time.

He saved the material to a memory stick, deleted what was on the computer, then switched off and went to bed.

Daniel wasn't rostered on the following morning, but he still rose early and eight fifteen found him next door in the vet's waiting room.

When he gave his name, the Saturday receptionist regarded him doubtfully. She had found him waiting on the doorstep when she opened the door.

'Do you have an appointment?' she asked now, scanning the screen in front of her. 'It's appointment only.'

'I think he'll see me. Tell him it's about Norman Boyd.'

'I don't understand . . .' she said, perplexed.

'That's OK,' Daniel told her. 'You don't have to, but Mr Symmonds will.'

Casting another doubtful look in his direction, as if unsure whether he should be left alone in the building, the receptionist slid off her stool and disappeared through a door into a back room.

There was a sizeable pause. Daniel imagined the elderly vet's dismay upon receiving the message and wondered if he would try to delay by refusing to see Daniel.

After a minute or so, however, the receptionist returned and told Daniel that Mr Symmonds would see him in his consulting room.

Daniel found the vet apparently busily engaged in sorting through the stock on his shelves.

'I can only give you a minute. I have a client arriving at any moment,' he said over his shoulder.

'Why did you agree to see me?' Daniel asked.

Ivor Symmonds turned.

'Well, because . . . I mean, you're a friend of Jenny's, aren't you? I treated your dog.'

'Not because I mentioned Norman Boyd, then?'

Symmonds looked flustered. 'I don't understand why you think that would interest me.'

'Even if I said that I've seen him and his son leaving here by the back door, after hours.'

'Vets work long hours, Mr Whelan. There is no "after hours" as such.'

'So it was a consultation?'

Symmonds shrugged, with an attempt at nonchalance. 'I expect so.'

'You don't remember? It was only a few days ago. I had it in mind that it was more of a dispensing issue. I thought they might have been picking up a few bits and pieces for their own use, if you know what I mean.'

'Don't be ridiculous!' The words were coldly hostile, but Daniel could read the fear in the older man's eyes.

'I think we both know I'm not,' he said quietly. 'Why don't you tell me what's going on? I know the Boyds own and use fighting dogs, and I know you know. But what I don't know is why you're keeping quiet about it. What have they got on you? Jenny has a lot of time for you, and I'm willing to believe that you aren't doing this for monetary gain, but you need to be honest with me.'

The vet hesitated, but just as Daniel felt he might be about to open up, the receptionist put her head round the door.

'Your eight thirty is here, Mr Symmonds.'

'Er, thanks. Won't be a minute.' Symmonds nodded to the girl, who withdrew, apparently unaware of the tension inside the room.

The vet planted his hands firmly on his examination table as if taking a stand. 'I really don't have a clue what you're talking about, Mr Whelan, and, as you can see, I'm very busy, so I shall have to ask you to leave now.'

Daniel sighed.

'Fair enough. If you prefer to talk to the police . . .' he said as he turned away.

For a moment, he thought his threat hadn't worked, but just as he reached the door, the vet said urgently, 'No, wait a minute! I need to think.'

Obligingly, Daniel waited, but he didn't move from his position by the door. For what seemed an age, Symmonds stood with his head bowed, rubbing one hand across his brow. Finally, he came to a decision.

'OK, I'll tell you,' he said, suddenly looking several years older as the fight went out of him. 'But you have to promise you won't go to the police.'

Daniel shook his head.

'I can't promise that. You know as well as I do that this can't go on, and the police are bound to be involved on one level or another.'

'It's not so much for me, but my son,' the vet pleaded.

'Tell me, and then I'll see what I can do.'

Silence stretched over several seconds as Symmonds looked down at the tabletop and then up at Daniel once more, despair in his face.

'You're right. It has to stop. *I* can't carry on like this, either; it's been a living hell. You've no idea.' He glanced up at the clock, which showed half past eight.

'They can wait a few minutes, I'm sure,' Daniel said, interpreting the look.

Symmonds nodded. 'It started last year. My wife, Enid, had been diagnosed with cancer. The doctors said it was inoperable and it was just a matter of time. We were devastated – we'd always been close; childhood sweethearts, married nearly forty years, and now they were saying we might only have six months. Then we heard about a treatment – a new drug, only just coming on to the market from America – but the doctors wouldn't prescribe it. It was too expensive, they said. If we wanted it, we would have to go private, but we couldn't afford to do that. Don't get me wrong, I'd have done anything to raise the money, but things have been tight and the house was already mortgaged, and, with the state of the economy, my bank wasn't keen to remortgage. Enid accepted it, but I couldn't. I felt so helpless – useless.

'About that time, the Boyds approached me, wanting me to supply them with drugs, dressings and suturing materials.' He paused and looked at Daniel. 'My first instinct was to show them the door and report the matter to the police, but Norman had done his homework, damn him! He knew about Enid and the treatment we wanted – I suppose it was fairly common knowledge around the village. We'd even had offers of help from well-wishers, but nowhere near the amount we needed. Anyway, Boyd offered me the exact amount if I'd supply him with what he needed and turn a blind eye. What was I to do? I told myself if I didn't supply him, someone else would, and that wouldn't help Enid, would it?'

Daniel didn't answer. He couldn't condone the vet's actions, but he could sympathize with his dilemma. Who could say what one mightn't do if put in that position?

'It made me sick to the stomach, but I took their money,' Symmonds continued after a moment. 'I told Enid it was a bequest from a distant relative. I'm not sure she believed me, but by then she was too ill to care very much. She died before the treatment could start.' His voice cracked a little, and he stopped to take a deep, steadying breath. 'I tried to give the money back and put a stop to the whole thing, but it was too late. I had already given them one batch of stock, and Norman Boyd said if I didn't honour the agreement, they would tell my son. And if I told the police, they would claim that I had been supplying them for years.'

'But surely your records would show that wasn't the case,' Daniel protested.

Symmonds smiled sadly. 'It's not quite that simple. It might sound clichéd, but I'm an old-fashioned vet, in it for the animals, not the money. One or two of my clients struggle to pay from time to time, and I have been known to waive my fees occasionally, just to see that an animal gets the treatment it needs. Usually the client finds some other way to settle the debt – payment in kind, you know the sort of thing. It's part of village life and it works very well on the whole. I never thought it would be a problem, until now.'

'I heard you had a row with your son. Was that about the Boyds?'

Symmonds nodded. 'Yes. He found out. Saw Taylor leaving one time with a bagful of stock and checked the records. He was furious. I couldn't make him understand. He just wouldn't listen. That's when he walked out. It was a huge blow, but I couldn't blame him. It's what I would have done in his place, and in a way I was relieved. If anyone did find out, at least he wouldn't be involved.'

'What did you do with the money?'

'I gave it to charity. To the RSPCA – anonymously. I didn't know what else to do. I sent a note saying I hoped they might use it in their campaign against dog fighting. I even mentioned the Boyds.'

'*Did* you?'

'Yes. It made me feel a bit better, but not much. But, then, noth-ing's come of it.'

'You never know. These things take time,' Daniel said.

Symmonds looked curiously at him.

'So, what's your interest in all this? I've given you enough information to get me struck off and yet I don't even know who you really are.'

'My interest is in getting these evil bastards stopped,' Daniel stated. 'If I can do it without dragging you into it, I will, but I can't make any promises.'

'I remember you were asking about the missing cats and dogs, last time you were here.'

'That's what initially started me thinking, but I've found out a lot since then.' He paused. 'I have to trust that you won't mention my visit to the Boyds.'

Symmonds looked offended.

'Of course I won't. I want this stopped as much as you do.'

'But you have a lot to lose if the truth comes out.'

The vet shook his head. 'I made my decision when I told you the truth. I won't go back on it now. I'll just have to take my chances. Whatever the outcome, whether the truth comes out or not, it's time for me to retire.'

Watching the man closely, Daniel was inclined to believe him.

EIGHTEEN

'**D**on't you trust me?'

Daniel stopped, his hand on the door handle of the drivers' lounge, and listened. It was Monday evening and he'd finished work a good half-hour before but had called in at the farmhouse on his way past.

The voice he'd heard was Dek's, and he waited with baited breath for the answer.

'It's nothing personal.' The reply, as he'd expected, came from Taylor. 'We don't trust anyone with that kind of information; it's the only way to be sure. All I can tell you is that it'll be soon, and I shouldn't even be telling you that, so keep it under your hat, OK?'

Dek's next remark was muted, but Daniel heard Boyd's response.

'Ricky? Christ! I don't know. Sometimes I think he must have been swapped at birth. The bloody cottage and now this. And to make matters worse, the dog's dead. Got bitten through the neck, apparently. I mean, he wasn't anywhere near pit-weight. The old man's spitting fire! He had plans for that dog. It was supposed to breed some size into the Butchers' strain. Any fool could see it was going to be a late starter – any fool except my fucking brother, that is. He's a loose bloody cannon! He could have blown the whole operation.'

Once again, Dek's reply was inaudible. Boyd's tone became placating.

'I know you wouldn't. Personally, I'd sooner trust you than him, but he's family, and family means a lot to the old man. Look, I'm gonna get going. I'm gagging to see this new machine he's bought. It's fuckin' massive, by all accounts. Wanna come?'

His voice grew louder as he approached the door, and Daniel was startled into action. Moving swiftly to the outer door, he opened and then slammed it shut, so that Boyd's first sight of him was walking towards the lounge. His quick thinking worked. Boyd looked mildly surprised to see him but not alarmed.

'You're late,' he commented.

'So are you,' Daniel countered.

'Been cosying up to the boss again?'

'That's right.' Daniel wasn't going to rise to the bait.

'Good luck there, mate. She's got another admirer now, so I hear.' With this parting shot, Boyd was gone, with Dek on his heels, leaving Daniel to wonder how it was that McCreesh's visit had become common knowledge.

Thursday was a half-day for the Summer Haulage drivers, the afternoon being set aside for Gavin Summers' memorial service.

The numbers at Great Ditton parish church were good, most attending, Daniel suspected, out of respect for Jenny, whose family were well known and well liked in the area. From what he could gather, Gavin had made few real friends during his time at the farm.

One surprising member of the congregation, as far as Daniel was concerned, was Jenny's neighbour, Liam Sellyoak, whose presence caused a stir among the younger football enthusiasts attending.

Drifting to Jenny's side during the reception afterwards at The Fox and Duck, Daniel quizzed her on it.

'I don't know. I had no idea Gavin even knew him. I was as surprised as you.'

'Perhaps he's trying to win brownie points with you,' Daniel suggested wryly.

'Well, he's wasting his time. But whatever the reason, it's made Harry's day. He's going round with stars in his eyes.'

Daniel looked through the window to where the children were amusing themselves on the mini adventure playground in the pub's garden area. As far as he knew, Drew had never shown any sign of worshipping sporting heroes. He seemed to have been born without a sporting gene in his make-up, for which Daniel wasn't overly sorry.

'I thought I saw George and Marian at the back of the church,' he said then. They had slipped in unobtrusively just as the service was about to begin.

'Yes. I was hoping to have a word with them, but they seem to have gone,' Jenny said, looking round the room.

Daniel felt he could make a shrewd guess as to the reason for that but he said nothing. His gaze tracked across to where Taylor, Dek and Terry MacAllister were taking full advantage of the hospitality. Reg stood a little apart, looking morose and depressed, as he had ever since the loss of his dog. Of Summer Haulage's former drivers, Mal Fletcher and Dean Stevens, there was predictably no sign.

Ivor Symmonds approached, patently ill at ease and just as obviously trying to avoid catching Daniel's eye.

'Jenny, my dear. I must be going. Patients to see, you understand. I'm so sorry for your loss. If there's anything I can do.'

Jenny took his hands in hers. 'Thanks for coming. It means a lot. I know how busy you are.'

The vet muttered something about old friends being more important than work, kissed her cheek and hurried from the room.

'He looks tired,' Jenny said with concern. 'It's such a shame he and Phillip fell out. It's a busy practice for a man of his age to cope with alone.'

'It must be hard,' Daniel agreed.

Eight o'clock on Friday evening found Daniel and William sitting in William's car in the shady lane outside Boyd's Salvage Spares once more, watching the image transmitted by the spy camera to Daniel's laptop. They had been there for half an hour, and so far there had been no movement on the screen to lift the tedium.

'Even a stray cat wandering past would be something,' William complained. 'I can't believe I let you talk me into sitting here again after last week, and especially with that hairy creature of yours breathing hot doggy breath down my neck.' He looked over his shoulder to where Taz was sitting on the back seat and was rewarded with a wet nose thrust at him. For some reason, the shepherd seemed to have developed a fondness for him. 'As if it wasn't warm enough in here without him fugging it up,' he added.

'Jenny's taken the kids out this evening, and I didn't want to leave him on his own for hours at the farmhouse,' Daniel explained. 'Anyway, you never know when he might come in handy.'

'What for? Blowing out candles on a birthday cake?' William replied dryly.

Daniel ignored him, and after a few more uneventful minutes, the young editor closed his eyes and gave all the appearance of being asleep.

Forty minutes later, Daniel was fighting the urge to follow suit when a movement on the monitor brought him wide-awake in an instant. He shook William's shoulder.

'What? What is it? Have we got a stray cat at last?' he asked, stretching his back muscles and sitting up.

'Better than that. Norman Boyd. In fact, all the Boyds *and* Dek.'

'Who's Dek?'

'One of the drivers at work. Remember, I told you – very pally with Taylor Boyd.'

'Do you think there's going to be a fight tonight, then?'

'I'm not sure.' Daniel answered abstractedly, his eyes glued to the screen. 'Now, what's going on here?'

The slightly distorted image provided by the camera showed the back of Norman Boyd's head and the front view of the three other men, with Dek standing between and slightly in front of the two Boyd siblings. Although there was nothing overtly threatening about Ricky's or Taylor's body language, something in the positioning of the three made Daniel's eyes narrow. Dek didn't appear to notice anything amiss; he looked relaxed and was apparently listening closely to what Norman was saying.

Moments later, the mood had totally changed. Norman turned and pointed up towards the camera lens.

Dek looked bewildered and then deeply alarmed as he realized the significance of the device and what he was being accused of. He shook his head and protested vehemently. Behind him, the two brothers closed in, Taylor's face grimly intent, Ricky's wearing an unpleasant grin. Norman then held up a small device towards the camera and the picture fizzed into oblivion.

'Oh, shit!' Daniel muttered.

'What did he do?'

'Scrambled it. Jammed it.'

'But they think this Dek character planted it,' William observed with amusement. 'So, that's all right, isn't it?'

'It's not good news for him.'

'Why does that matter?'

Through the open window of the car, they heard a crash of metal and a sudden outbreak of shouting. Daniel couldn't hear what was said, but it wasn't hard to guess what had happened. Faced with the evidence against him, false though it was, Dek had decided to cut his losses and run for it. The trouble was that the salvage yard was a secure premises with the gate the only way in – unless you knew of the hole in the fence that Daniel had engineered. Unfortunately, Dek wouldn't, and if the Boyds had blocked his exit, it would only be matter of time before they hunted him into a corner.

Daniel wrenched the car door open. 'I'm going in,' he told William.

'What?' He was astounded. 'Are you mad?'

'It's my fault they're after him. Call the police. Get them out here as quickly as you can.'

'But what do I tell them?'

'I don't care, just get them here!' Daniel said, shutting the door in Taz's eager face. 'No, Taz. Not this time, mate. It's too dangerous. Stay there.'

'You're not taking the dog?'

'There's too much sharp metal,' Daniel explained. 'Call the police, then wait here. I'll try and get Dek out this way, if I can.'

'But I don't understand. *Why?*'

'Tell you later.'

'Daniel!'

Ignoring him, Daniel sprinted the short distance up the lane to the hole in the fence, bent the corrugated panel back and squeezed through, scraping his back painfully. As he straightened up on the inside and looked round at the maze of heaped metal and alleyways, he wondered if he'd been overprotective in leaving Taz behind. His tracking ability might have come in very useful before this business was over. However, it was an injury sustained while searching a scrapyard that had ended the dog's police career, and although he had eventually made a full recovery, it had been a close run thing for a while. Daniel wasn't prepared to put him at that kind of risk again if he could help it.

Running down the clearway between two heaps of scrap, Daniel was aware that this time the CCTV cameras were likely to be fully operational. He could only hope that there was no one free to man them and his presence would remain undiscovered for as long as possible.

At the junction between alleyways, Daniel paused, straining his ears to make out what was happening from the sporadic shouts and sounds of metal shifting. Someone shouted away to his right, and then Daniel jumped as there came the boom of a shotgun, shockingly close and quickly followed by a second.

'For fuck's sake, Ricky, are you mad?' That was Norman's voice, away to Daniel's left.

'I saw Edwards,' came Ricky's reply.

'Did you get 'im?'

'Nearly.'

'Nearly's not good enough! Keep that bloody thing quiet till you're sure, or we'll have the fuzz down on us,' came the furious retort. 'Go and cover the gate like you were told.'

Daniel hesitated. Should he head in the direction that he'd heard the shotgun, on the basis that Dek must have been nearby? But surely, if he had any sense, he'd now be heading the opposite way, as fast as he could. The salvage yard was a maze of piled-up metal junk and interlinking passageways. He could, potentially, bump into Dek around any corner, but he could also just as easily bump into one of the Boyds, which was not a prospect he relished.

It was a sobering revelation that Papa Boyd's only worry about his son shooting someone was that the police might have heard the gun. And what kind of man would let a borderline psycho like Ricky loose with a firearm in the first place?

Moving cautiously, Daniel made his way to the end of the alleyway he was following and paused. The air was still and humid, and he could feel perspiration trickling down his back under the grey T-shirt he wore. Grey was a lucky choice, for although the sun had slipped below the horizon, covering darkness was still a fair way off, and grey blended reasonably well with the background mass of metals, painted, rusty and bare.

He had come to a crossroads. Glancing quickly to right and left, he crossed the broader alleyway and continued in his original direction, keeping his ears open for any tell-tale conversation between Dek's pursuers.

Suddenly, closer than was comfortable, Daniel heard the jingle of a pop song on someone's mobile and a voice answered, 'Yes?'

He froze, listening, and after a moment or two Norman Boyd said 'Is he now?' then raised his voice and called out, 'Hey, lads. Whelan's in here, too. Melody's just seen him on the cameras.'

Daniel cursed silently. How much had she told her father? Did Norman know where he was? He glanced around but could see no covering CCTV. As he waited, he could hear Boyd's heavy footfalls continuing up the adjacent clearway and decided to backtrack.

Reaching the junction once more, Daniel paused, half-hidden behind a pile of rusting oil drums, to scan the available options. As he did so, he caught sight of Taylor Boyd approaching down the alleyway to his right. His heart rate stepped up a notch. There was a one in three chance that Taylor would choose to turn left at the crossroads, and those were odds he didn't especially like, but it was too late to move.

Just as he reached that decision, he glanced behind and saw something that changed the odds completely. Dek was making his way down the same alleyway behind him, entirely unaware that in a matter of moments he would come practically face to face with his erstwhile mate, Taylor. At the moment, Dek probably couldn't see Daniel, concealed as he was, but when he did, would he recognize him as an ally? Daniel had a feeling that in the heat of the moment he would be reluctant to trust anyone, for which he couldn't blame him.

In the absence of any better idea, Daniel picked up a lump of twisted metal from the ground at his feet, rose up from concealment and lobbed it as far as he could into the piled up metal behind Taylor.

Risking a quick glance to see if his unoriginal ploy had worked, he saw that Taylor had indeed stopped and turned. It might not trick him for long, but it might have gained them a few precious seconds.

Unfortunately, upon seeing Daniel, Dek had taken to his heels and was now sprinting in the opposite direction for all he was worth. Wishing he could yell out to him, Daniel set off in pursuit.

Running blindly felt all wrong. Playing cat and mouse in a

labyrinth was scary enough, without scuttling willy-nilly towards
the waiting paws of the cats.

Ahead of Daniel, Dek swung left and disappeared from view.
Sod's law that he should turn away from the potential escape route
provided by the hole in the fence. Running after him, Daniel
wondered if William was having any luck with motivating the
authorities. He had no illusions that it would be easy, especially in
such a rural area where there would be little manpower available
at the best of times.

Turning the corner in pursuit of Dek, Daniel ducked just in the
nick of time as an oil drum flew at his head. The drum bounced off
his shoulder and he straightened up to find his quarry coming at
him with a length of angle iron raised high to strike.

'No, wait! Dek!' Daniel gasped, ducking again as the metal
swished past. 'I'm here to help you.'

Missing Daniel, the bar crashed into the door of a rusting white
van behind him. He dodged to one side, trying to put space between
himself and his misguided attacker, saying urgently as Dek whirled
to face him, 'Listen to me! I'm not the enemy. I can show you
another way out.'

Dek took no notice, raising the angle iron for a second attempt.

Bending low, Daniel launched himself in a rugby-style attack at
the other man's midriff, throwing him off balance and back against
the van with a hollow boom. The metal bar dropped, ringing on the
hard earth.

Taking advantage of his moment of dominance, Daniel tried once
again to convince Dek of the benevolence of his actions, but he
wasn't in a listening frame of mind and began to struggle violently
against the armlock Daniel had placed on him.

Suddenly, the July evening air was split asunder by the deafening
roar of an engine. Not Ricky's quad bike – this was something much
more powerful and it wasn't far away. Even Dek stopped, struggling
to listen.

'What the . . . ?' Daniel breathed.

'They've got this massive bulldozer-type thing,' Dek gasped,
panting. 'German. Taylor was showing it off yesterday. It can go
through absolutely anything. If they catch us with that, we're dead
meat!'

'Well, I'm getting out of here,' Daniel yelled as the roar grew
even louder. 'Come with me if you want. It's up to you . . .'

He released the lock on Dek's arm and stepped back, trying to gauge where the machine was in relation to their own position, but the racket it made was all-encompassing and it was difficult to pinpoint. With no idea of the Boyds' whereabouts, the only strategy that suggested itself was to head for the hole in the fence and the waiting car as directly and quickly as he could.

Turning, Daniel headed back the way they had come, not stopping to see whether Dek was following. At the first junction, he caught sight of Taylor approaching from his right at a run and sprinted forward down the only clear route. After a short distance, he became aware of Dek running at his shoulder.

The alleyway swung left, away from his target, and Daniel cursed inwardly. They traversed two more intersections, turning first right and then left, before coming face to face with the white transit van beside which the spy camera had been placed. With no sign of Taylor behind them, he slowed to a halt.

'Shit!' Dek exclaimed, stopping beside him. 'Back where we bloody started!'

'At least I know which way is out from here,' Daniel told him. 'I just wish I knew where that bloody machine was.'

The noise of the engine seemed louder than ever, and suddenly the reason for this became obvious. Dek shook Daniel's shoulder and pointed behind them.

Turning into the end of the clearway, a scant fifty yards distant, was the biggest construction machine Daniel had ever laid eyes on, bar none. Liveried in green and white, the wheels were as tall as a man and the bucket, which at the moment was raised like the head of some huge alien insect, looked big enough to accommodate a minibus. The machine's width was such that its wheels were crushing the edges of the piles of scrap that bordered the trackway as it started to advance towards them.

For the space of several heartbeats, both Dek and Daniel gazed in frozen fascination before their survival instincts cut in again and they turned and ran with one accord.

The alleyway they were following was taking them further away from the hole in the fence, and when they rounded a corner to be faced with the choice of another left turn or a cul-de-sac, Daniel caught Dek's arm and pointed at the wall of scrap on their right.

'We need to go that way,' he yelled, and with a glance behind at the approaching horror of the machine, Dek nodded. 'OK.'

Together, they launched themselves at the mound of rusting metal, climbing from the roof of a long-dead car to the precarious slope of a sheet of corrugated iron and on up over the booming hollowness of an oil tank. Their frantic progress was slowed by other items of junk slipping and sliding away under their weight, and Daniel was very aware of the multitude of ragged metal edges that threatened horrific injury should a step be misplaced.

Descending the other side of the metal mountain ridge was, if anything, more perilous than the ascent had been, as their momentum carried them faster than they could plan their route. Daniel caught his foot as he neared the bottom and landed sprawling on the gritty surface of the track. Dek reached a hand down under his armpit and hauled him to his feet. Apparently, their alliance was now sealed.

'Where now?' he shouted, and Daniel pointed right.

Barely had they started in that direction when they faltered to a halt, their way blocked, not only by Taylor but also his brother Ricky, baseball cap turned back to front, sitting astride his quad bike with the shotgun across his knees and an expression of evil glee on his spotty face.

Daniel hesitated. To go the other way meant they would be heading away from their goal once more and it would very likely bring them to a dead end, just as the parallel track had done. He looked unenthusiastically at the mound of scrap metal that stood between them and where they wanted to be. They had no choice.

As if to underline the fact, the machine behind them geared down, revved up and attacked the pile of metal they had just scrambled over.

'He's coming through!' Dek yelled, and, galvanized into action, they threw themselves at the second mound.

As he climbed, Daniel consoled himself with the thought that the proximity of the earthmover should at least keep Taylor and Ricky off their backs for the time being. However, unless he and Dek got a move on, they might well find the Boyd siblings waiting for them on the other side.

A glance back as they gained the top wasn't reassuring. The monster machine was surging through the metal debris, pushing a tide of scrap ahead of it with its lowered bucket, like the bow-wave from a boat.

Throwing caution to the wind, he and Dek charged down the other side, leaping and bounding from one semi-stable object to another, trying desperately to keep their footing. Something sharp grazed Daniel's ankle and a spike pierced the thick sole of his shoe, but by some miracle he reached the ground safely.

Dek wasn't so lucky. As he touched down seconds after Daniel, he was clutching his leg just below the knee where the fabric of his jeans was rapidly darkening with blood. He looked up at Daniel, his face contorted with pain, and uttered one short, sharp expletive.

'It's just over there,' Daniel shouted, pointing. 'Here. Lean on me.'

Dek draped his arm across Daniel's shoulders, leaning heavily as he hopped at his side, dragging his left leg uselessly. Behind them, the machine's engine roared once more and the pile of metal shivered as the onslaught began. Taking much of Dek's weight, Daniel hurried down the narrowing trackway towards the last corner, behind which – if his sense of direction hadn't let him down – should be the perimeter fence with its comforting triangle of bent back panel.

A quick look over his shoulder revealed the shifting mass of metal gaining on them with a grinding, squealing cacophony, and he redoubled his efforts. They were too close to fail now.

With their breath coming in hoarse gasps, they rounded the last corner and saw the fence just a few yards ahead. Relief flooded Daniel. It was the right stretch of fence. The problem now was how to get an incapacitated and rapidly weakening man through the gap.

From this side, Daniel couldn't see the car. Was William still there? Or had he driven to the entrance to meet the hoped-for police?

Reaching the fence, Daniel dropped his shoulder and thankfully lowered his burden to the ground. Dek groaned and appeared barely conscious. The leg of his jeans was soaked in blood, and Daniel feared he must be losing a huge amount.

Trying to put the oncoming earthmover out of his mind, Daniel bent the loose corner of the corrugated iron fence further back upon itself with shaking hands and then turned to take hold of Dek once more. This was where he could have done with William to pass the injured man through to, but there was no time to waste in phoning him. Daniel would just have to go through the gap himself and then drag Dek through after him.

If you're asleep, William, my friend, I'll murder you! he swore under his breath as he positioned Dek close to the escape hole, leaning him up against the metal post that supported the fence.

'You go on,' Dek muttered, half opening his eyes.

'Save your breath – you're coming too,' Daniel told him. 'I didn't drag you all this bloody way for nothing.'

The combined noise of the earthmover's revving engine and the mountains of scrap metal it was pushing ahead of it was unbelievable, and, risking a glance back, it seemed to Daniel as though everything in his field of vision was on the move, relentlessly forced forward by the unstoppable might of the massive machine.

Oil drums were rolling and bouncing along, the rusting hulks of cars, vans and a powerboat were being tumbled end over end, and household appliances gouged deep furrows in the gritty earth.

What was Norman Boyd thinking? Daniel wondered desperately, as he turned to wriggle through the gap in the fence. He seemed to be in the grip of a temporary madness. How did he suppose he would ever get away with such an obvious murder? The penalty for his dog-fighting crimes would have been a fraction of what he was laying himself open to now. It was overreaction on a ridiculous scale. Easy to see from where Ricky had inherited his crazy streak.

The gap between Daniel, Dek and the tide of metal debris was closing too fast, and Daniel had no hope of Boyd stopping the earthmover merely to save his fence.

As he pulled his feet out on to the verge and turned to reach through the triangular hole and grasp Dek's jacket, Daniel knew that time had run out.

NINETEEN

Feverishly working to drag Dek through the fence, it was a second or two before the significance of the sudden silence dawned on Daniel.

A rolling oil drum bounced up against the fence just feet away, and a motorbike with no engine and one wheel flopped on to its side in the dust. There was the sound of metal sliding and settling, but the only sound from the machine that had caused all the mayhem was the heavy ticking of its hot engine.

Had Norman Boyd finally recognized the madness of his actions, just in the nick of time? Daniel wondered, but moments later the engine coughed and spluttered as he tried to restart it with no success.

'Dad? What you doin'?' That was Ricky.

'What d'you think I'm bloody doing? Fucking thing's stalled!' Norman shouted back, as if he had no part in its failure. 'Don't just stand there – get the bastards!'

Daniel hadn't been idle. Dek was now clear of the fence but it was twenty or thirty yards to the car and there was nothing to stop the Boyds following them. With Dek's dead weight to carry, he had no illusions about his chances of reaching it ahead of them.

'William!' he yelled, but the youngster had seen his predicament and had already started the car's engine.

Draping Dek's arm round his neck once more, Daniel hauled him to his feet.

'Come on, mate. Hang on in there,' he told the injured man, but although Dek murmured something in response, he was clearly too weak to be of any help.

William's arrival in the car coincided with that of Ricky at the hole in the fence. He was a few strides ahead of his brother and put his boot to the loose panel, elongating the triangular hole. As the gap widened, to his dismay Daniel saw that Ricky still carried the shotgun. With an evil smirk, he lifted the barrel and levelled it at Daniel.

Shock washed over Daniel like a cold shower as he stared at the twin black holes. There was nowhere to run or hide, and, of its own volition, his whole body tensed in a futile effort to defend itself. In the same instant, a furry torpedo rushed past Daniel and Dek and squared up to the fence, barking furiously.

Lifting his lip in a snarl, Ricky started to alter his aim.

'Taz, no! Off!' Daniel shouted, desperate with fear for the dog.

Taz took a step backwards but continued barking, while Ricky Boyd's knuckles whitened as his finger tightened on the trigger.

Mesmerized by the horror of what was happening, Daniel didn't see Taylor arrive at his brother's side and reach for the gun. Both the shotgun's barrels discharged with a shattering report. Daniel flinched, but now the muzzle was pointing skywards and somehow, miraculously, both he and the dog were unharmed.

Ricky rounded on his brother, wrestling for control of the gun.

'What did you do that for?' he demanded furiously.

'Because you can't just shoot people!' Taylor replied through gritted teeth.

Hurrah for the voice of reason! Daniel cheered silently, but Taylor rather spoiled it by adding, 'Not here, anyway.'

William appeared on Dek's other side and, leaving the dog to oversee the ongoing defence of the hole in the fence, he and Daniel managed to get the injured man round to the rear of the hatchback, where the door had already been raised to allow Taz to get out.

Climbing into the back of the car on the folded-down rear seats, Daniel pulled Dek in after him, William lifting the injured man's feet. A sharp command brought Taz reluctantly to his side and, in seconds, William had slammed the hatch, slipped into the driver's seat and was accelerating down the lane.

Daniel turned his attention to Dek, who looked to be in a bad way, his face the colour of putty and clammy, eyes only half open.

'Have you got any rag or a cloth?' Daniel asked William urgently, and moments later a ragged dishcloth was passed back. It had been used to wipe condensation from the car windows and was somewhat soiled, but there was no time to be fussy. Rolling it lengthways and wrapping it round Dek's leg just above the wound, Daniel fashioned a tourniquet using a spanner to twist the cloth until the bleeding slowed and stopped.

'Dek. Can you hear me?' he asked loudly, and the man's eyelids flickered. 'Stay with me, OK? We'll soon be at the hospital. How far is it?' he added to William.

'About fifteen minutes, barring hold-ups,' William replied, concentrating hard on negotiating the narrow roads at speed. 'Is he OK?'

'Not great. What happened with the cops?'

'Oh, God! I tried,' William groaned, as he slowed for a junction. 'I got stuck with some jobsworth who was highly suspicious and wanted all the details before he was prepared to do anything. All I got were bloody questions – half of which I couldn't answer – until I lost my temper and he finally said he'd send someone as soon as they had someone free. I'm really sorry.'

'It's not your fault. Some of these rural stations might only have a couple of officers on duty overnight, even at the weekends.'

Beside him, Dek stirred and muttered something.

'What's that?' Daniel asked, bending low.

'Football match,' Dek repeated faintly, and Daniel relayed the information to William.

'Of course,' William said, annoyed with himself. 'I should have remembered that. I covered the build-up in my own bloody paper! It's a local grudge match. A lot of bad feeling.' With a quick glance right and left, he pulled out on to a main road and floored the accelerator. 'Hang on to your hats! Next stop A and E.'

When Daniel and William were finally allowed into the curtained-off cubicle in the A&E department, they found Dek attached to various monitors, with a bag of blood infusing into each arm. A nurse stood at the head of the bed making notes, but as they entered, she hung the clipboard on the bed rail and smiled at them.

'He'll be going in to surgery shortly,' she said. 'He's had his pre-med so he's a bit sleepy, but it should be OK for you to see him. Are you relatives?'

'No. Friends,' Daniel replied. 'We brought him in.'

When the nurse had gone, William looked at Daniel quizzically. 'Since when did we become his friends?'

'Oh, we've been friends all along. We just didn't know it.'

'I see.' He plainly didn't.

'I didn't know for sure until tonight when he cut and ran, but Dek's on our side.'

'So that's why you took off after him. I thought you'd gone mad.'

'Yeah, sorry. There wasn't time to explain. The thing is, he played his part well but there have been one or two things, right from the start, that didn't quite sit right with the character he was portraying. Because I've been in the same situation myself, I suppose I'm extra-sensitive to inconsistencies. For instance, I caught him doing the cryptic crossword in the paper one day. Now, I know it's dangerous to generalize, but the dregs of humanity that frequent the dog-fighting world aren't usually academic, and it just didn't fit in with his persona. Then, I think he let his guard down when he was alone with Drew in the drivers' room the other day. Drew told me he liked him, and I've found that kids can be quite shrewd judges of character.'

'So are you saying he's an undercover cop or something?'

'Undercover, certainly. I'm not so sure he's police. I had a look at the office computer and took the liberty of chasing up his reference. My query threw the people at the other end into some confusion. I imagine they'd dealt with the initial enquiry from Jenny and hadn't expected any follow-up. It took a moment for them to get their act together. If it had been a police operation, they'd have had a dedicated line that would have been kept for the duration. I suspect he works for a newspaper or an animal welfare organization.'

On the bed, Dek stirred.

'RSPCA,' he murmured weakly.

'Thought it might be,' Daniel said. 'How do you feel?'

'About a hundred and two.' The rough edge had slipped from Dek's voice.

'Is there anyone we should call?'

'The number's on my phone. Nurse put it somewhere.'

'I'll find it. What name am I looking for?'

'Dad.' Dek managed a faint smile. 'He's not really. Name's Lou Danvers. You have to say, "I'm ringing about the red canary." He'll get things moving.'

'I didn't know you could get red canaries,' William commented.

'You can't,' Daniel said shortly. 'That's the point.' Then to Dek, 'I think Taz and I owe you a huge thank you for that night at the cottage.'

'Almost blew my cover,' Dek muttered. 'Good job the old guy turned up.'

'You've lost me again,' William complained.

'Taylor paid me a visit at the cottage in the middle of the night, with the aim of persuading me to go home,' Daniel explained. 'They trapped Taz in a net, and I imagine Dek was supposed to finish him off while Taylor and his mate delivered a warning off to me, but old Woodsmoke, the poacher, put a crimp in their plans. Afterwards, he told me that the guy he took the dog from seemed glad to give him up, and at first I thought it might have been Dean – the young lad from work, but he swore he hadn't been there. Turns out it was Dek, so I owe him, big time.'

'Nearly blew it with Taylor, that did,' Dek said. 'So I take it the camera at the Boyds' place was yours. Fine way to repay me.'

'Yeah, sorry about that. I did my best to make up for it.'

Dek nodded and closed his eyes. 'Guess we're quits, then.'

The nurse twitched the curtain aside and came back in, her experienced eyes flickering over the monitors and checking the progress of the transfusions. She turned to the visitors.

'I'm sorry, you'll have to leave now. Mr Edwards needs to be kept quiet until he goes to theatre.'

With an effort, Dek opened his eyes once more. 'Can Daniel have my phone, nurse? I need him to phone someone for me.'

The nurse looked Daniel and William up and down as if assessing whether they were fit to be entrusted with the responsibility, and Daniel smiled encouragingly.

'I suppose it's all right,' she said grudgingly, and found the mobile before practically shooing them from the cubicle.

When Daniel spoke to him, he found Dek's boss, Lou Danvers, to be decisive and efficient. He said he would make the call to initiate a police search but was, however, of the same opinion as Daniel; namely, that the Boyds would have been quick to cover their tracks and there would by now be nothing incriminating to be found at the salvage yard.

'So they get away with it?' William exclaimed indignantly, when Daniel relayed this piece of information.

'Not if I can help it,' Daniel said. 'But they'll be on their guard now, which'll make the job a whole lot harder.'

'Pity we didn't get any decent camera footage before it all kicked off,' William said despondently.

Daniel looked at him sharply.

'Camera footage. I wonder . . . The CCTV at the yard was running the whole time; it might have caught something. Let's just hope it's recorded and not just on a loop. William – you're a genius!'

Taking Dek's phone from his pocket, he called Lou Danvers once again.

Two days later, on the Sunday morning, an assortment of people were gathered in the kitchen at Maidstone Farm. It had started with a phone call to Daniel from Lou Danvers, just after nine o'clock, asking if they could talk.

'A debriefing?' Daniel queried with amusement.

'Something like that.'

Daniel suggested they meet at the farm, as he was on his way there anyway, and as William had been such a big part of the whole business, he felt it only fair that he should come along.

The three older kids were in the kitchen when they arrived but departed almost immediately for the stables and promised rides. Daniel watched Drew running out with Harry and Lucy, and was struck once again by how much he'd come out of himself. He was behaving like a child for the first time in a long while, and it served to highlight how sober and withdrawn he had become since Daniel and Amanda's break-up.

Jenny filled the kettle and stood it on the Aga to heat.

'Oh, Daniel, this came for you yesterday,' she said, picking up a smallish padded envelope and handing it to him.

Daniel turned it over in his hands, mystified. His first thought that it was divorce paperwork from Amanda or her solicitor was quickly proven wrong. The envelope contained something solid and he didn't recognize the writing, which was in black felt-tip, large and rather childish.

Slitting the end with a sharp knife, he tipped a mobile phone and a folded piece of notepaper out on to the table. Unfolding the note he read, *Hope this helps but I won't testify!* It was written in the same felt-tip and initialled, *MF*.

'Well, well,' Daniel murmured.

'Whose is that?' William wanted to know.

'I'm about to find out, but I'm hoping it may once have belonged to Taylor Boyd.' Daniel switched the handset on and scrolled through its phonebook memory. 'Bingo!' he said with quiet triumph.

'So, who sent it?'

'Mal Fletcher. He used to work here.'

'Mal? Why on earth would he have Taylor's phone?' Jenny asked.

'I presume he either found or nicked it,' Daniel replied. 'It doesn't really matter. What does matter is that it has an extensive list of contacts stored on it that make very interesting reading.'

'Like who?' William came round to look over Daniel's shoulder, but he was saved from answering by the arrival of a car sweeping into the yard. It wasn't Inspector Danvers, as they expected, but McCreesh, the fire investigation officer.

McCreesh looked a little less than overjoyed to find Daniel there before him, but greeted him cordially enough, and when Danvers' RSPCA van pulled up in front of the house just moments later, he seemed resigned to the fact that any hopes he might have had for a quiet morning with Jenny were destined for disappointment.

The door opened to admit not only the RSPCA inspector but also Dek, on crutches. He looked pale and a little tired but otherwise fit enough.

'Discharged already?' Daniel asked, surprised. 'Last time I saw you, you were at death's door!'

'He discharged himself,' the inspector answered. A middle-aged, burly individual, he had grizzled hair and an impressive pair of bushy eyebrows, but a tell-tale crinkling at the corners of his eyes spoke of a sense of humour. 'The staff nurse phoned me. She was worried he'd collapse in the street, and even though I told her he's an ex-marine and ninety per cent gristle, she was having kittens about him, so I called by and picked him up.'

'I would have got a taxi,' Dek protested. 'I couldn't stay in that place another minute. They put me in the geriatric ward, and all the moaning and groaning was driving me insane. One man called out constantly the whole night through. I didn't get a wink of sleep. Anyway, I had no reason to stay there. I'm fine.'

Jenny pulled a chair out for him, and he manoeuvred himself round and sat gingerly in it, the caution of his movements and a poorly concealed grimace giving the lie to his confident claim.

Daniel stepped toward Danvers, holding out his hand and formally introducing himself and William. He said nothing of William's occupation; the two of them had agreed it might do better to remain undisclosed at present.

'Ah, the getaway driver,' Danvers said. 'The hero of the hour.'

William turned pink. 'No, that was Taz, I think. Without him, I doubt if any of us would have got away.'

Hearing his name, Taz looked up from his position on the floor.

'Good lad,' Danvers said approvingly. He turned to Jenny. 'And you must be Jenny Summers. I'm Inspector Danvers – RSPCA. Dek works for me when he's not working for you. I'm sorry about the subterfuge. A necessary deception.'

'No, that's OK,' Jenny said. 'I understand.'

Danvers raised his eyebrows in the direction of McCreesh.

'Paul McCreesh. Wiltshire Fire and Rescue,' he supplied, and the credentials obviously gave him the all-clear because Danvers nodded and said he was pleased to meet him.

Jenny brought a large cafetière of coffee to the table and passed mugs round.

'So what happened at the yard, Friday night?' The question had been burning in Daniel's mind for thirty-six hours.

'A monumental cock-up, I'm afraid,' the inspector said ruefully. 'Your efforts to mobilize the local boys in blue produced two community police officers on bicycles who arrived at the front gates and asked if everything was all right. Naturally, the Boyds assured them that it was and they went away.'

William groaned. 'I don't believe it! I talked myself hoarse trying to get them to understand how dangerous the situation was.'

'Surely they know the Boyds – by reputation, if nothing else,' Daniel added.

Danvers shrugged. 'You'd think so, wouldn't you? It seems that everyone available was policing a local football derby. Anyway, by the time I managed to get hold of someone with clout and they organized an appropriate response, there was nothing to be seen.'

'Nothing? What about the fighting pit they'd built? Did they at least find that?' Daniel asked.

'I'm afraid it no longer exists. I think they probably bulldozed it with that machine you told me about. We found plenty of rubble amongst the scrap, but nothing to prove what had been there. It could have been anything.'

'And the kennels? The dogs?'

'The kennels were still there, but the only dogs were a couple of Rottweilers. Guard dogs, they claimed.'

'But they had equipment,' William said. 'Stuff for training fighting dogs.'

'Yes, that was still there, but it's not illegal to use treadmills to get a dog fit or even hanging tyres to improve its bite. It's suspicious, yes, but without the dogs themselves, we have nothing.'

'That sucks!' William stated crossly.

'What about DNA?' Daniel wanted to know. 'We know the pit bulls were there, so can't they take DNA samples and prove that they don't match the Rotties?'

'That's been done,' Danvers confirmed. 'But unless we can find the actual dogs to match the samples to, we're no further forward.'

'Can't they tell what breed the dogs were from their DNA?' McCreesh wanted to know, but Danvers shook his head.

'DNA breed profiling with dogs is a very imprecise science, I'm afraid. It's a service offered to pet owners by several companies, but it hasn't been shown to be accurate – quite the opposite, in my experience. Even so-called pure-bred dogs are the result of many centuries of crossing and recrossing. It's a minefield. I'm afraid our only hope is to find the original occupants of those kennels and match the samples. However, with an organization like the Butcher Boys, the dogs have almost certainly been spirited away beyond our reach by now.'

'Didn't they even take the Boyds in for questioning?' Daniel asked. 'What about the CCTV evidence?'

'Norman Boyd claims he was after a couple of trespassers he found stealing from him. He admits that his reaction was rather extreme but insists he was only trying to scare them away, and as no harm was actually inflicted with the machine, there is nothing to prove otherwise. But in answer to your question – yes, they were taken in for questioning.'

'And released, I suppose?' Daniel said gloomily.

'In the absence of further evidence, they will be released this morning, so my contact tells me.'

'So there's a remote chance the dogs are still somewhere local?' This was Dek.

'Exactly what I was thinking,' Daniel agreed. 'Knowing the police were almost certainly on their way, they didn't have a lot of time to act, so surely they couldn't have gone far.'

'Unless they called one of their Butcher Boys buddies to come and fetch them,' the Inspector pointed out. 'But working on the supposition that they didn't, do you have any idea where they might have taken them?'

Both Dek and Daniel thought for a moment and then shook their heads.

'Mrs Summers?' Danvers asked. 'You know the area well.'

Jenny also shook her head helplessly. 'I'm sorry. There are so many barns and old farm buildings around. They could be anywhere. The Boyds have lived in these parts for ever. They know it like the back of their hands.'

'I suppose Radpole's Barn might be worth a look,' Daniel said, without much conviction. 'It's nicely remote and they've used it before, but, on the other hand, it's quite a long drive for them to have got there and back before the police turned up the other night.'

'How do you know about Radpole's Barn?' Dek asked curiously.

'I went along when Ricky organized his little meet last week.'

'*Did* you, indeed? I didn't even *hear* about that until afterwards.'

'Woodsmoke, the poacher, got wind of it. I got some video footage, too,' Daniel said, taking the memory stick from his pocket and holding it up. 'Sickening stuff. It'll definitely be enough to convict Ricky, but the others weren't there.'

'Christ! You took a chance!'

'Well, I thought something should be done to stop them. The police didn't seem to be getting off their backsides, and I didn't know about you at that point.'

'So, when did you realize?'

'Only really when it all started to fall apart for you at the salvage yard. Suddenly, things began to make sense. Shame it was a bit late. Between us, we might have got somewhere. As it was, I fouled it all up, big time, for which I can't apologize enough.'

Danvers shrugged. 'Things weren't going to plan anyway. Dek's brief was to find evidence of the funding behind the Butcher Boys. The organization seems to have money and to spare. We believe it's huge. Countrywide. But it's based round here, and although we'd had a tip off that the Boyds were heavily implicated, we don't believe they have the kind of money we're talking about. However, they run an extremely tight ship, and Dek wasn't making much headway.'

'Taylor is a cunning bastard,' Dek put in sourly. 'He let me see so much but never enough. There were dozens of little things we could have had him for, but none of them would have carried much of a penalty. We wanted the big hit.'

'You helped him bring a dog into the country, didn't you?' Daniel said.

'Two dogs, actually. Papers all correct. Labrador crossed with a boxer, and who could prove otherwise? No one even raised an eyebrow, and if they had, Taylor would've pleaded shock and innocence. He's a consummate liar.'

The farmhouse telephone rang and Jenny went to answer it.

'Oh, hello, Sue,' they heard her say, and Danvers began to talk quietly, revealing details of other suspicions the authorities held about the Boyd family's activities.

A minute or two later, his discourse was interrupted by Jenny saying sharply, 'Well, where are they, then?'

The conversation round the table hushed, alerted by the tone of her voice.

'She does, does she? Send her up to me, then, and tell her to make it quick,' Jenny continued. 'Yes, I know. It's not your fault. I'm not blaming you. OK, thanks.'

She put the phone down and turned back to the others with a crease between her brows.

'What's up?' McCreesh asked.

'That was Sue, down at the stables. I asked if the kids were behaving themselves and she said only Lucy turned up. She doesn't know where the boys are, and Lucy either doesn't know or won't say. I've told her to send Lucy to me.'

'I expect they've just gone off on some boys' adventure,' McCreesh suggested lightly.

'Probably,' Daniel agreed. He would have been surprised if that was the case, given how much Drew had been enjoying being around the horses, but he didn't want to add to Jenny's anxiety at this stage.

There wasn't much more to be said without Lucy's input, so they sat in silence until Jenny, who was standing by the open front door, said, 'Here she comes. She's riding Piper.'

Moments later, her twelve-year-old-daughter was in the room, standing in front of Jenny in denim jodhpurs and a pink T-shirt, with her strawberry blonde curls pulled back into a ponytail and a somewhat stubborn set to her mouth.

'If you know where they've gone, you tell me, young lady,' her mother said in a voice that brooked no argument.

Lucy looked mulish and said nothing.

'Lucy, it's important. If you don't know where they are, at least tell me which way they went.'

'I promised not to tell,' she said, turning pink under the scrutiny of so many interested persons.

'Well, I can promise you that if you don't tell, you'll be grounded for the rest of the holidays!' her mother warned.

Lucy appeared to consider this and come to the conclusion that loyalty had a price after all.

'They were going to see if they could get an autograph off that footballer they're so mad about,' she muttered after a moment. 'I told them you wouldn't like it, but they wouldn't listen.'

'They already knew I wouldn't like it,' Jenny said grimly. 'Or they'd have asked first.'

'What footballer?' McCreesh asked.

'Liam Sellyoak. He owns the house next door,' Jenny told him. 'Great Ditton Manor.'

'Well, surely the worst he'll do is send them away with a flea in their ear,' he said.

'I suppose so, but I don't like the man.'

'Did Taylor ever speak of him?' Daniel asked Dek, who frowned.

'I don't think so. Not more than in passing, anyway.'

'And yet he knew him well enough to have his number on a hotkey on his mobile phone,' Daniel mused.

'How do you know that?'

Daniel picked the recently acquired phone up off the table and explained how he'd come by it. 'I tried to get Fletcher to talk a couple of weeks ago but he more or less slammed the door in my face, so I posted him my number in the hope he'd change his mind. Looks like he has.'

Danvers looked interested. 'And are you sure the phone is Taylor Boyd's?'

'Pretty much. It's got all the members of his family on there, including one that says "Dad". Even if the phone's not registered, it'll be easy enough to check if that's Norman Boyd's number.'

'Excellent!' Dek said.

'What I'm interested in right now is the way Liam Sellyoak's name keeps cropping up through all this,' Daniel said. 'You're looking for someone with money who may be bankrolling the Butcher Boys, and here we have a millionaire footballer who lives just round the corner and whose number is on Taylor's old mobile. That seems quite a coincidence, and I don't know about you, but I don't like coincidences.'

'You think they might have taken the dogs there?' William asked. He had picked up the phone and was pressing buttons.

Daniel looked at him. 'I hadn't got that far, but it's possible, isn't it?'

'Worth checking out,' Danvers agreed, taking his own phone from his pocket. 'I'll give the DS a ring and run it by him.'

'Talking of checking out, check this out,' William exclaimed on a note of triumph, and passed the phone to Daniel.

William had accessed the phone's photo gallery, and on the miniature screen was a shot clearly taken at a dog fight. What was equally clear was that the photo had been taken not to record the action but to highlight one particular member of the watching crowd. Standing close to the ring, and clearly urging the participants on, was Liam Sellyoak in clear, sharp detail.

'Got him!' Daniel breathed, passing the phone to Dek. 'And I'm guessing this explains why Sellyoak is bankrolling the Boyds, if he is. Think what a picture like this would do to his career if it found its way into the papers. He has near-hero status with half the young

boys of Britain. It would ruin him. I'd say the Boyds have him
eating out of their hands.'

'The Boyds were released just over half an hour ago,' Danvers
reported. 'So it's a fair bet, if the dogs are being hidden at Sellyoak's
place, they won't waste too much time getting over there.'

'And Harry and Drew are on their way to see him.' Jenny looked
stricken. 'Oh my God, Daniel – we've got to stop them!'

TWENTY

'W hich way did they go?' Daniel asked, pushing his chair
back and getting to his feet. 'By road? Or is there a
shorter way?'

'There's a shortcut,' Jenny told him. 'Through the woods behind
us. They could be there in twenty minutes if they went on their
bikes. Did they?' She fired the question at Lucy who still stood
nearby, eyes round as she listened. Now she nodded, looking scared.

'I'll go after them,' Daniel said. 'Can you show me the path?'

'Yes, it's pretty easy to follow,' Jenny said, heading for the door.

'I'll get things moving,' Danvers said, keying numbers into his
mobile.

Outside, Jenny had paused and Daniel almost ran into her.

'What's wrong?'

'You could take Piper,' she said, and Daniel saw the quarter horse
patiently standing tied to the garden gate where Lucy had left him.
He was wearing a bridle but no saddle, and Daniel knew from what
Drew had told him that Sue was very keen on improving grip and
balance by teaching the kids to ride bareback.

Hoping that his own grip and balance were up to the challenge,
Daniel untied Piper and vaulted on to his glossy chestnut back.
Gathering up the reins in one hand and a hunk of mane in the other,
he urged the horse to follow Jenny who was already moving towards
the side of the house.

Passing the office, she showed him where a rather overgrown
path ran alongside the field behind the house, heading for the dark
line of the copse, some fifty yards away.

'Just stay on the path. It's signposted as a bridleway. It comes out in Well Bottom Field and crosses the river. Watch Piper with the bridge. When you go up the track on the other side, you'll see the house on your right. Please find them, Daniel!'

'I will.'

Guiding Piper through the narrow opening to the bridleway, he applied his heels firmly and was rewarded by a surge of power that almost caught him napping. Glad of his handful of mane, he regained his balance and leaned forward as the horse thundered along the path, the straggling hedges on either side whipping Daniel's lower legs as they passed.

In the copse, which had once been a working hazel coppice, he had to lean even lower to avoid being scooped off the animal's back by low branches. He could feel Piper's muscles rippling under him as he gripped the smooth satiny coat with his knees, and was grateful that the path was, for the most part, straight.

Bursting out of the cool dimness of the wood a minute or two later, Daniel and Piper were suddenly faced with a narrow picket gate leading into a meadow. Moving fast and with only a stride or two's warning, Daniel took the only option available and urged the horse on, twisting both hands into his thick mane and sending a prayer skywards.

Piper took the gate in his stride, bunching his quarters and leaping neatly over to land with hardly a jolt on the soft turf beyond. Daniel landed a little less gracefully, with his face buried in the animal's mane. Finding himself rudderless, Piper veered left for a stride or two but Daniel soon regained his balance and straightened him up, heading downhill towards a gap in the far hedge.

This time, he pulled the horse up in time to avoid the necessity of jumping the five-bar gate, a feat he didn't feel confident of attempting. Luckily, the gate was easily opened, and they were soon cantering down a grassy track towards the bottom of the valley.

Rounding a bend, the river came into sight, crossed by the bridge that Jenny had warned him about. It was narrow; not much more than a footbridge, with a handrail on one side. Daniel slowed the horse to a walk and steered him towards it, but as soon as his hooves touched the wooden planking, Piper baulked, swinging round and away from the structure.

Daniel turned him back again, with the same result. He could feel the horse's coat growing warm with sweat as he became agitated. Slipping off his back, on to legs that had become strangely jelly-like, Daniel attempted to lead the horse forward, but Piper was having none of it. He dug in his toes and threw his head high, looking at Daniel through white-rimmed eyes. He clearly had issues.

'OK, fella. I guess we'll just have to go round it, then,' Daniel said soothingly, looking to the side of the bridge where vegetation grew tall on the river bank, masking the transition from solid ground to water. To his eyes, the prospect looked far more daunting than twelve feet or so of wooden planks, but then he wasn't a horse.

Vaulting on to Piper's back once more, he rode him towards the river's edge, quite prepared for him to dig his toes in again but the horse breasted the vegetation without hesitating, sliding a little as the ground gave way beneath his hooves and plunging knee-deep into the water where Taz was already cooling off.

Feeling that he would never completely understand horses, Daniel patted Piper's neck and urged him forward across the stony riverbed. Piper stumbled as his feet met the rising ground unseen beneath the reeds, then lurched upwards, almost losing Daniel out the back door.

They rejoined the path, and he sent Piper on into a gallop, seeing the trees flitting by on the edge of his vision. After a few hundred yards, the path left the wood and split into two, the left fork, which was signposted as the bridleway, hugging the lee of the trees, and the right one leading to a gate. From there, across the open parkland beyond, Daniel could see the impressive Georgian facade of Great Ditton Manor. His hope that he would see the two boys pedalling across the last stretch of grass was dashed. They were nowhere to be seen.

The main gate was padlocked, but beside it a smaller one swung in the breeze. Making a mental note to reprimand the boys for leaving it unlatched, Daniel pushed it wide and rode through, doing the same thing himself as he tightened his legs on Piper's sides and sent him into a gallop once more. Out to one side, Taz stretched into a run.

This time they went like the wind, thundering across the open grassland with the wind whipping through the horse's mane and rippling Daniel's shirt. There was no chance of approaching unseen, so speed was the best option, and within a very short time they had reached the low hedge that bordered the gravel drive, jumped it and pulled up in a spray of shingle.

Daniel caught sight of movement through an archway to the side of the house and turned the horse that way. It led through to a large quadrangle formed by the wall behind him, covered stables and a coachhouse to the right and ahead, and the house on the left. It appeared there were no horses in residence as the yard was bare of the usual signs of occupancy, but he could hear dogs barking somewhere.

A familiar blue van was parked alongside several other vehicles, including Liam Sellyoak's black Porsche, and the sound of Piper's hooves crunching on the gravel brought the footballer hurrying from an open doorway, followed closely by Taylor Boyd.

Boyd initially glanced past Daniel, but then, apparently satisfied that he had come alone, said with a sneer, 'Well, if it isn't the lone fuckin' ranger!'

Daniel ignored the taunt, his eyes searching, without success, for any sign of the boys. What he did see, in the open back of the van, was a number of wire-mesh crates, such as are commonly used for transporting dogs. One of the cages was already occupied. It seemed their guess had been right.

'Looking for the kids?' Boyd asked.

'What have you done with them?'

'Well, see – we caught them trespassing . . .'

'Don't be bloody stupid! They're only kids – football mad. They came to try and get Liam's autograph. They don't know anything about – all this.'

'Ah, but they saw too much, and kids chatter, don't they? And we couldn't have them chattering – at least not until we'd finished our business here.'

'Where are they?' Daniel demanded. 'The police are on their way. You don't want to add kidnapping and unlawful imprisonment to the list of charges.'

'If the police are on their way, why the heroic charge across country? I don't think so, Mr interfering busybody. They've got nothing on us, or why did they let us go, eh?' Boyd stepped towards Daniel. 'Now, get off the little pony and hand over your mobile, and we might let you see your precious kids.'

From beside Daniel there came a rush of black and tan, and suddenly Taz was between the horse and the approaching man, hackles up and teeth bared. Boyd recoiled instinctively.

'Call off the fuckin' dog!' he ordered, fear in his eyes.

'I don't think so,' Daniel replied. Even though the man was used to handling fighting dogs, they were quite often soft with their owners. Taz was a different matter altogether, and Boyd was understandably less comfortable when the aggression was targeted at him.

Taylor hesitated, then, turning his head, he bellowed, 'Dad! Bring the kids out.'

For a moment nothing happened, and then Daniel tensed as Norman Boyd appeared in the doorway of one of the stables holding Harry Summers on one side and Drew on the other. Drew was pale and stony-faced – his usual reaction to anxiety. Harry was sniffling as he manfully tried to repress sobs.

'Dad!' Drew cried out. 'I knew you'd come.'

Being there was one thing, Daniel reflected ruefully. Being able to effect a rescue was quite another. The sight of Boyd senior with his grubby hands on the boys made his blood boil.

'It's OK,' he reassured them quietly. 'I'll sort this out.'

'They took our phones,' Drew said, greatly aggrieved. 'We didn't do anything wrong. We only wanted an autograph . . .'

'Shut up!' Norman Boyd said roughly, shaking the boy's arm.

'It's not your fault. I'll sort it,' Daniel told him.

'No,' Taylor cut in. 'I'll tell you what's going to happen. You're going to call off the dog, get off the pony and hand over your phone. If you try anything fancy, the kids'll suffer, got it?'

Daniel hesitated, but only for a moment. He had had first-hand experience of what Norman Boyd was capable of, and he had no reason to suppose he would have any more scruples just because his captives were children.

Calling Taz to heel, he slid off Piper's sweaty back, trailed the reins and took his mobile from his pocket. It was vibrating silently. No doubt Dek or Danvers wanting an update. Too bad. He hoped his silence would hurry them on their way.

Taz was reluctant to come to his side. He had just caught sight of Drew being restrained by the enemy, and his doggy brain knew it was a situation he should do something about. Drew was family and therefore his responsibility. He stood his ground and continued to growl menacingly.

'Taz! Heel! Now!' Daniel reiterated sharply, and glancing from one to the other in agitation, the dog did as he was told.

'Throw the phone over,' Taylor instructed. 'And don't even think about trying anything!'

Daniel had been toying with the idea of lobbing the phone hard towards Taylor's face and making a play for the two boys, but Norman Boyd was just too far away, and although the footballer was standing slightly apart, looking miserably unsure, Daniel couldn't rely on him not to enter the fray if Daniel went on the offensive. Sighing inwardly, he tossed the phone in an underarm action to Taylor, who caught it deftly. Taz took a step forward, watching like a hawk, but a word from Daniel stopped him in his tracks.

'So, what now?' Daniel asked.

'Now we load up the van and be on our way.'

'What about the boys?'

'Oh, I think we've got a spare crate. They can come along as insurance.'

Daniel turned cold with fear. 'You can't do that.'

'Watch me.'

Daniel looked at Liam. 'And are you OK with this? You're a hero to these kids.'

The footballer shrugged unhappily, and Daniel grew impatient.

'Think what you're doing, man! There's a world of difference between owning fighting dogs and kidnapping children. You'll be behind bars for a long time. You can kiss goodbye to your career, that's for sure.'

'Shut up!' Taylor said sharply, but Daniel's words had clearly hit home with Liam.

'Look, couldn't we just leave the kids?' he asked. 'They haven't done nothing.'

'Bit late for a conscience now,' Taylor replied with a sneer. 'You're in this as deep as we are. Shut up and go get one of the dogs. You,' he added to Daniel. 'Into the stables.'

Daniel assumed a resigned expression and, leaving Piper standing obediently with his reins trailed, began to follow the footballer towards the nearest open door with Taz at his heels and Taylor a step or two behind.

His path took him closer to Norman Boyd and the two boys, and as he came level with them, Drew said desperately, 'Dad?'

It was now or never. Swivelling on his toes, Daniel pointed at Taylor, and shouted, 'Taz, get him!' In the next instant, he'd launched himself at Boyd senior with his head down and tucked into his shoulder like a prop forward with his eye on the try line.

Faced with a human battering ram, Norman Boyd's survival instincts took over and he released his two captives in favour of protecting himself. Even so, Daniel's shoulder hit him squarely in the midriff, sending him staggering back to land sprawling on the gravel with Daniel on top.

'Run!' Daniel shouted at the boys, shifting his weight to pin Norman Boyd down as the bulky, salvage yard owner tried to throw him off. Out of the corner of his eye, he saw Drew take Harry's arm and drag him away. Somewhere behind him, Taylor was shouting obscenities as Taz silently and efficiently took care of that particular business.

Gritting his teeth with the effort of restraining his captive, Daniel glanced round and saw Liam Sellyoak standing irresolute in the stable doorway. He was looking at the two boys.

'Stay out of it!' Daniel warned. 'Don't make things worse for yourself.'

'I never wanted any of this,' the footballer complained weakly, advancing a step or two. 'Not the kids . . .'

'So do something about it. Give me a hand.'

'I can't. You don't understand . . .'

Norman Boyd unleashed a stream of expletives in Sellyoak's direction. Daniel bounced on him.

To one side, Taz had his man floored on the shingle with a classic hold on his right forearm, and Taylor was clearly not happy, screaming for Daniel to call his dog off.

'Stay still and he won't hurt you – much,' Daniel advised him dispassionately. Now they just needed the cavalry to arrive. Surely Danvers couldn't be far away.

A door banged in the direction of the house, and suddenly there was a new player on the scene.

'Don't just stand there, you fool!' Taylor screeched, loud and furious. With a sinking heart, Daniel glanced up to see the younger Boyd break into a run towards them.

Not overjoyed at the prospect of being caught on the ground, Daniel swung a haymaker at Norman Boyd's jaw and scrambled to his feet.

He almost made it.

Reaching him a fraction before he straightened up, Ricky lashed out with his foot, catching Daniel on the shoulder and spinning him helplessly around to measure his length on the ground. Instinct had him rolling and coming to his feet in an instant – just in time to see Ricky reach into the back of the transit and withdraw a familiar shiny blue baseball bat.

Daniel's spirits sank still further. He had had ample experience of the damage that particular weapon could do.

To one side, Norman Boyd was scrambling groggily to his feet, and behind him, Daniel heard the scrunching of footsteps on gravel as Liam Sellyoak stepped forward. He was surrounded.

'Call your fuckin' dog off or I'll smash your fuckin' head in!' Ricky threatened, slapping the baseball bat into his open left hand and advancing menacingly towards Daniel.

Aware that he had little option, Daniel nevertheless still hesitated, playing for time.

'Ricky – for God's sake!' Sellyoak protested. 'You can't do that. What about the kids?'

'Too late to get squeamish now,' Ricky sneered. 'You're in this as deep as anyone.'

'No one was meant to get hurt,' the footballer said.

No, just the dogs, Daniel thought fleetingly, but his mind was toying with another idea. With Ricky Boyd's attention temporarily on Sellyoak, was it worth trying for the baseball bat? It was a slim chance – so slim as to be anorexic – but it might be the only one he got.

He tensed himself for the attempt, but, even as he did so, help arrived from a completely unexpected quarter.

With a scrunching of hooves on gravel, Piper charged into the fray, accelerating with the speed of a drag racer, guided by a slight figure that clung grimly to his bare back.

With many other breeds, the ploy wouldn't have worked; horses naturally avoid collision, but a quarter horse is bred for working cattle in the way that a sheepdog is for sheep, and shouldering aside a running steer is all part of a day's work. Although, as far as Daniel knew, Piper had never worked cattle, the instincts were all there, and he thundered into the midst of the group without flinching.

Ricky's bravado deserted him. Dropping the bat, he dived for cover behind the van, and his father, who was halfway to his feet, leapt to the side with such haste that he stumbled and fell once again.

The horse charged through the gap he had created and on for some way before the boy on his back managed to pull him up, but the diversion gave Daniel all the time he needed.

In three swift strides he had reached and wrenched open the driver's door to Taylor's transit. The keys hung in the ignition, as he'd expected, and within moments he had the vehicle started, in gear and heading for the archway. Accelerating across the quadrangle, he swung it into a handbrake turn that finished with the van almost completely blocking the stableyard exit.

The spray of shingle was still filtering down through the climbing roses on the wall when Daniel leapt out of the vehicle, taking the keys with him. Piper was already on his way back, and, recognizing the figure on the horse with a rush of pride, he yelled, 'Drew! Over here!' and was ready to catch Piper's rein as the horse came to a propping halt in front of him.

Over by the stables, the Boyds were beginning to recover their equilibrium, and, mindful of the baseball bat, Daniel shouted to Taz to release his captive and come to heel. There was no way out for those in the yard except on foot through the gateway or the house, and whichever they chose, they wouldn't get far. Daniel could already hear the welcome sound of approaching police vehicles, including a helicopter overhead.

Still holding Piper's rein, he reached up and lifted Drew off the horse's back. The boy put his arms round his father's neck and slid sideways to cling to him, shaking and half sobbing with what Daniel suspected was a mixture of shock and relief.

'I've got you. It's all going to be all right. You were brilliant, Drew,' Daniel said into his hair. 'Where's Harry?'

'Outside,' Drew said, pointing beyond the van, where several sets of blue lights could now be seen flashing.

'Let's go find him,' Daniel suggested, taking his hand. Taz circled them, still on a high from his part in the action.

As they made their way past the front of the transit van, with Piper trailing in their wake, a succession of police cars and vans burst from the driveway at speed, followed closely by an ambulance and a paramedics' car. One by one, they drew up on the gravel sweep in front of the scaffold-clad Elizabethan manor. Blue lights reflected in the numerous diamond-paned windows as a bewildering number of uniformed personnel spilled out on to the stones.

'Where are they?' one of the police officers shouted, and Daniel pointed through the archway behind him.

'In there. Four of them. And the dogs are in the stables.'

At least eight men wearing riot gear charged through the gap into the stableyard, and a half-dozen more were set to follow. Daniel was impressed with Danvers' influence. It seemed a huge turnout for a rural force to accomplish at such short notice. As the second phalanx approached, he held out the keys to the transit.

'You might need these.'

'Thanks, mate.'

Behind the ranks of official vehicles, Daniel saw Danvers' van arrive, followed by Jenny's Land Rover, and headed thankfully in that direction.

'Where's Harry?' Jenny was out of the vehicle almost before it stopped, her eyes searching the parked vehicles.

'Mum!' A small boy torpedoed from behind a police van and threw himself into her arms, sobbing hysterically.

All of a sudden, Daniel felt stiff, sore and unutterably weary.

TWENTY-ONE

Both the Boyds and Liam Sellyoak gave themselves up without a struggle, falling back on their claims that the pit bulls were in fact boxer-cross-Labradors with papers to prove it, though – as Danvers pointed out – if that were the case, why had they been so anxious to hide them from the police?

Although statements would in due course be needed, Jenny and Daniel were allowed to take the two boys back to the farm as soon as the arrests had been made, but it wasn't until the evening of that long, long day that things began to settle down.

Finally, the door closed behind the last uniformed officer, and the remaining company heaved a collective sigh of relief.

At the big kitchen table, the children were eating their meal, chattering to Jenny's mum, who had once more stepped in to help.

On the sofa and chairs at the other end of the room sat Daniel and William, Jenny, Lou Danvers, Dek and Paul McCreesh. Taz lay asleep on the floor at Daniel's feet.

'You Whelans make quite a team, don't you?' Danvers observed.

'Drew was amazing!' Daniel said proudly. 'God knows what would have happened if he hadn't done what he did. If we'd still been in the thick of it when the troops arrived, we could have had a really nasty hostage situation on our hands.'

'I still don't think they should have let them go in the first place. If they knew they were guilty, it seems a huge risk to take,' Jenny said. After her initial euphoria at finding Harry and Drew unharmed, she had become increasingly subdued as the day had gone on. Not surprisingly, in Daniel's opinion. After all, it had been a hell of a day, and she had only just lost her husband.

'They had to give them enough rope to hang themselves,' Dek told her. 'It was a calculated risk. Chances were they would go straight to where they'd hidden the dogs and move them to somewhere safer, and, sure enough, that's what they did. Of course, what they didn't know was that the police had planted a tracer on their van.'

'I wondered how you managed to mobilize such a response in such a short time,' Daniel said to Danvers. 'I was well impressed. When I found out they were on their way all the time, I'm afraid you were relegated back down to the realms of us mortals.'

'So, what will happen to the Great Ditton Mafia, now?' William asked. 'Have we seen the last of them for a while?'

'Hopefully the police have enough on them to put them away for a good few years this time,' Danvers said. 'They didn't do themselves any favours this morning. As traumatic as it was for the boys – and I wouldn't have had it happen for anything – the Boyds managed to add kidnap and false imprisonment to their rap sheet in the space of half an hour or so. Add to that aggravated assault, and they should be looking at a lengthy custodial.'

'With any luck we might be able to get them on arson, too,' McCreesh put in. 'Forensics are working on that pick-up of the youngster's.'

'What'll happen to the dogs – the pit bulls?' Jenny asked. 'Harry wanted to know, and I had to tell him I wasn't sure. I suppose they'll be put to sleep, won't they?'

'They are classed as evidence, at the moment,' Danvers said, 'but yes, in the long term there's nothing else we can do. They're a banned breed in this country. They're fighting dogs. Through no fault of their own, I admit, but fighting dogs all the same.'

'It's so unfair. They can't help what they are.' Jenny looked sad.

'And what about our football hero?' McCreesh wanted to know. 'What'll happen to him?'

'I think his days of public adoration are well behind him,' Danvers stated. 'At the very least I should hope he'll lose his job, and I imagine the various lucrative advertising deals he's got going will be cancelled. The companies involved will drop him like a hot coal; they won't be able to distance themselves quick enough. You know, that mobile phone has turned out to be something of a gold mine. Not only did it have a useful list of contacts on it that were pretty damning for Taylor and his family, but there were a good few incriminating photos, too, besides the one of Liam. Even the girl – Melody – was on there, holding on to a dog in the fighting pit.'

'The end of your romantic dream, mate. I'm sorry,' Daniel said to Dek. 'You must be gutted.'

Dek responded with a choice expletive.

'Melody was a means to an end,' he said. 'As I'm sure you are well aware.'

'There was a picture of Gavin on the phone, too,' Jenny said flatly, ignoring the repartee. 'Sergeant Paige told me earlier. She asked me if Gavin was involved in dog fighting. As if I would have stayed quiet if I'd thought he was. The whole idea of it sickens me!'

'How dare they even suggest that?' McCreesh said angrily. 'The man's only been dead a couple of days.'

'But, you see, it turns out he *was* involved,' she said with tears in her eyes. 'There was a picture on that phone and they faced Taylor with it. He told them the whole story. He said Gavin was at a dog fight the night he . . . I mean, when he . . . Did you know?' she demanded, rounding on Daniel.

'I was beginning to suspect,' he admitted unhappily.

'But you promised to tell me. You promised!' she said, tears flowing freely now.

At the table, her mother noticed the breakdown and distracted the children with an offer of ice cream.

'I didn't know for sure,' Daniel said in his own defence. 'And I hoped I was wrong. I didn't want to upset you while there was still a chance it wasn't true.'

'So, do they know what happened to your husband?' Dek asked gently. 'Did the Boyds have something to do with it? They never spoke about it when I was around.'

Jenny took a deep steadying breath.

'They claim it was an accident.'

'They *would*,' McCreesh said.

'Well, the police think they might actually be telling the truth. It fits the forensic evidence they have. The Boyds say Gavin had gone with them to a fight, but, unbeknownst to them, the police had got wind of it and it was raided. The Boyds managed to get away, and they say Gavin jumped on the back of their pick-up truck. But it was a rough ride, and further down the track he fell off, which is how he got his head injuries. The police say that he did have traces of oil on his clothes that might well have come from the truck bed.'

'But how did he end up here?' Daniel asked.

'Paige's superior reckons they thought he'd died and were panicked into dumping him. I don't suppose we'll ever know for sure,' Jenny said wearily.

A knock at the door brought Taz to his feet and everyone else to attention.

'Oh no. Please don't let that be them again,' Jenny begged. 'I can't bear it!'

'You stay there. I'll get it,' her mother said with a martial light in her eye. She opened the door and moments later those listening heard a deep voice asking for 'Miss Jenny'.

'It's Woodsmoke,' her mother reported, keeping the door half-closed.

'*Woodsmoke?*' Jenny repeated, looking mystified. 'What on earth . . . ?'

'Shall I send him away?'

'No, I'll come.'

At the door, she invited Woodsmoke to step inside, an offer he declined.

'Reckon I won't stop,' he said. 'The thing is, Gypsy's got pupses and I juss got to thinking about your liddle ones an' how they've had a rough time of it lately, and I wondered iffen they'd like a liddle pup when they's weaned.'

Whatever Jenny's thoughts might have been on the matter, Lucy and Harry had overheard the offer and the decision was taken out of her hands.

Jumping down from their chairs, they ran to the door and demanded to know when they could see the puppies.

'Reckon not yet awhile,' Woodsmoke said, looking uncomfortable in the proximity of such eager intensity. 'They's only liddle. Be a week or two afore they's fit fer visitors. I'll let ee know, soon enough.' With a nod of his wide-brimmed hat, he turned and melted into the darkness.

Jenny knew when she was beaten. Closing the door, she attempted to calm the children down, warning them that it was nearly their bedtime.

Drew was standing a little behind the others, unable to share fully in their excitement, when his mobile emitted a passable representation of a barn owl's call. He took it from his pocket and answered it, turning away to gain a little privacy.

A minute or two later he ended the call. 'That was Mum,' he told Daniel, who had followed Jenny to the kitchen end of the room.

'Oh, was it?' Daniel's heart sank. He had meant to have a word with the lad about how much it was prudent to tell her about recent events. 'Did she not want to speak to me?'

'No. She said to tell you she's staying in the Maldives for another week.'

'She did, did she?' Typical of her to give Drew the job of passing on what she felt might be unwelcome news.

'You don't mind, do you?' Drew asked anxiously.

'Absolutely not,' Daniel assured him. 'So, she didn't ask what you'd been doing, then?'

'Yes, she did, but I just said riding and stuff,' Drew said blandly. 'I told her it's been pretty quiet.'

Daniel shook his head and smiled a slow smile.

'You, my lad, are a legend,' he said. 'But I'd hate to think you got that devious streak from me.'

Monday morning in the drivers lounge was a strange affair. With Taylor missing from the rota, they would now have been two drivers down if Jenny hadn't contacted Dean Stevens and persuaded him to return to his job. Even though explanations had been made, he, Reg and Macca all looked slightly askance at Dek's alter ego, as if they couldn't believe he was the same person, which, Daniel supposed, he wasn't.

So far the investigation had found nothing to suggest that Terry MacAllister was involved with the Butcher Boys in any way, and with no evidence to the contrary, Daniel had to admit that his initial suspicions regarding Macca's participation in the midnight assault on himself were probably groundless.

Talking with Dek and Daniel late into the previous night, Jenny had decided to give the business a few months more, and although, in the short term, both Daniel and Dek agreed to stay on to keep the lorries on the road, she failed to persuade Daniel to accept a permanent position as supervisor.

'I'm sorry. I can't. What about Mal Fletcher?' he had suggested. 'He was with Gavin from the start. He knows the business.'

'I suppose I could ask him,' she said reluctantly. 'If you're sure you won't change your mind.'

Daniel had shaken his head. 'You need continuity. Someone who'll stick with you for the long haul. I can't give you that assurance – I just don't know where my life is going at the moment.'

As Jenny outlined her plans for the future to the drivers gathered in the lounge on that Monday morning, Dek got up and slipped from the room.

'So, it won't be easy and I'm relying on you to help me through this rough patch, but I believe that Summer Haulage has the potential to be a thriving business if we all pull together,' she finished. 'Are there any questions?'

Dean cleared his throat. 'Um . . . I could really pull my weight if I was allowed to drive one of the bigger trucks,' he ventured hopefully.

'And I think you should,' Jenny replied. 'We need all the capacity we can get. I'll get on to the insurance company and see if I can negotiate a reasonable deal.'

Dean stammered his thanks, positively glowing with pride at the thought of his promotion.

At that moment, the door opened and Dek reappeared. All eyes glanced his way but without any special interest until he announced, 'I've got someone here who's a bit keen to see you, Reg.'

'Me?' Reg asked, puzzled.

A sharp yap answered the sound of his voice, and the veteran driver's expression changed to one of shocked disbelief.

'Skip?'

Dek leaned down and moments later straightened up with the Jack Russell terrier held in his arms. The little dog's eyes sought and found his master, and he wriggled and whined in his efforts to be free.

Smiling broadly, Dek put the dog on the floor and, with a

scrabbling of claws, Skip shot round the side of the sofa and made a beeline for Reg, leaping into his arms, covering his face with frantic licks and squeaking with excitement all the while.

Reg pushed his face against the dog's warm body, his eyes shining with unshed tears.

'How?' he said wonderingly. 'I mean – I saw his collar . . . The blood . . .'

'I'm sorry we had to do that to you,' Dek said. 'But it was necessary to prove myself to the Boyds, and I couldn't risk telling you the truth at that stage. Too much was resting on it.'

'You bastard!' Reg said with quiet fury. 'If you only knew . . .'

'I do know,' Dek assured him. 'I have a dog myself and I longed to tell you the truth.'

'Where has Skip been all this time?' Jenny asked. Her eyes were suspiciously bright, too.

'Living the life of Riley at the home of one of the kennel maids at the local RSPCA,' Dek told her. 'Apart from missing his dad, he certainly hasn't suffered.'

Reg didn't comment. Carrying Skip, he left the room, face buried in the little dog's fur.

Dek looked wistful and Daniel went to his side.

'Let him go. He needs time but he'll get over it.'

'I hope so. The thing is, Taylor had it in for that dog after it bit him, and if I hadn't taken it, he would have done it himself. I'm sure I don't need to tell you that if he had, the outcome would have been very different.'

'Absolutely. When Reg realizes what you've actually done for him, he'll come round, I'm sure.'

Jenny joined them.

'You didn't look particularly surprised,' she said to Daniel. 'Have you known all along?'

'Not at first,' Daniel admitted. 'But since I found out about Dek and realized what a chance he took to save Taz, I knew he couldn't have harmed Reg's dog. The only thing I can't work out is how you squared it with Taylor,' he added to Dek. 'Didn't he want to see the evidence?'

'It was a tricky one, but I set it all up in advance with Lou's help. When I snatched Skip, I was supposed to hand him over to Taylor straight away, but obviously that wasn't going to happen, so we swapped him for another Jack Russell that had had to be put down at one of our rehoming centres. When I showed Boyd the body, I told him Skip must have had a weak heart. I knew he wouldn't know whether it was Skip or not, and it was a pretty good match, to be honest.'

Behind him, the door opened, and Reg came back in, Skip now trotting happily at his feet. Taz wandered over and sniffed him, waving his tail gently.

'I don't know whether to knock you down or shake your hand,' Reg said, his face ruddy. 'But just so's you know – if you *ever* do anything like that again, I'll personally beat you to a pulp or die trying.'

'I understand,' Dek said, looking down from his six-inch and thirty-two-year advantage without a trace of amusement. 'And you have my word that I won't.'

Reg nodded shortly, then headed for the door, saying, 'Come on, Skip, you lazy varmint. No time for socializing. We've got a day's work to do, my lad.'